ALSO BY CHELSEA ICHASO

Dead Girls Can't Tell Secrets

Little Creeping Things

THEY'RE WATCHING YOU

THEY'RE WATCHING YOU

CHELSEA ICHASO

sourcebooks
fire

Copyright © 2022 by Chelsea Ichaso
Cover and internal design © 2022 by Sourcebooks
Cover design by Esther Sarah Kim
Cover images © kertlis/Getty, Greg Courville/Shutterstock, Mélanie These/UnSplash
Internal design by Tara Jaggers
Internal images © Yongcharoen_kittiyaporn/Shutterstock

Published by Sourcebooks Fire, an imprint of Sourcebooks
P.O. Box 4410, Naperville, Illinois 60567–4410
(630) 961-3900
sourcebooks.com

Cataloging-in-Publication data is on file with the Library of Congress

Printed and bound in Canada.
MBP 10 9 8 7 6 5 4 3 2 1

To my parents, for all the scary movies

ONE

"You do realize you're going straight to detention," I say to my lab partner Gavin Holt. He's wearing a white button-down shirt adorned with his signature bow tie—all the boys wear ties. It's a requirement, though Gavin is the only guy on campus who insists on the bow variety.

But this time he's gone off the rails and paired it with plaid pajama pants. Strictly against dress code. Torrey-Wells Academy, named after its two founders, has a bit of a double standard when it comes to attire. Guys have to wear slacks and a tie to classes, chapel, and to the dining hall; girls can wear pretty much whatever they want as long as it covers the necessary parts. For example, I'm wearing sweatpants and a ratty TWA sweatshirt—my daily uniform—and am in no danger of violating the code. Apparently, when the school opened up to girls back in the seventies, the board found altering the academy handbook too much of a bother.

Which is fine with me.

Gavin shrugs but scoots his stool closer to the lab table to hide his lower half. "I woke up late."

I roll my eyes.

"And then I had a small Pop-Tart smoke alarm emergency."

"Well, you look like you're ready to crouch by the Christmas tree and unwrap a package of Hot Wheels."

"You're one to talk, Sweatpants Girl."

Fair enough. I scan the list of ingredients again. "I guess this means I'm getting the water. Try not to blow anything up while I'm gone." I grab the beaker and head over to the sink. There's a sixty-six-point-six percent chance that Gavin will ignore my warning and blow something up while I'm gone, if we're basing this on stats from our last three assignments.

With a wave of my hand, the fancy steel faucet turns on. The Lowell Math and Science Building, constructed four years ago thanks to a rich donor named Lowell who made his money genetically modifying crops, is a state-of-the-art facility. No penny was spared, from the touch screens the teachers use in place of whiteboards to the observatory fit with a massive telescope. Handle-less water faucets were important too, I suppose. Water starts spewing out the sides of the beaker before I realize I've been gazing off into space. I shut it off with another wave and dump some of it, glancing over my shoulder at Gavin.

His lips are quirked, eyes squinting at the tray full of materials. He's definitely contemplating lighting something on fire. I watch as he adjusts his glasses, picks up the spatula, and begins prodding at the sodium metal without his gloves on. A sudden wave of frustration rolls through me. My best friend, Polly St. James, should be sitting here next to me, not Gavin.

If she hadn't left, I wouldn't be so stressed about my grade in this class. Whereas some teachers tend to show leniency toward the athletes, Dr. Yamashiro is extra strict. To keep the GPA required for my financial aid, I can't get anything less than an *A* on this experiment. Or on any assignment, for that matter. But with Gavin for a partner, I might have to settle for getting out of the building alive.

I return, setting the beaker onto the glass tabletop with a clank. Water droplets splatter the ingredients list as well as our findings sheet.

"You okay?" Gavin asks, leaning closer, his jade eyes narrowed behind his lenses. His scent is sweet with a hint of smoke, like he downed an energy drink on the way here or tried to ignite a Jolly Rancher.

"Fine. Put your safety goggles on."

He obeys, placing the goggles over his glasses, and I add a few drops of phenolphthalein indicator to the beaker. But he nudges me with an elbow, and I almost fumble the dropper. "Well, you don't look fine."

I take a deep breath and steady my hand. I'm not about to tell Gavin that life pretty much sucks now that my only friend has abandoned me. I'm not about to tell Gavin that I suspect something bad might've happened to Polly—that she didn't just up and run away like her parents and the police say.

I would never tell Gavin Holt that my eyes are stinging with tears because even the best-case scenario means my closest friend chose to leave me and never return my calls or texts again.

"I'm just tired and sore. Still recovering from hell week." Every year, at the start of lacrosse preseason, Coach makes us attend 5 a.m. practices before classes, and again at 5 p.m. after classes. It helps to get us in shape. It also makes every inch of my body feel like it's melting off.

"And maybe a little upset that Polly is…" Gavin pushes a strand of dust-brown hair off his forehead. "You know, gone."

"Maybe." But the truth is I started losing Polly months ago.

A few weeks into our Form III school year (Torrey-Wells Academy can't very well call us juniors and seniors like every other school in the United States), Polly was suddenly too busy for me. Even though we're roommates—we've been roommates since Form I—I didn't see her as much. Polly's straight As always came with a healthy dose of cramming; this year, she never felt like studying. Then there was the staying out and sneaking back into the room after curfew, reeking of booze. It wasn't like her.

At least, it wasn't like the Polly who was friends with me. She'd vaguely mentioned her wild-child days, but people change. We were content to drink soda from the vending machines and spend Saturday nights in our pajamas.

Until she started getting buddy-buddy with Annabelle Westerly and joined chess club. This has to be the only school in the country where chess club is cool, and it's all thanks to Annabelle. Polly and I used to joke about how Annabelle Westerly's endorsement could probably make pin the tail on the donkey the next school fad. But suddenly, Polly wasn't laughing much with me anymore.

She was laughing with Annabelle, who's trouble veiled in designer labels and a posher-than-thou lexicon.

Then two weeks ago, Polly wasn't laughing with anyone. She was gone.

I tried to tell Mr. and Mrs. St. James about Polly's new habits, so they'd do more to try and find her. But my claims only supported the police's conclusion. Polly had left a note, after all, telling her parents she'd taken a break from school to clear her head.

Authorities ruled her a runaway.

I'd seen so little of her this semester, I could hardly argue with them. I wasn't exactly an expert witness on Polly's habits or state of mind.

I put on my gloves and slap Gavin's hand as he reaches for a small green vial he must've stolen from the supply cabinet, because it has nothing to do with this experiment. Then I remove a tiny piece of sodium metal from the container with the spatula, drop it into the water, and thrust my arm to the side to keep Gavin back as the liquid sputters and reacts, leaving a pink trail through the beaker.

Across the room, Dr. Yamashiro eyes us, having learned from past experiences. Gavin pulls off the whole clueless thing so well that he hasn't been busted yet. Take, for example, whatever happened in his dorm this morning with a Pop-Tart.

But I'm on to him.

I think Gavin is actually a freaking genius.

He scribbles down our findings, just as Dr. Yamashiro starts to wrap up class. It's probably for the best, considering Gavin's fingers are spider-crawling across the table toward that green vial.

"Lord, help me," I whisper into the fumes.

"Maren, you know I'd clean up," Gavin says, "but if Dr. Y saw me…" He glances down at his PJs.

"You wore those stupid pants on purpose," I say, snatching the beaker off the table. Gavin grins, grabbing his books. He waits for Dr. Yamashiro to turn to the fancy screen that looks like a portal into another dimension, then shoves himself into a cluster of students headed for the door.

Gavin could probably come to class in no pants and still

end up with a clean record. My cheeks heat suddenly at the thought, so I rush to the sink and stick my hands beneath the cool water.

———————

Back in my dorm room, a cozy cube still plastered in Polly's vintage Hollywood photographs and my lone Lionel Messi poster, I throw myself onto the bottom bunk. My gaze drifts toward the photo collage—the one we made together last year—hanging on the wall between our desks, but I force myself to stare at the bedframe slats above me.

Polly's top bunk remains empty; the school hasn't forced a new roommate on me yet. It should be nice having the place to myself, except I loved living with Polly. We used to study together in here, comfy on our beanbag chairs, our dusty desks neglected. We'd lie in our beds, chatting for hours after lights-out, keeping our voices low to avoid shushing by the Form IV proctor.

Polly's parents came by and picked through her things. They took what they wanted but left the majority. Like they're convinced she'll regret her decision and return any second. I've been through everything dozens of times, hoping I'll find some clue concerning her whereabouts.

I shut my eyes and replay our last conversation. It didn't happen in this room—over the past few months, we never spoke more than a greeting to one another in here. I'd spotted her out at the Commons, across the large expanse of pristinely cut grass. I watched her for a few seconds, the way she walked with her head tucked into her shoulders. The sun bathed the campus in a warm glow, but she tugged the hood of her expensive new coat—most likely a gift from Annabelle—over her auburn curls.

When it came to money, Polly was like me. In fact, money was the way we'd met. During Form I orientation, we both attended the financial aid seminar with our parents. Torrey-Wells is ridiculously expensive, and my parents are not rich. They had to figure out how to send me here through a combination of payment plans and scholarships. There are only a handful of us scholarship kids at Torrey-Wells, and something about sticking together made sense. It felt safe. After a few minutes of listening to the droning financial aid advisor at our parents' sides, we stole through the side doors of Henning Hall, giggling as we explored our new campus, inventing histories for every statue, giving imaginary freshmen the tour. Bonding over lattes in the café.

During our first two years, while the other students were out gallivanting all over town on weekends, throwing around wads of cash, Polly and I were content to hang out in the dining hall and watch movie marathons in the common area of our dorm. At least, I was content. I guess Polly had her sights set on Annabelle and the rest of them.

That day on the grass, I called her name and waved her

down. We were both headed to chemistry. But she turned and spotted me, and for a split second, I thought she might keep walking.

"Hey," I said, jogging to catch up. "Can I walk with you?"

She nodded, and up close I could see beige-colored patches where her attempt to conceal the dark purple bags beneath her eyes had failed.

"Where'd you sleep last night?" I asked, though it was obvious she hadn't slept at all.

She shrugged, pursing chapped lips. "In a friend's room."

"So, Annabelle's room."

Another shrug, but she wasn't running away from me. Her fingers fidgeted and her gaze floated away, searching the grounds. My chest pricked. She was probably worried about being seen with me.

"Are you okay? You look...stressed," I said.

"I've had a lot on my mind. Chess isn't going so well."

"Chess?" I asked, wondering how a club could be the cause of whatever I was witnessing in my normally lively and fresh-faced friend.

"It's not really working out. There's a lot more to it than I thought." She hitched her bag higher on her shoulder and massaged her temples with her fingertips. The hood fell back, and her tousled curls glimmered bronze in the spring sunlight. Then the words came out in a jumbled rush. "It's not just pieces and a board. It's...more. Too much, maybe." Her eyes widened as she finished, shining with something like terror.

At first, I was too stunned by her rambling to respond. Had the sleep deprivation really gotten to her? Was it drugs? Or was this something more? Finally, I reached out to touch her arm. "You don't have to play chess anymore, Polly. Is Annabelle pressuring you to stick with something you hate?"

She exhaled through her teeth, rustling her curls. "No, it's—forget I said anything." She reached up, removing my hand from her arm, and slowly, her fingers began to squeeze. "*Please*, forget it."

"Yeah, fine." She dropped my hand, and another pang shot through me.

"Polly!" a voice shouted from across the grass. I glanced over to find Annabelle Westerly, dressed in a slouchy sweater and tall leather boots.

"I've got to go," Polly said softly, looking at the ground.

"I miss you." I cringed at the way my voice cracked. "I miss our movie nights and our beanbag chats. I miss—"

"Let's meet tonight," she interrupted, spinning around to face me. We reached the end of the grass, and a large statue of Lord Torrey himself towered behind her on the cobblestone walkway. The cathedral bell tolled in the distance, reminding us to hurry along. "We can catch up."

"Okay," I said, the word dragging. "We don't have to

meet. You could just come back to the room for a change—
your room."

She shook her head and glanced over her shoulder. "I
want to show you something. Meet me at the fountain." I
knew which fountain she meant. *Our* fountain. The one with
the white iron bench where we always had a quick coffee
while waiting for our next morning class. "I'll see you in
chem," she said, rushing over to Annabelle.

My heart buoyed in my chest. The meeting. It meant
something. She was coming back to me. She'd seen the error
of her ways.

After dinner, I sat on the bench by the fountain. Beneath
the glow of the lamppost, I waited for an hour, checking
my phone every ten seconds for a text from Polly that never
came. I thought about texting her, asking if she was on her
way, but it felt even more desperate than sitting alone in the
cold night air.

When she never showed, I was furious. Hurt too, but
mainly incensed that she'd gotten my hopes up. I made my
way back to my dormitory, panic streaking through my
chest that I would miss curfew and be locked out. Torrey-
Wells is one of these sprawling New England establishments
built on two thousand acres, complete with two orchards,
four ponds, and fifteen student housing buildings; ancient,
ivy-laced brick buildings stitched occasionally with newer
models, like the Hamilton Fitness Center, to keep up with the

times. I had to sprint to make it, and when I did, a cocktail of anger and adrenaline pumped through my veins, making sleep impossible.

As I lay there, the silent hours passed as I prayed for the beep of the room key. I hoped the door would click open and I would find Polly standing there, an apology ready on her lips.

Instead, in the early hours of the morning, I finally drifted off, and the top bunk remained empty. No creak of the door. No soft steps on carpet.

The next day, Polly missed all of her classes. When she didn't come to dinner, Annabelle Westerly started asking around, and eventually Headmistress Koehler reported her missing. The academy's state-of-the-art security cameras failed to pick up anything useful, so the police were brought in. Being her roommate, I was soon questioned. Her teachers were also questioned. Polly's parents were notified, and by the time their plane landed, the police had discovered Polly's note in the top drawer of her desk.

I voiced my concerns to the police. To her parents. Polly was supposed to meet me. Why would she run away?

But her parents took one look at the note, in Polly's own handwriting, and their faces fell. They pressed the cops to look for her, but even their pressing was half-hearted. Apparently, Polly had run away before. Back in middle school. Part of the reason they'd opted to try private school in the first place was to keep her on the straight and narrow. Yet here they were again, thousands upon thousands of dollars later, their daughter wandering somewhere out there in the wide-open world.

Now I force my lids back open and stare up at the wooden beams strung beneath the top bunk. The white of Polly's mattress peeks between the beams, edged in mauve-colored roses from her sheets. I've called her at least ten times. Left half that many messages. *Please, Polly. Call me back. Let me know you're okay.*

She never has. I can't stop thinking about that flicker of fear in her eyes that day. Her incoherent words. *It's not just pieces and a board. It's...more.*

I sit up so fast I nearly whack my head on the top bunk. *Polly's words.* They echo in my head with the thunderous force of lacrosse cleats on concrete. What if they weren't supposed to make sense? What if they weren't meant to communicate her feelings about chess?

Because they were meant to communicate something else.

I get down from the bed and pad over to the closet, sliding open Polly's half. After two weeks of digging through the leftover contents, I know her chess set is buried at the bottom of a box of random paraphernalia. I remove her playbill for the academy's performance of *The Crucible*, in which Polly played Abigail, and dig the heavy, wooden folding chess set from beneath a blow-dryer, a tattered copy of *The Iliad*, and a black ballet flat.

The chess set—another gift from Annabelle—is engraved *Polly St. James* at the bottom. I undo the two golden latches and open it, lifting the flap and dumping the marble pieces out. They tumble over Polly's gray IKEA rug; queens and kings, pawns and rooks, all elaborately carved. I don't know what I'm looking for, so I take up every piece in hand, inspecting one before casting it aside to grab the next.

When I've checked the base of every piece, only to find the same set of initials left by the artist, embarrassment creeps from my neck up to my cheeks. I examine the board next, unfolding and flipping it. But there's nothing. Polly's babbling the day she disappeared was simply a symptom of the stress she'd written about in that note the cops found. She'd had enough. Of chess. Of school.

Of me.

I start to tuck the board back into its case when my eyes fall onto a ripple in the red silk lining. A ripple that seems out of place in a chess set worth as much as all of my belongings combined. I tug at it, and my heart skitters.

The fabric is loose. I remove it, uncovering a little white envelope that lies flush with one corner.

The envelope's seal, a heavy wax emblem of a circle slashed through the middle, has been broken. I tug out a sturdy white card, printed with the same emblem, which sort of reminds me of this T-shirt clip I found in my mom's old junk. She said they used to wear them in the eighties. The print on the card is an embossed gold that looks like it was meant for the Queen of England.

Dear Polly,

You are cordially invited to attend the semiannual initiation meeting of the Gamemaster's Society, located in the old cathedral. Please wear your finest attire and arrive promptly at 11 p.m. on Friday, the 17th of September. Within this envelope, you will find the tokens required for entry.

Do not forget your tokens.
Do not tell anyone about the meeting.
Do not mention a word of the society.
VICTORY OR DUST.

Sincerely,
The Gamemaster

I dump the envelope over and shake it. But nothing falls out. Polly must've used whatever was in here to get into this meeting. This meeting that was months ago.

I've only heard the vaguest whispers of a secret society. One with access to liquor and parties after curfew, like the fraternity over at Langford School. This must explain why Polly was so distant this past term. It even explains that trip she took to the headmaster's office a couple months back, a trip she refused to explain to me. She must've gotten in with the wrong crowd—some weird club that forced her to break lots of rules.

But why wouldn't she tell *me* about it? Sure, the fancy card says it's a secret. But we shared everything—at least, we did back in September. Did this society really want only Polly? Or did she simply choose not to include me?

Then a thought hits me so hard I drop down onto a beanbag chair.

If Polly was spending all her time with this society, someone in it might know where she is.

TWO

WHEN YOU'RE DIGGING FOR INFORMATION ON A SECRET society, it's good to have a lot of contacts.

I have three. First up, my lacrosse teammates, who basically count as one collective contact. They're also a contact I'm sort of on the outs with; instead of bonding with them during Form I, I bonded with Polly. Still, the relationship is amicable and they value my offensive skills on the field. After practice that afternoon, I gather up enough courage to interrupt their conversation about Saturday night's masquerade ball to ask them.

"Secret society?" our Form IV captain, Valeria Reyes, asks with a smirk. "Of course, there's a secret society."

"Well, great then—"

"And if we knew anything about it," she adds, "it wouldn't be secret." She yanks off a muddy cleat and tosses it into her bag.

"So nothing?" I ask, feigning disinterest as I peel off my disgusting sock. "Not even a name?"

I'm not stupid. I know Suspect Number One is Annabelle Westerly. She must know something about this Gamemaster's Society. Or else why would she and Polly have been so buddy-buddy?

But I can't just waltz up to someone like Annabelle without a plan of attack. Without a plan—without leverage—she'll deny everything.

"Not a name," says our goalkeeper, Mari DeJong. "But when my aunt was a student here, a rumor went around that a society was responsible for the fire in the old cathedral. Like a prank gone wrong or a night of debauchery gone wrong or"—she shrugs—"something gone wrong." Valeria giggles, but Mari stays somber. "A kid died that night."

"That's horrible," I say. But it makes sense. A bunch of drunken students, hanging out in an ancient building.

It was also ages ago. I need to talk to someone who's in the society now.

"There's no secret society," Larissa Gaines says, rolling her eyes. She shoves her goggles into her bag. "Unless you count those kids who play Dungeons and Dragons in the corner of the dining hall every Friday night. But that's more *exclusive* than secret." She waggles her brows. "You might be able to get in, though, Maren. If you practice."

"Thank you, Larissa," I say, giving her a tight-lipped smile and making a mental note to accidentally trip her with my lacrosse stick at tomorrow's practice.

"Well, I heard they have this password or something about dirt," Diana Willis offers, wiping her sweaty forehead on the hem of her practice shirt. The line from the invitation flashes through my head: *Victory or Dust.* "And the only way you pass the initiation is if you spend the entire night inside a casket that they literally bury—beneath the ground. If you freak out or refuse to do it, they don't let you in."

My breathing gets shallow at the thought. "Okay, but how do you even get invited to the initiation?"

I'm met by silence. Shrugs ripple around the group like they're doing the wave at a sporting event. The invitation is tucked inside my lacrosse bag, and my fingers itch to whip it out. Maybe if they saw it, someone would be spurred to spill more information.

"Just give it up, Maren," Valeria says. "How can you even think about joining a secret society with our schedule?"

"No, it's not—I'm not trying to join. It's more like...a friend of mine was asking."

She slings me a dubious look and zips her bag shut.

Contact number two is Jordan Park, the girl who got paired with me for an English assignment when Polly did the unthinkable and paired up with Annabelle Westerly right in front of me. Jordan's been my friend ever since. She's a little uptight, but sweet, and she's kept me from having to eat alone in the dining hall this year.

Currently, she's behind me in the salad bar line at dinner. "A secret society?" she whispers, casting a paranoid look at the security camera in the corner of the room. "What kind of secret society?" Her salad tongs halt in midair, and the girl behind her grumbles about moving things along.

I sigh audibly and then feel a little bad about it. My poor detective skills aren't Jordan's fault. "I don't know," I say, scooping up sunflower seeds and sprinkling them over my ranch-doused lettuce. "The kind that possibly buries kids underground as part of some initiation ritual."

Jordan's eyes widen as she tucks a shiny black strand of hair behind her ear. "Why would anyone want to do that?"

"Why does anyone join a secret society? There must be perks." Polly certainly climbed to a higher social ranking, at least. The only other perk seemed to be vanishing.

Unless Polly never made it past the initiation. I shiver, imagining her trapped inside a dark casket, grains of dirt sifting through the cracks as she struggled for air. What if Annabelle was wooing Polly, trying to get her to join the society? But something happened during the ritual?

Jordan opens her mouth to say something, but my third and final contact passes us on the way to the soft-serve ice cream.

"I gotta go," I say, lifting my tray. "Talk to you later."

"But I thought we were—"

Jordan's words are drowned beneath dining hall chatter as I chase after Gavin Holt.

Sure, Gavin knows as much about a secret society as my grandma knows about Kanye West. But he's the only other person at Torrey-Wells I can ask.

"Hey, Gavin," I say, sounding overly cheery.

Gavin looks over his shoulder, lowering his empty cone. "Hey, Maren. What did I do now?"

"Nothing," I say, eyes brushing over his lean frame, clothed now in black slacks and a clean button-down shirt the same sea green as his eyes. "In fact, I'm very impressed by the way you managed to put on real pants."

Gavin starts loading his cone with chocolate and vanilla swirl. "I did have to trek all the way back to my dorm to change, so thank you for the words of affirmation."

"Can we sit for a sec?" I motion to a nearby table.

Gavin's brow arches as he licks his ice cream. We're not exactly friends outside of chemistry lab. Still, he assents.

I set my tray down across from him and lower onto the bench. Inadvertently, my gaze wanders to the table in the corner where Polly and I always sat during Form I and II, now occupied by some field hockey players. "I think Polly might've joined a secret society before she left."

Gavin keeps licking his ice cream as if my conspiratorial accusation never happened. A strand of golden-brown hair flops over his frames.

"Did you hear what I said?"

"Mmhmm," he says, still focused on that stupid cone.

"Well, do you know anything about this society?"

Gavin finally pauses, placing both elbows on the table. He lowers his chin onto a fist, the ice cream clutched in his free hand like Lady Liberty's torch. "You're not supposed to talk about the society," he says matter-of-factly.

At first, I think he's going to add some sarcastic remark like Valeria did, but he doesn't. "Or what?" I ask, lowering my voice as a gangly boy maneuvers past our table. "What happens if you talk about it?"

Gavin shrugs and crunches on the sugar cone. "That's just what they told me."

"*They? You know* these people?" I practically plant my palm in my salad as I lean in. "How?" This absentminded goof might actually know something useful.

"I tried to get an invitation," he says through the munching. "But I was denied."

I might snatch the remainder of his cone and chuck it across the dining hall. "How? How did you even know who to ask for an invitation?"

"I found the Gamemaster," he says, like it's obvious. And it should've been. *The Gamemaster's Society.* Even the invitation was signed *The Gamemaster.* "That's how it works. You have to find the Gamemaster and challenge him to a game. If you win, you get an invitation. If you lose, it's tough luck. The Gamemaster swears you to secrecy on pain of death or some mumbo jumbo and sends you on your way."

"If you were sworn to secrecy on pain of death, then why are you telling me?"

Gavin laughs lightly. "The kid beat me at a game of cornhole. I hardly think he's going to carry through on the death threat."

"So then, you think it's all a joke?"

"I don't know. I'm kind of glad I failed, to be honest. Bunch of kids playing games and pretending it's life or death. Sounds like a waste of time."

"Unlike blowing stuff up."

He shrugs again, but a grin forms on his lips. Lips that I'm definitely not thinking about because he's Gavin.

"I heard the initiation is some sort of burial ritual involving a casket," I say. "Not a game."

"The game isn't the initiation." His eyes finally fasten on mine. "That comes later. First you have to win an invitation to even make it to the initiation. I obviously wasn't given the opportunity to see the inside of a casket." He frowns, like he's truly disappointed.

"Well, who's this Gamemaster person?"

"No idea." He pops the last bit of cone into his mouth and I'm forced yet again to wait for the chewing to stop. "I found him back in Form I—a somewhat reckless Form IV tipped me off. This year it could be anyone."

But there's only one person at this school who befriended Polly right before she disappeared. My eyes trail over the bustling room, past Jordan—who's sulking off in a corner, stabbing at her salad—and land on my target.

In the center of the hall, Annabelle Westerly perches on a bench, back straight as she lifts a silver soup spoon to her lips. As usual, a flock of beautiful people surrounds her.

"Thanks, Gavin," I say, remembering my untouched salad and gobbling up a couple quick bites.

"No problem, m'lady. Just remember." I look up from my salad to see his usually playful eyes eerily stoic as he reaches to touch my hand. "Be careful."

I freeze, incapable of chewing the lettuce trapped between my teeth as the noise of the hall suddenly fades away.

But Gavin chuckles and pulls his hand back. "'Cuz you might get hit in the head with a bag of corn." He shakes his head gravely. "Dangerous sport, cornhole."

I toss a lettuce leaf at his chest, stand up, and walk my tray to the dirty stack.

I met Annabelle Westerly last year while we were waiting for our parents to pick us up for winter break—well, *I* was waiting for my parents. I soon learned that Annabelle was waiting for a shiny black limousine to chauffeur her to the airport. We were seated on a bench beneath the bare cherry blossom trees at the main entrance. The air was sweet with the scent of Dr. Theodore Lowell's prize rosebushes, which had won some award for their virus-resistant foliage.

"Are you going to stay local, or does your family have plans to holiday abroad?" she asked. Her words carried a lazy, almost Mid-Atlantic intonation I'd heard only in old movies.

"Oh," I said, startled that a Form III, let alone someone like Annabelle, was talking to me. "Staying home, with my parents in the city." Immediately, I felt like an idiot. *The city?* Students come to this New Hampshire academy from all over New England—hell, from all over the country—and I said I lived in *the city.* "Providence," I added quickly, feeling my chest constrict. "What about you?"

"We always spend Christmas in London," she said, applying red lipstick in her phone's camera before blotting audibly. Her blond hair was twisted up into an effortless bun, and she wore a long black peacoat, jeans, and leather ankle boots. I, by contrast, was wearing soccer sweats that weren't warm enough for the weather, so I'd thrown my ratty old snow jacket on top. We must've made quite the picture sitting side by side. "We lived there until I was eight. But my father grew up here—he was a student at Torrey-Wells, you know." I didn't know. But the moving around explained the accent. "He moved us back here for his company, but kept our country house there."

Annabelle spoke to me for a solid five minutes, during which time I learned what a country house was and how many servants it takes to keep it running.

"It sounds amazing," I said, fascinated by her perfect posture.

"You'll have to come for a visit," she said, as if we'd been long-time friends rather than schoolmates who'd just met on a bench. "Yes, over summer holiday." She clapped, smiling over at me. "It's so lovely with the garden in full bloom. And you'll be able to meet Beatrice—she's my horse." Annabelle then went on to tell me all about her grueling schedule as a prima ballerina for the academy. She asked me about my extracurriculars too. "Three sports?" She looked genuinely impressed. "Which one's your favorite?"

"Soccer," I answered, wondering if I should've called it 'football' in her presence. "It's the one I'm best at. Coach says I could get a scholarship someplace."

"Where's someplace?"

I shivered and zipped my puffy coat up higher. "Maybe California. UCLA sounds nice and warm."

When we exhausted the topic of our futures, she tugged

a pack of cards from her designer handbag. "Do you play rummy?" she asked.

The truth was I hated cards, but I would've done anything to please her at that point. It's probably the reason I've never faulted Polly much over the past year. If it had been me instead, I'm not sure I would've been able to resist Annabelle's charm. I've never cared about the money; still, there was something about her attention that day beneath the bony cherry blossom trees that made me feel special. It might've been all too easy to slip away from my best friend, fading into oblivion as sharp curfews turned to hazy mornings and hangovers.

I never got to play the card game that day. Annabelle's car arrived and the driver scuttled over to take her bags. With a smile and a wave, she tucked her long legs into the spacious back seat. No promise to hang out after the break before the car drove off.

Back then, I didn't know there was a secret society.

I still don't know for sure. But if Annabelle has any information, I'll have to start with her. Unfortunately, her giggling groupies are still swarming her table across the room. Instead of discarding my tray, I turn left to the drink station, my mind swimming with bad excuses to interrupt her dinner. *Hi, Annabelle. I believe we met once? Before you stole my best friend and then managed to completely lose track of her?*

I have to pass her table to get to the soda dispenser, and as I do, her distinct, softened vowels drift into my ears. "You'll have to excuse me. I'm off to bed. Early morning at the studio tomorrow."

I start to turn, ready to abandon my plan in order to catch her alone. She stands, bringing her iron-curled hair in front of one shoulder with a grand flipping motion, and my eyes catch on a wink of metal at the nape of her neck. There's something unusual about the clasp on her necklace. It's only a second before her hair tumbles back down to cover it.

My heart beats faster, and I press on before Annabelle's tablemates can catch me staring. Continuing to the drink station, I set my tray down to give my now-shaky arms a rest.

Annabelle more than *knows* about the secret society. She's in it.

The clasp at the back of her neck might not have caught the attention of some random observer. But it caught mine. It was shaped like a very particular symbol. A circle with a thick bar through the center. I've seen it before: the wax seal on Polly's society invitation.

And it's just the leverage I need.

THREE

THE NEXT MORNING, I WAIT FOR ANNABELLE OUTSIDE THE
dance studio, but I have to head to my first class before she
ever emerges. I try throughout the day to get her alone, but
people are always stuck to her like barnacles.

After lacrosse practice, I throw my warm-ups on over my
sweaty workout clothes and head across campus to where I
learned (thanks to all my eavesdropping) she'd be at this hour.

She's seated on the marble steps of the performing arts
center now, clothed in tights and leotard, a fluffy gray scarf
her only protection from the afternoon wind. She must've
just finished rehearsals for the spring ballet. I'm not sure what
they're performing this year, but I have no doubt Annabelle's
the star. Last year, she got the lead in the Christmas production,

even though she was only a Form III and the role always goes to a Form IV.

She's engrossed in a textbook as I tiptoe up the steps, my lacrosse bag heavy on my shoulder. Up close, Annabelle's blond bun is pristine, and there's a barely there post-workout sheen to her airbrushed skin. When I stop in front of her, clearing my throat, her gaze flicks up, and then she's back to reading.

"Hi," I say, smiling as I lower my bag onto a step. "I don't know if you remember me, but I'm—"

"Maren Montgomery," she says, the strange accent drifting off her tongue in a way that makes me want to copy her. "Form III. Soccer, basketball, and lacrosse. Last year, you were the leading scorer for both the soccer and the lacrosse teams. You were also the only Form II in the ISL to be named All League for soccer."

A wave of relief rolls through me. She remembers. "I think you know my friend. Polly St. James?"

Annabelle's perfectly straight neck dips in the world's curtest nod.

"She talked about you all the time," I lie.

Annabelle doesn't move, but I can tell by the slightest twitch of her eye she's no longer reading. "Did she?" My heart sinks at her skeptical tone. Polly must've told her we were barely on speaking terms this year.

"Well, I'm trying to get ahold of her," I say, my attempt

at posh talk coming out like a lousy attempt at an English accent. "She isn't answering my calls, though."

"That's a pity."

A knot forms in my throat. It's pathetic, begging someone who only knew Polly a few months to get her to speak to me. "Can you help me get in touch?"

Annabelle looks up at last, and her finely sculpted features soften. "I would if I could," she says, the words dusted with compassion. "But Polly hasn't answered my calls either. I think she needed to make a clean break. At least for a while. She'll return, though. Like she did before. Polly told me all about the last time this happened."

My neck heats, because I believed I knew everything about Polly St. James, and she never once confided in *me* about running away from home in middle school. I didn't even find out until her parents mentioned it. "It doesn't make sense. She had plans to meet me that night. Why would she ask to talk one minute, and then just...*leave* the next?"

Annabelle shrugs, brushing a fallen leaf off her tights. "Couldn't handle the pressures of a school like this."

Anger needles at me. If that's true, it's because of Annabelle. The Polly I knew had no problem handling her course load on top of debate club and theater. The Polly I knew loved this school.

I dig my fingers into my warm-up jacket pocket to grasp the edge of Polly's invitation to the Gamemaster's Society.

"Yeah, I guess all the late nights and partying might make it difficult to hang in there." I lower onto the step beside Annabelle as I pull out the card, setting it on my lap. She isn't wearing the necklace today, and a worry that she'll simply deny knowing anything about the society plants itself in my head. "Are you sure there isn't anything else you want to tell me about Polly before I take this to the headmistress?"

Annabelle's blue eyes cut to mine like a blade. For a moment, I think she's going to whack me in the head with her textbook. Instead, she laughs. Her gaze, her cheeks, her entire face lights up. "Maren Montgomery," she says, like she's learning my name for the first time again. "You think some parties drove Polly away?"

"I think you and your *society* are bad news, and now my friend is gone."

"That little card in your hand is hardly proof we're responsible."

Disappointment feathers in my chest. She's right. If I go to the headmistress now, maybe they'll keep a closer eye on things around campus for the next few months, but it's not going to get Polly to speak to me. It's not going to convince anyone to open an investigation after having found a note written in Polly's own hand.

Annabelle waves at someone across the courtyard and then leans an elbow back onto the step behind us. "I honestly haven't heard from Polly. I miss her as much as you do, but the best thing is to give her some space." She stills for a moment. "I do have a theory, though, about where she went."

"You do?" This I wasn't expecting.

"Well, she spoke so often of becoming a television star, like her favorite actress—what was her name?"

"Mona Perkins."

"Right. Well, what if she decided to go for it?"

The idea sends pinpricks of sadness through me. They spread until my insides are just a swollen mess of pain. Polly and I used to binge-watch *Stolen Hearts*, a show about a genetically engineered monster teen who can't allow herself to fall for anyone out of fear she'll eat them. One night, when Polly and I had finished rewatching the season 4 finale, where Hetty accidentally kills Zane, Polly shut off the TV and just sat there, staring at the black screen. "What's wrong?" I asked, confused, since she'd already known Zane was going to die.

"She didn't go to college, you know."

"Hetty? She's only a junior."

"No, Mona Perkins. She was just walking around Venice Beach with her friends one day when some film director spotted her and invited her to an audition."

"Wow."

"Yeah." Polly sat still, arms wrapped around her knees for another minute. Finally, she shrugged. "Guess we'll have to take a trip to Venice Beach after graduation." Grinning, she chucked some popcorn at me, and I whined, because we were going to have to clean it up before the next group who'd booked the common room TV came in.

I clear my throat and glance up to find Annabelle watching me, warmth in her expression.

But I don't trust her. The Polly I knew wouldn't have quit high school on some reckless mission to become a Hollywood star. She might've had a momentary lapse of judgment in middle school, but she'd changed after spending two years at my side. She'd learned that good things only come from hard work. And Polly works just as hard as anyone. At her grades, at theater. Annabelle knows something about my friend.

My friend, who looked terrified a few hours before she "ran away." My friend, who wanted to show me something the day she was last seen. Could it have had something to do with this society?

I have to speak to more members. But if Gavin's right, the only way to find out who they are is to earn an invite.

After tucking the invitation back into my pocket, I reach for my bag, removing the deck of playing cards I stole from my dormitory's common room. "Any chance you're up for a game?" I ask, waving the deck.

She tosses me an incredulous expression before glancing back down at her book. "Occupied at the moment." Her mouth barely parts as she speaks. Like she can't be bothered to move it.

"Really? It would be a shame for everyone on campus to see this invitation," I say, letting the playing cards spill from the box down into my palm. "Not much of a secret if everyone knows about it." My hand trembles, but I do my best to match her icy glare. "One game. You win, my lips are sealed about your special club. I'll give you the invitation and you can light it up in whatever drunken ritual caused the cathedral to burn down." A hint of amusement lights her eyes at this. "I win, and"—I shrug—"you give me a chance to become one of you."

"Why?" she asks simply.

My head draws back. "Why what?"

"Why do you want to become *one of us*?" Her hand makes a furling gesture through the air. "You just said we were bad news."

I bite my lip, not having thought through this part. "*Bad* doesn't bother me," I say, which is a complete and utter lie. I haven't been late for class once during my entire time at Torrey-Wells. "I guess if Polly comes back, I want to be a part of whatever she's part of. To be honest, I'm a little hurt she never invited me." The truth of this statement falls on my ears with a weight that presses down, slipping through my throat and landing on my chest.

"It wasn't her place," Annabelle says.

"I could use the excitement too," I add, struggling for words. For air. "When you run on adrenaline, being bored most of the time—especially the past few months without Polly—is a major soul crusher."

An eternal moment passes as Annabelle stares, her shiny lips pursed. "It's not what you're thinking," she says finally. "The society." She tugs the elastic from her bun, letting her majestic hair tumble down her back. "But I do admire a competitive spirit."

"Rummy, then?" I push the cards between us on the cold marble, thankful I made Jordan play a few hands with me last night in preparation for this moment.

"Afraid I'm not in much of a mood for rummy." Despite Annabelle's word choice, her tone conveys no fear. My stomach drops. She pauses to think and then her eyes flash. "Texas Hold'em. For coin."

"Oh." I dig into my pocket, even though I know exactly what I'm about to find inside: a hundred bucks my parents gave me to buy new cleats for when the small holes in my current pair become massive craters. My parents don't just hand out spending money. Every latte I buy, every movie I attend, every pack of socks I purchase, gets charted in this budget spread-sheet my dad wrote up. Each penny eventually gets paid back through summer jobs. If I tell my parents I gambled this money away, there will be no cleats. Which means I'll be playing lacrosse in my socks by the end of the season.

Annabelle reaches out to stop me. "No need to flash that filthy thing around," she says, indicating the threadbare FC Barcelona wallet my aunt brought back for me years ago. "You can settle your account with me later."

Settle my account? What's going on? Either Annabelle and her fancy society friends like to pass the time by gambling away their rich parents' money, or she's messing with me. Maybe *coin* isn't old-timey speak, and she actually means we're playing for pennies.

But, she adds, "One hand. One hundred and two hundred-dollar blinds." Then she moves up to the top of the marble steps where there's more room to play.

It's a kick to the gut. Let's hope one of my teammates has an extra pair of cleats.

Annabelle digs into the Prada bag she uses for ballet, her hand emerging with a fistful of colored, glassy stones. "We'll use these for chips," she says, as if it's perfectly natural to have a collection of rocks in your expensive gym bag. She lets half of them drop into my palm before tossing two blue stones in between us. Guessing I'm the small blind, I add one.

"I'm dealer." Anabelle shuffles the cards and deals two to each of us, facedown.

She never asked if I knew how to play the game. Maybe not knowing the rules is an automatic forfeit of your shot at an invitation. The truth is I learned Texas Hold'em from a ten-year-old during a babysitting gig a couple summers back. We used Halloween candy as ante. Even if that kid taught me the game correctly, I'm not sure I remember the rules.

But I don't tell her that. I simply pick up my cards and analyze them. A four of hearts and an eight of spades. I remember enough about the game to know that this is a crappy hand. My shot at infiltrating this society is dwindling before my eyes like a dying fire. And everything rests on this one round. With no other option but to call, I toss my second stone in to match hers.

There goes two hundred bucks.

Next, Annabelle flips three cards faceup between us: ace of hearts, seven of clubs, and ace of diamonds. She smiles. "I'll bet." A surge of fear has me jittery. She must have pocket aces. She lifts two stones, a pink and a red, in her perfectly manicured fingers, and I resist the urge to glance at my bitten and likely dirty fingernails. Whatever. Maybe it's true what they say about ballerinas, and her toes look worse than my fingers do.

I've got nothing. I'm going to lose hundreds of dollars I don't possess, and my dad is going to freak and withdraw me from the academy.

Annabelle stares pointedly at me, and I jerk to attention. This could be my only shot at finding Polly. Something kept her from confiding in me that day on the lawn, but she wanted to. She planned to show me something. She wanted me to find this invitation. If I get in, someone in the society could help me contact her, so I can put my fears to rest, once and for all.

Another thought pushes in my head—one I try desperately to ignore. That maybe I'll find out exactly what had Polly so terrified before she vanished. Images flicker now of caskets and dirt-coated air. Of smoke and flames and a fiery roof crashing down. I push two bright blue glass stones out in front of me. "Call."

She flips over the next card, which has a name that's completely escaped my memory. The turn? The burn? *Burn* wins for most accurate, because it's a five of spades. If Annabelle has even one ace, she's going to trample all over my crummy hand.

Annabelle checks this time, making me feel slightly better. She can't be too confident in her hand if she's checking, can she?

Suddenly, a thought punches my gut: What if she's trying to make me *think* she has a poor hand? To get me to throw more money away.

I inhale slowly, drawing any ounce of recklessness and negligence from my responsible girl bones. I can't fold. I have to keep going. "Check."

My stomach roils as Annabelle turns over the fifth and final card. This one I remember: the river. Maybe I remember because my stomach feels like it's going over a series of rapids as I calculate the total number of hundred-dollar stones I'm about to lose.

The card is a six of diamonds, and suddenly my riotous stomach settles as something like hope smooths it over. A four, a five, a six, a seven, and an eight. Holy crap.

I've got a straight.

The second Annabelle checks, I push a rock into the pile. Then, for good measure or because my parents are going to kill me when they find out I lost all this money, I toss in one more stone.

Annabelle peers down at her cards, her expression unreadable. A moment later, her limber frame lifts and falls in a loud sigh as she tosses her cards. "Fold," she says, frowning and gathering up all her chips. "You'll get your money shortly."

"No, that's okay," I say, so relieved and excited I can barely speak. "I honestly just wanted—"

Annabelle's eyes dart to mine like a falcon to a mouse. "What *did* you want, Maren Montgomery?"

My gaze falls to the cards, and I start stacking them back into the box. "The deal was a shot at becoming one of you."

Annabelle stares at me, her gaze slipping over my hoodie and my sweatpants like a cattle rancher surveying his product. She's about to go back on her word. Clearly, I'm not society material. She stands, dusting herself off and slinging her bag over a shoulder. "You'll find what you require in your dormitory. Good day."

Does she mean the money? I don't care about her money. I open my mouth to call after her, still clutching the little glass stones. But I stop. Because she cranes her delicate neck back and says, "Well played, Maren. I think you'll do nicely for us. And keep the pebbles. You'll be needing them."

And she winks.

FOUR

WHEN I RETURN TO MY ROOM AFTER DINNER, THE INVITATION is lying on my pillow. Which is creepy. Either my hall proctor is in the society, or someone broke in.

I flop down onto my beanbag chair and tear the little wax seal in half. Tucked inside is $400 cash and an invitation almost exactly like Polly's.

Dear Maren,

You are cordially invited to attend the semi-annual initiation meeting of the Gamemaster's Society, located in the old cathedral. Please wear your finest attire and arrive promptly at 11 p.m. on Friday,

the 25th of April. You already possess the tokens
required for entry.

    Do not forget your tokens.

    Do not tell anyone about the meeting.

    Do not mention a word of the society.

    VICTORY OR DUST.

Sincerely,

The Gamemaster

Friday, the 25th. That's today.

It's probably for the best. Less time to think means less time to overthink and back out. I'm not claustrophobic, but that doesn't mean I'm eager to get stuffed inside a casket.

The invitation refers to tokens again; this time it says I already have them. I rack my brain for what it could mean, and Annabelle's words from this afternoon ricochet back to me: *And keep the pebbles. You'll be needing them.*

So weird.

I scramble over to my dirty clothes hamper, where my sweats are dangling over the edge. Some of the "pebbles" have fallen inside the hamper and scatter the floor. A couple more are still stuck inside the pocket. I gather them and pace over to my closet, but my eyes snag on the collage hanging between my desk and Polly's. The one filled with photos of the two of us.

Every year, the Form II class takes a trip to Europe as part of the school's World History program. While the members of the sophomore class at East Derry High across town were stuck inside their plastic chairs, reading about the Renaissance in their crusty textbooks, Torrey-Wells Form II students were strolling the Louvre. Of course, there was no way my parents could afford the trip. Polly couldn't afford it either, but she managed to win the academy's lone scholarship, which meant I'd be the only Form II stuck at school for two weeks.

Except Polly refused to leave me behind. She gave up the scholarship to stay with me. I couldn't believe it—no one could believe it. Her parents and Headmistress Koehler tried to convince her that she was forfeiting the opportunity of a lifetime. But Polly didn't care.

The final project for the Europe trip is always a scrapbook of everyone's travels. The perfect way to rub all those gorgeous photos in our faces. So Polly decided we'd make our own memories. Over those two weeks, we took a million selfies of all the stupid stuff we did—movie marathoning in the empty common room, illegal apple picking in the campus orchard, downtown shopping in our pajamas.

It's all up there on the wall. The two weeks that forged an unbreakable bond between us.

At least, I thought they did.

Wrenching my eyes away from the collage, I focus on the invitation again. My *finest attire*. It takes three seconds of shoving my "fancy" dresses around to grab the most suitable option.

Then I slide the door over, exposing Polly's half of the closet to find the black wool maxi coat she always let me borrow for athletic banquets. An assortment of sparkly dresses fit for a princess dangle from the rack; more gifts from Annabelle. My eye stops on a silver one with a deep V, but there's a knock on the door.

I scurry over to open it, finding Jordan in the doorway, holding a box of Funfetti cake mix.

"Hey, Maren. I thought we could bake." She smiles expectantly, glancing beyond me like I'm supposed to invite her in.

"Oh." My mind zips to the invitation still lying on my desk in plain sight. "That would be fun, Jordan, but I have to study. For English."

"No problem," she says, the hand holding the cake mix lowering to her side. "I'll study with you. I have this essay—"

"I can't, sorry. It's a reading assignment, and I need total silence or I can't concentrate." Jordan's brows angle, probably because she knows I have no issue reading in the café across campus that's been known to play Taylor Swift on repeat while its patrons sing along.

"I get it," she says, and it hurts, because I think she really does get it.

"You know what?" I reach out just as she spins around to face the hall. "I'm getting all stressed because of my scholarships, and it's making me overreact. Let's go bake that cake."

I peek over my shoulder again and add, "I'll meet you down in the kitchen."

———————————

At a quarter 'til eleven, I'm ready in my knee-length, navy blue dress, and my hair smells of sugar and vanilla. Jordan is tucked away in her own room, suffering from a slight stomachache due to all the cake she scarfed down. I was too nervous to eat anything other than my fingernails, which are chewed to the point of pain.

I've never stayed out past curfew before. It never seemed worth the risk, considering everything my parents have done to get me into this place. Supposedly, the front door is locked from both sides. Last year, a girl complained about trying to meet her boyfriend, only to be thwarted by that lock.

But Polly got in and out tons of times. There has to be a way. I ease my room door open, shutting my eyes as it buzzes. Then I peek out into the dark corridor.

The coast is clear, so I grab Polly's cheap, faux leather handbag packed with my phone, my room key card, the invitation, and the glass stones. I tiptoe down the hall, my heart thumping and my lids half-shut. My hall proctor is a horrible Form IV named Mary Elizabeth Sweeney. If she catches me dressed like this, I can hardly use the bathroom as an excuse.

But I pass her room, and the door remains shut. Hunching my shoulders, I take the stairway down to the dormitory's main floor. At the entry of the building is a large room with a brick fireplace, a front desk only manned during the day, and a looming set of double doors.

Doors the school claims are electronically locked at night.

I scan the walls and ceiling for cameras, and sure enough, one blinks red light down on the room. It's all over. As soon as I step in front of that camera, security will catch me trying to escape. The school will call my parents in the morning.

But suddenly, the camera crackles, its red light dying.

My eyes fall shut in relief. It malfunctioned.

I approach the door, my legs shakier than they are at the end of two forty-five-minute soccer halves. When I reach for the handle, I'm holding my breath. I turn it, waiting for some sort of alarm to go off and wake up the entire building. Waiting for the lever to resist my hand.

But it turns.

I breathe again, checking over my shoulder one last time before I push and skitter out into the night.

A half-moon sits above, spilling soft light over campus. The air has a bite to it, so I button Polly's coat as high as it will go. Beneath me, my black kitten heels clomp along the path unnervingly, past the lanterns that line it. I keep scanning ahead and behind, even off the path into the grass. I'm actually out here past curfew. The lock on the doors was nothing but an academy legend.

As soon as my heel touches the grass, a beam of light

swings in front of me, cutting just short of my toe. I back up, searching frantically for somewhere to hide as the light draws a wide oval around the lawn. There's a statue a few yards away on the cement, but my clackety heels would give me away in an instant. Ducking low, I slide them off and tiptoe behind the base of the statue.

My heart's thumping is soon echoed by the sound of footsteps along the path. Whistling. The light swerves and bounces on the cement, and sweat breaks out on my forehead, despite the cold. What's my excuse if I'm spotted? I just happen to be sleepwalking in a semi-nice dress and heels?

The footsteps approach, and I shuffle around to the back of the statue. The whistling nears. After a moment, my leg muscles ache from the strain of crouching. And this security guard decided to camp out right next to the fountain. I try to adjust my position, but my foot slides. I topple, my thigh smacking the cement.

My nerves singe. The clomping gets closer, the whistling seemingly over my head. When his light slings by again, it illuminates a rock beside my foot. I reach out, grab it, and windmill chuck it off to the side. It clatters over the cement, and the guard's light flicks off in that direction.

His footsteps follow, the light slings by for a final time, and the whistling soon fades.

Letting out a breath, I slide my dirty feet back into Polly's heels and scurry through the grass with my head down. Then

I stalk along the path between the Stanley Health Center and the Hamilton Fitness Center, stopping to scan the Commons before racing across it along the tree line.

On the banks of Mills Pond, a hedge rustles and my heart lunges. Stopping, I squint into the dark, regretting ever coming out here. But the noise dies. Must've been an animal. I continue past Harrington Dormitory, the building's hulking shadow my only cover.

The old cathedral looms ahead now, a monstrous, gray, brick establishment with a spired bell tower, flying buttresses, and stained glass windows. Of course, it's condemned. During that fire back in the seventies, the windows burst and the brick was charred. Eventually, the bell was stolen. The building still stands, merely as a monument to the academy's long history. The cathedral we actually use is a replica on the other side of campus.

The last time I got anywhere near this place, the doors and windows on the ground floor were boarded shut. We must be meeting outside the cathedral and heading elsewhere. I spot the door, which is still boarded, but there aren't any society members huddled around, awaiting my arrival.

A thread of terror spins through me. Was this a setup? Did Annabelle only invite me here to humiliate me? Or worse. Is a pack of drunken society members about to rush out from behind that copse of trees and jump me?

My chest tightens. I want to turn on my phone's light to

get a better view of my surroundings, but I can't risk getting caught by security.

I reach the door, hoping for a note instructing me where to go from here.

Nothing.

Five minutes. I will wait exactly five minutes for someone to show up. If no one does, I'll head back to my warm bed.

I stand with my back to the door, so I can see whoever—or whatever—is coming. The campus is eerily silent at this hour. Crickets chirp in the distance, and occasionally, an owl hoots off in the woods that border the school. I cup my hands, blowing in them for warmth and ducking my head as far down into my coat as it will go.

When I start to pull out my phone to check the time, a grating sound slices through the night. I freeze. It sounded close. I force myself to breathe, and the tendrils of air swirl visibly before me. Another grate comes, like metal against concrete, followed by a clack.

I keep my head ducked low and step around the front of the building. Leaning slightly around the corner, I glimpse the place where the noises are coming from.

Propped against the side of the tower is an industrial-sized ladder. A dark figure stands on the cobblestone path, holding the base of the ladder while another figure climbs up, his feet banging on the rungs. From my concealed position, I watch this person reach the top and slide in through the tower's empty window frame, just below the space for the bell.

My vision spins. This is how to get to the initiation meeting. It's not enough that they bury you alive. They also expose you to extreme heights in the dark. And what happens on the other side? It's too high to jump.

I blink away the dizziness. I have to do this. These people know something about Polly's whereabouts. It's what she would've done for me. I force myself into the open, striding ahead toward the figure on the ground, who wears a long black cloak with a hood. I rifle through my purse, pull out as many of the pebbles as I can, and thrust them forward.

He or she—I still can't tell in this light—gives a curt headshake and motions toward the ladder.

I stuff the pebbles back into the purse and sling the strap across my chest to secure it. Gritting my teeth, I step onto the ladder, which is no easy feat in these kitten heels. Why the hell did they tell me to dress up if I was going to be scaling cathedrals and climbing through broken glass?

When I reach what I think is halfway, the ladder shifts. I glance down, finding that not only is the world spinning, but someone else is climbing up behind me. Someone who's not even bothering to wait for me to make it to the top. I turn my attention back up the ladder, trying to cinch my dress so I'm not flashing whoever's down there. My next step is quick, but as I put my weight on it, the heel slips off the rung.

Yelping, I slam into the ladder. I grip the rails with every ounce of strength in me. The darkness, the brick cathedral wall, the rungs—it all rotates until I'm not sure what's up or down.

But I hold on tightly, and a moment later, I regain my footing. Below me, Mr. Impatience lets out a serpentine "Shhhhh."

Sorry if my near-death experience almost blew your idiotic club's cover.

I take my time on the next step, struggling to catch my breath and to get these ridiculous heels to land on the rungs. At the top, I heft myself onto the windowsill and maneuver my body so that I'm perched in a sitting position, ready to face whatever death-defying stunt comes next.

But it's another ladder leading down. The darkness thickens inside the cathedral, with only the half-moon glow spilling in from the topmost windows to light it. I can't make out what awaits me below. The top few rungs of the ladder are visible, but the night washes the rest of it away.

I stretch my leg out onto the back side of the ladder. Praying another mysterious figure stands below to hold this one, my pulse pounds in my ears as I lower myself onto a rung I can't see. Above me, the ladder clanks as Mr. Impatient starts down.

If I survive the descent, maybe I'll shake the ladder a little.

Soon I touch ground, where I still can't see anything clearly. But I hear something.

Breathing.

My skin prickles. I don't know exactly how many others are in this condemned building with me, but there are people. Silent ones. They lurk in this space like an army of gargoyles slowly waking to life.

Mr. Impatient makes it down, slithering up behind me without a word, and now I'm positive coming here was the worst idea I've ever had.

Suddenly, a light blazes, illuminating the space.

Annabelle Westerly stands in the middle of a small crowd, holding a lantern—the ancient kind you light with a match. The base of the bell tower is in complete disarray, and I take care to avoid the holes in the ground as well as the collection of cobwebs. The small space leads to an ambulatory identical to the one in the new cathedral. Nine or ten group members seem to leak out of this small space into that one. Their faces are shrouded by black hoods, just like the figure outside. Only Annabelle and a few others, like Mr. Impatient, who has shifted into the shadows, are uncovered.

"Welcome," Annabelle says, a faint curve to her lips. She drops down onto her knees, setting the lantern onto the warped stone. Reaching toward the floor, she grasps something I can't quite distinguish, and tugs.

With a groan, the floor lifts.

One of the hooded figures approaches, dropping what I can only assume to be pebbles like mine into a basket beside the trapdoor. He whispers something before disappearing beneath the floor.

The other members line up, repeating this procedure over and over until only the uncloaked students remain.

We exchange uncertain glances, which I find strangely comforting. The guy beside me steps up to the trapdoor. I don't know his name, but he's always in the coffee shop. Orders a double espresso every time like a forty-five-year-old Wall Street executive. I consider stopping him to ask about the whispered words, but that might be against the rules. He drops his pebbles into the basket, whispers to Annabelle, and then ducks beneath the floor.

A girl is up next, Kara something or other. A Form II. I make an effort to press closer and listen, but I can't make out the words.

Think. Think. Think. The guy to my left, Mr. Impatient, steps forward, and my cheeks heat. I recognize him now as Remington Cruz, a Form III. Back in Form I, we were discussing donuts while waiting for a perpetually late professor, and I mentioned liking the cream-filled kind they sell in the coffee shop. The next day, he brought me one, and we ate our donuts together until Professor Gross showed up. I actually thought Remington liked me. So stupid. He got together with completely gorgeous Jane Blanchard a couple months later.

I start to ask something, but he steps forward, leaving

only me. Panic locks my jaw. Annabelle didn't say anything about a password.

But Diana did. At lacrosse practice. She mentioned the word *dust*.

The line from the invitation rolls back into my memory.

As soon as Remington disappears, I inch closer to Annabelle, massaging my sore jaw muscles with my thumb. "Victory or dust," I whisper, tossing the words like a shot on the buzzer. Annabelle doesn't respond, so I let the glass stones clink into the basket.

Then, placing my foot onto what appears to be a staircase, I lower myself down into a dark abyss.

FIVE

My foot touches ground and I wobble on my heel. A firm hand takes my arm and steadies me. I find myself looking up into Remington Cruz's dark features. I flush in embarrassment, but he smiles, his piercing brown eyes meeting mine. My stomach ripples the way it did when he handed me that damned donut.

Torches line the walls, illuminating a stone vault, its roof formed of several pillared arches. The tunnel stretches out ahead, its depths seemingly endless. The air is frigid. "What *is* this place?" I whisper to Remington, whose eyes are as wide as mine in the muted light.

"Some sort of crypt," he mutters.

A crypt. Meaning a place full of dead bodies. Buried bodies. This must be the place where they stuff us into a sarcophagus and wait until we cry mercy. I glance back at the trapdoor, only to see one of the hooded figures pull it shut.

There goes my way out of here.

"Welcome to the catacombs," Annabelle says, stepping into the center of the narrow vault, "a Gamemaster's Society secret. This series of underground tunnels was erected in 1850, before the academy was established, for this very society's purposes. If you should fail your initiation challenge, you must carry this secret to your grave. On pain of death."

Death? Catacombs built for a secret society? I scan the stone walls, searching for the sarcophagi or whatever it is they keep down here, and my gaze lands on a familiar symbol carved into the stone wall. The one from the wax seal: a circle slashed through the middle on a diagonal.

"A linchpin," a hooded boy beside me says, noting my focus. "The society's emblem."

"What's a linchpin?" I ask, keeping my voice low, but the boy flicks his chin toward Annabelle.

"I'm pleased and honored to announce that tonight we have a special guest member here to commence our initiation ritual." Off to the side, one of the figures lets her hood fall back, revealing a head full of glossy brown hair. When the woman's face pushes into the candlelight, a series of gasps resounds throughout the chamber. "Wait a minute," I say to Remington, whose lips are parted in awe, "isn't that—"

"Everyone, please give a warm welcome to Gianna Guardiola."

Everyone applauds as the actress moves to the front of the room. "But how?" I whisper, unable to process how I'm seeing the star of *Lady Legend* and countless other blockbusters a few yards away from me. In real life.

"I've heard she's a Major Supreme," whispers the hooded boy, as if that means something to me. "And when she was a Minor Supreme, the society worked some deal to keep her out of prison."

"What'd she do?" asks Kara, who presses in closer, standing on her tiptoes to get into this discussion.

But at the front, Gianna flashes her big-screen, professionally whitened smile at us, and the boy shushes Kara. "What an exciting night," Gianna says, gaze flitting from the hooded members and stopping to rest on the initiates. "You've been called here because we believe you may possess such values as our society upholds. Values such as competition, strength, cunning, and drive. To put it plainly, we esteem *winners*." She begins pacing in front of the display table, her heels clacking against the stone. "The society looks to our patron saint, the Greek hero Pelops, whom many scholars credit with the mythological origin of the Olympic games. Pelops sought the hand of Hippodamia, the daughter of King Oenomaus of Pisa. But the king feared an oracle foretelling his own death at the hands of his daughter's husband. The king challenged his daughter's suitor to a chariot race under the guarantee that if Pelops won, he could marry his daughter." Gianna's head tilts, her eyes narrowing. "If Pelops lost, however, his head would decorate the king's palace."

"Now, Pelops was not only handsome, but quite cunning. He bribed the king's charioteer, Myrtilos, into aiding him. Myrtilos exchanged the bronze linchpins that held together the king's wheels with wax ones. When the wax melted, King Oenomaus's chariot fell apart. The king was dragged to his death by his horses."

"To honor the fallen king and to thank the gods for his victory, Pelops held the first Games. The Gamemaster's Society was built upon this legend."

Obviously. Because this society is nuts. I glance at Remington, gauging his reaction, but he seems to be eating it up. "We prize neither legacy, nor seniority, nor sheer intelligence, nor wealth. All of those things will turn to dust the moment a stronger or cleverer opponent comes along. Just like the king."

Victory or dust. What the hell did Polly get herself into?

"Take me, for example," Gianna continues. "When the society found me, I was one bad binge away from expulsion and jail time. But they saw my true potential and unlocked it. I discovered my home and my forever place in this world." An almost palpable energy buzzes in the room as her chemically plumped pink lips arch. "Good luck, everyone."

Annabelle makes her way toward the display now, and Kara turns to the hooded boy. "You said something about Major Supreme. Is that the highest level?"

The boy stares out at her from beneath the dark fabric and then lets out an airy laugh. "Of course not. The highest you can achieve is to become the Gamemaster."

"Thank you, Gianna," Annabelle says, clapping lightly. She waits for the room to quiet down before motioning with an outstretched hand to a display of chalices, each ornamented with a small colored jewel. "Just as Pelops held the Games to honor those he credited with his success, we now hold our own games to honor him."

"And because they're fun!" shouts a hooded figure from somewhere at the back of the vault.

Annabelle's features pinch momentarily, but she laughs. "And because they are extremely diverting, of course. Now, it's time to see how strong and clever you are. Will my initiates please step forth?"

Here it comes. The part where she tells us to step into a sarcophagus. I move with the other three initiates, each of us stopping before a set of two chalices. Yellow and black jewels dangle from mine. Remington stands behind two chalices strung with green and red jewels. Kara is positioned on his other side, followed by Double Espresso on the far end.

"You have two chalices before you. One contains wine. The other..." Her lips curl deviously. "Poison."

My stomach squirms. She must be using the word *poison* for dramatics. It's probably a laxative—something designed to make us miserable for a few hours.

"You will be given a card with a clue. A scavenger hunt, so to speak. Your clue may lead you anywhere on the academy grounds. Be forewarned: getting caught by security will be an automatic disqualification. No two clues are alike, so don't bother attempting to cheat. If you solve your clue, it will lead to another card that will inform you which cup is safe to drink. All you have to do is return and drink the proper chalice's contents."

This doesn't sound so bad. She didn't even mention burying us alive.

"However," Annabelle continues, "as with any competition, there must be winners and losers. Only the fastest three contestants will be initiated into the Gamemaster's Society tonight. The fourth contestant will not."

My nerves buzz. If I'm last, I'll never be allowed back in. Other than Annabelle—who refused to comment on my best friend's whereabouts—I have yet to uncover the identity of a single member apart from Gianna Guardiola. I'm no closer to finding Polly than I was before I won the card game.

"Oh," Annabelle adds as an afterthought. "And think again about guessing. The wrong chalice will *kill* you."

Remington leans over to whisper something in my ear, but before he can say a word, Annabelle's hooded minions start passing each of us an envelope. When Remington and I try to accept ours, a low voice emerges from beneath the hood. "Phone first." He lays a palm out in front of us, shaking it impatiently.

I bite the inside of my cheek, but beside me, Remington is already handing his phone over. Taking a deep breath, I tug my phone from my purse and slam it into the guy's hand.

No sooner does he pass me the envelope than Annabelle says, "On your marks, get set..." Her hands unfurl at her sides—"go."

I tear open my envelope, letting it fall to the floor as I squint at my clue in the phantom light.

LOOK FOR THE BARD'S BOOK. YOUR ANSWER LIES SOMEWHERE ON THE PATH BETWEEN FLIES AND GODS.

The bard's book? My feet seem glued to the stone floor as the others spin around and head back through the tunnel. The swarm of hooded figures parts like the Red Sea to let them pass, pressing up against the walls as I race after them to the trapdoor.

I scramble to the top of the staircase, and my throat dries up.

I'd forgotten about the leaning ladder of doom.

The other three are already scaling it, one after the other. And this time, nobody's standing below, holding the base.

I force a swallow and peel off Polly's heels. Expensive leather or not, I can do this quicker barefoot. And I have to be quick. Discarding the heels, I step onto the first rungs. The entire thing quivers from the weight and movement of the others, but I'm a million times more stable without the heels. I make it up and over just after Double Espresso.

At the bottom, the others disperse, their shadowy shapes darting through the grounds. I start off barefoot in the direction of the library. Other places on campus with books exist—the bookshop, for example. But I have a feeling the creepy, seven-story library in the dead of night is more the society's style.

Fortunately, I recognize "the Bard" as a nickname for Shakespeare, thanks to Form II World Lit. But that's the extent of my progress. I figure I'll just pick up the Shakespeare collections and dump them all over, one by one, until the card with my answer falls out.

The bigger question is: how do I break into the library after hours?

My feet throb as I continue barefoot over the cobblestones, darting onto the squishy grass rather than sticking to the path, which takes a wide, scenic course to my destination. These mangled feet are going to kill during tomorrow's practice. Remington plays as many sports as I do, so he's in equally good shape. But my speed may be an advantage over the other two initiates.

The lawn ends in another path, which I take around the mail center before abandoning it to push through one final copse of trees.

Shadows bleed from the library building as I slink up to the doors. To my disappointment, no society member is waiting to congratulate me on deciphering half the clue and wave me in with a key card. I'm alone with the shadows.

I scan the front of the building for another ladder or some way to breach it. With no answer, I reach for the door handle with a stiff arm and turn the lever.

It clicks and opens. My head sinks forward in relief. But there isn't time to celebrate. I've got to find the Bard's books.

An elevator looms to the left, but I can't risk getting caught on the cameras. Instead, I take the staircase up to the fourth floor, where the classical collections are kept. Back in World Lit, we had to write a research paper comparing a Shakespearian play to a modern retelling. I mainly used the online databases, but I borrowed a couple sources from this aisle. I approach it, the sheer volume of Shakespeare's works on the shelves pushing on my chest like smog-filled air. I reread the clue, hoping it will spark some memory from World Lit: YOUR ANSWER LIES SOMEWHERE ON THE PATH BETWEEN FLIES AND GODS.

Between flies and gods. The line sets off a nagging thought at the back of my brain. I've read something about flies and gods before, but I'm too hyped up and panicky to remember. I stuff the clue back into my purse and reach for the nearest tome: Shakespeare's comedies. I riffle the pages, turn the anthology over, and shake. Nothing. I drop it to the floor and move on to the next one.

Five collections later, I'm just wasting time. My mind tumbles and spins. If I could just slow down, maybe I could solve the clue systematically. It does sound familiar.

What did we read during World Lit? The focus was histories and tragedies, so I pull out that anthology and skim the table of contents.

Richard III. We read that one, but it's not stirring a fly-related memory.

Hamlet. We read that one too. Maybe that's it. I locate a copy of the play itself and flip through rapidly, giving it a good shake. Nothing.

Grinding my teeth, I return to the table of contents, my finger tracing the titles. *Macbeth*. We read selections from it, but I don't know. I keep going, skimming title after title until my finger stops. It trails back up, landing on *King Lear*.

Hope expands in my chest. There's a beggar in the story. Gloucester. He makes a comment—something about flies and little boys pulling off their wings. In class, we read the play aloud, and when we came to this line, a few guys snickered and Liana Gerard went off on them, calling them bullies.

I reach for the play, my hope wavering: three copies stand on the shelf. I yank all of them down and start riffling toward the back of one. I don't remember exactly which act, but it was near the end. Nothing tumbles from the first one, so I grab the second copy and search.

Sure enough, in act 4, a minuscule, arrow-shaped tab clings to the page, in the center of a line:

"'As flies to wanton boys are we to th' gods.'"

I remove the sticky tab, shoving the book into a stream of moonlight coming from the window. The words are written in tiny script.

Choose ye black, poison lack. One sip of yellow shall kill a fellow.

It's a warped play on that saying about snakes. I shut off my light and make for the stairs.

Down in the open air, I sprint with everything in me toward the old cathedral. Still barefoot, I keep to the shadows of the mail center, Polly's purse flapping against my waist. My once-combed hair whips into my eyes and sticks to my lipstick. I fly through the cool, prickly grass to the final stretch of cobblestone.

Off the path, something barrels like a wild animal over the hill leading to the lawn. My heart stops and my feet skid to a painful halt against the rough stone.

But it's only another initiate, about to beat me back to the ladder.

I ignore the pain in my toes and sprint over the stone

until my lungs nearly burst, reaching the bottom of the ladder seconds before my competitor.

I scramble up, feeling the ladder jolt as the other initiate starts behind me. A new fear suddenly spikes in my chest, and I grip the rails with sweaty fingers. The society is all about winning, no matter the cost. What if this person tries to pull me off?

I hurry, struggling against the horrible thought that I'm about to be overcome. I wait for the inevitable feel of a hand on my bare foot.

But it doesn't come, and I reach the window. Making use of my strategy from earlier, I flip myself around to the front of the ladder and descend.

I jump the last few feet, landing with a thump. Only the moonlight guides my path as I fly to the trapdoor and clamber down the staircase.

Below, the lanterns still flicker, highlighting hooded figures posed in clumps along the walls. I peer past them to the display of chalices, and my entire body heaves in a sigh of relief.

I'm the first initiate to make it back.

But steps clunk behind me, and I race for the cup.

Lifting the ink-jeweled chalice to my lips, I push aside the screaming doubts and gulp it down.

My competitor, who I now see is Remington, pulls up next to me, slamming his hands down on the table and turning to me, eyes wide, the warmth drained from his face. "Which of these jewels is red?" he asks, voice frazzled. "Please, I can't tell."

Startled, I point to the chalice with the crimson-colored jewel dangling from the stem. Remington hesitates, having placed his life completely in the hands of his competition. But he reaches for the chalice I indicated and downs it with one flick of the wrist.

The wine works its way into my stomach, warming it. My head spins with what I hope is alcohol and not a lethal poison.

"Congratulations," Annabelle says, gliding across the stones to shake our hands. She reaches toward me with some sort of necklace. I realize she expects me to bend down. I submit, and she fastens a silver chain around my neck. While she repeats the gesture for Remington, I straighten, letting the pendant lie flat in my palm.

A silver linchpin.

"Keep the pendant on you at all times," Annabelle says, "but wear it discreetly. You are now members of the Gamemaster's Society. Victory or dust."

"Victory or dust," Remington repeats without missing a beat.

"Victory or dust," I mumble, still shaky from the wine and all the running.

Behind us, the staircase rumbles and Kara spills down into the crypt. Her face is pale as she lurches toward us. "Do you—will you tell me the answer?" she calls out to us. "I couldn't solve my clue, and that other guy, he's right behind me."

In horror, I look to Annabelle.

"She doesn't care if we cheat," Kara presses. "Remember Ponchus? Or Pepcid? Or whatever his name was. He won by cheating!"

And sure enough, Annabelle stays silent, a sly curve to her mouth.

"Please," Kara begs. "I need this more than you can imagine."

"Remember the rules?" Remington asks, almost apologetically. "We can't cheat because all of our clues were different."

Kara's head tips back in desperation. "Fine, then." I'm certain she's going to concede; instead, she marches straight up to her pair of chalices, takes a deep breath, and grabs the one with a green jewel.

"Do remember," Annabelle warns, an unsettling calm to her voice, "the wrong chalice will kill you."

Kara sets the chalice back down, gnawing on her bottom lips. Her hand remains on the stem as her eyes flood with tears.

Behind us on the staircase, the final initiate, Double Espresso, clambers down.

Kara's hand darts to the other chalice, this one strung with a purple jewel.

"No!" I shout, and Remington is already lunging for her.

But she gulps it down, terror flooding her eyes as she spins to face us.

SIX

I RUSH TOWARD KARA, FEAR AND WINE FOGGING MY BRAIN. *Please be okay. Please, please be okay.*

She staggers, and Remington catches her. "Why would she do that?" I shout, helping Remington lower her to the stone floor. The final initiate blazes down the tunnel, darting wide eyes at Kara before lumbering on to the display. Clutching a stem with a garnet-colored jewel, he guzzles the thick, red liquid and slams the chalice down victoriously.

On the floor, Kara inhales a deep, wheezing breath. She exhales slowly, her lids fluttering.

Then she sits up. "I...I think I'm fine," she says, peering down at her extremities uncertainly. My body sinks in a wave of relief. "Would I know by now if I drank the poison?" Kara asks Annabelle.

"Oh yes," she answers through a laugh. "You'd be writing and spasming on the floor. Your lungs would essentially be melting, so you'd be spitting them out, not speaking." Smiling, Annabelle bends down to place the final chain around Kara's neck. "You're a bit winded—a bit dramatic too, for that matter. But not dying. Congratulations, you three. Welcome to the Gamemaster's Society."

After what Kara just put us through, I'm far from proud. I help her to her feet with a shaky hand, even though I'd like to shove her back over.

Annabelle's attention falls onto Double Espresso, whose real name I still haven't learned. "Unfortunately, you are not society material." She frowns. "You will be escorted out and must take our secret to the grave, on pain of death."

A hunched-over Double Espresso barely has time to grunt before a swarm of hooded minions prods him toward the trapdoor.

As soon as they've gone, our phones are returned and the remaining society members begin to push back their hoods, revealing some familiar faces; Torrey-Wells Academy only has four hundred students. The nine members vary in age. This surprises me at first, until I remember what Gianna said about not valuing seniority.

But shock bolts through me when I spot Larissa Gaines from my lacrosse team, who denied the society's existence at practice, standing with her back pressed against the nearest pillar. She offers a small wave, and I force one in return.

I continue squinting into the dim light until my gaze lands on one face that forces my lips to part.

Freaking Gavin Holt.

He's slouching against the stone wall with a smug grin, his brown hair disheveled, ridiculous robe draped over him. I'm tempted to march over and slap him in front of everyone. He was a member this entire time. He could've told me what I needed to know about Polly and saved me from this entire night of terror.

Annabelle begins her gliding gait toward the trapdoor. "Tomorrow night, the three of you will get to experience a real meeting of the Gamemaster's Society. We'll assemble here promptly at 8 p.m., before the Masquerade Ball. Dress in your finest."

That's right. The ball is tomorrow night. Are we dressing up because we'll be attending? Or is this meeting in place of the dance? Before I get a chance to ask the more pressing question—how we're supposed to climb that massive ladder in front of a campus full of ball-goers—Annabelle adds as an afterthought, "Oh, and you'll be admitted through the members' old cathedral entrance from now on. You'll find it on the south side of the building, if you look hard enough."

My fists tighten. Of course there's an easier way inside this place. One more deadly exhibition I could've avoided if Gavin hadn't lied to me about being denied membership.

Annabelle climbs the staircase, the hem of her immaculate gown clutched between slender white fingers, and the other members line up behind her. Beside me, Remington inches closer. "Hey, Maren." He smiles, and the firelight flickers over his dark eyes.

"Hey," I say, trying not to get squashed by the herd in this small, airless space.

"It's a relief to have a friend in here."

"Yeah," I say, and my insides completely overreact to the way he called me a friend.

"I guess congratulations are in order." He extends a hand.

"You too." I shake his hand, finding it astonishingly warm compared to my frigid one.

"And thanks for what you did back there."

"What else was I going to do? Point to the green one and let the color-blind kid ingest lung-melting poison?"

Stunned, he chokes out a laugh. He places a hand on my back, using his sturdy frame to help steer me through the others. "It's all pretty bizarre, huh?"

"Thank you for noticing!" I glance behind us, tucking a loose strand of hair behind my ear. "I felt like I was on some prank show the entire night."

"It's definitely odd. But I guess...worth it, right?"

"You've been wanting to take up acting?"

He laughs. "No, but my dad was a member, and he credits the society with all of his career success. According to him,

every Ivy League school has a member on its board. As long
as we make it to Minor Supreme, we're pretty much guaran-
teed a place wherever we want to go. And if we make it to
Majors"—he shrugs—"the sky's the limit."

I guess that's why someone like Remington Cruz would
want to get into the society. And it explains why someone as
brilliant and lazy as Gavin Holt would use a secret society
to cut corners. But it doesn't explain why Polly joined. She
wasn't seduced by pomp or flash. Her giving up Europe was
proof of that.

Unless I was only fooling myself, believing she'd changed
from that person she was in middle school because of me.
Maybe Annabelle was right. Maybe the money—the dreams
of Hollywood and camera lights—became an obsession she
was willing to risk everything for.

We reach the staircase, and Remington motions for me to
go first. I scramble up, conscious again of my dress dangling
open as he waits below. I grapple with it, attempting to cinch
it tight, and my face heats despite the chilly air.

Up on the ground floor, I lean down to inspect my battered
feet. "Well played," comes a low voice behind me that isn't
Remington's.

"You are dead," I snap, spinning on Gavin.

"Shhh." He leans closer, and it takes everything in me
not to shove him. "Would you just calm down?" Beneath the
moonlight that pours in through the empty windows, he lifts

his hands in an act of passivity. Slower this time, he nears me, his warm breath tickling my neck as he whispers into my ear, "You can't let it slip that I told you about the Gamemaster."

I jerk away, too mad to think. I stride toward the towering ladder, but he grabs my wrist and pulls me along in the opposite direction. Remington and a few others dot the wall ahead, ducking under a section that hinges like a flap. Must be the members' entrance.

When we reach the wall, Gavin lifts the flap, holding it while I crawl through. Outside, black figures shift through the night and break off toward various dormitories. I slink over the cobblestone, trying to ditch Gavin—my heels are still on the far side of the cathedral—but he catches up to me, reaching for my arm again. "Maren, I'm sorry, okay?" he hisses. "But I did break the cardinal rule just by telling you how to get an invitation."

"Tell me about these levels."

"Stations," he corrects, and I dart him a murderous glare. "Sorry. There are five. First, Initiates." He makes a grand gesture toward me and I kick him in the ankle. "Minor Supreme is the second station," he says, hopping momentarily on one foot. "Then there's Medi Supreme, Major Supreme, and Gamemaster. You usually move up by winning select competitions."

"And what do the stations mean?"

"Initiate just means you're in. But Minor Supreme means

you've proven yourself. You get to call upon the society for favors."

"Like Gianna and the prison thing?"

"Possibly."

"Like the numerous explosions that have magically gone unnoticed by the school?"

Gavin bites his lower lip and makes to turn onto the grass of the Commons, but he stops, thrusting a hand out in front of me. Before I can sock him in the arm, he turns, raising an index finger to his mouth.

I listen until the sound of footsteps on cement reaches my ears. A low hum follows. A few yards away, a security guard is pacing the grounds by the vending machines along the side of the cement quad.

Gavin grabs my hand and lightly tugs me back the way we came. "We'll have to go around the pond," he whispers.

I nod, even though the idea of trekking all the way around Mills Pond makes my tired head hurt. I shake off Gavin's hand, trying to play back his words about Minor Supremes, and my mind flashes to Polly the day she was called into the headmistress's office. Maybe something happened. Something she later needed to call in a favor for. "What do you know about Polly?"

Gavin shrugs. "Every year we have two initiations, fall and spring. Each one has a tournament. Back in the fall, Polly was quite a competitor, one of Annabelle's favorites." Our feet squelch along the muddy bank, and Gavin takes a route straight through the tall grass and hedges. "But she couldn't hack it."

"Meaning she didn't want to compete in potentially life-threatening games anymore?"

"That back there wasn't *life-threatening*, Maren. Nobody forced Kara to drink anything. But the games are highly competitive. And taxing. They can wear on a person."

"Why not just drop out of the society, then? Why leave the academy?"

"It can be"—he pauses—"complicated. Especially if she already called in her favor. Which I'm pretty sure she did."

"What do you mean?"

At the fitness center, Gavin glides along the side of the building, avoiding the lamplight, and I copy him.

"I don't know, Maren. But she was a scholarship student, right?"

"Yeah."

"And the last few months, she wasn't dressing like one, was she?"

"Oh." Maybe I was wrong to assume all those expensive things in Polly's closet were gifts from Annabelle. "So you're saying the society gave her money?"

"It's a thought. Maybe she felt an obligation to give the money back if she stayed at Torrey-Wells."

A fear spikes in my head, high and sharp. He could be right. This whole past year, Polly abandoned me for someone better—some*thing* better. And wealthier. Did she simply take it a step further that night? If she was planning to escape with the society's money, it would explain the jitters I saw out on the lawn.

"She's not a thief," I finally spit, batting the idea away. There has to be more going on here.

Gavin opens his mouth to argue, but a whistle drifts on the breeze, and we duck behind the health center. The first rays of sunlight glimmer in the distance. The path to my building is clear, but it won't stay that way for long.

"I have more questions," I say. "You're going to tell me everything about Polly. Tomorrow night, when you walk me to the meeting. I'll see you outside my dorm at a quarter 'til."

Gavin grins. "Like a date."

"Shut up," I growl, eyeing his stupid cloak again. "And for once in your life, wear something halfway normal, please."

SEVEN

AFTER MY SATURDAY MORNING ELECTIVE, THE ONLY THING I want in life is a nap. But we've got a preseason lacrosse scrimmage against Meadow Green Prep.

My head is completely out of the game from the get-go, and it shows. By the end of the first half, I've missed a dozen shots, and Meadow Green is up by two goals.

Frustrated, I slump down on the bench and jab at the grass with the shaft of my lacrosse stick, avoiding my teammates' stares. Coach is so baffled by my performance, she barely even yells at me during the halftime talk. I've never been this unfocused on the field before. I've allowed everything going on with the society to interfere with my game, and now the whole team is paying for it.

"What's up with you today?" asks Valeria as the others wander back onto the field.

"Sorry, I was up late studying." I adjust my goggles. "I'll pick it up."

"You'd better." She takes one last gulp of water and picks up her stick. "We're counting on you."

As we get into position for the second half, I replay Valeria's short-winded pep talk in my head. I let it consume my thoughts, pushing out my tiredness, the distractions. *Get in the game, Montgomery.*

The whistle blows for the opening draw, and I sprint toward the loose ball, snatching it up for my team. Ball in pocket, I sprint down the field, weaving in and out of the opposition, my teammates' voices cheering me on. My heart pumps and my vision tunnels, everything blurring by in my periphery, only the goal in focus. Dodging another defender, I spot my opening. I release the ball, which sails past the goalie into the back of the net.

The crowd erupts, and my teammates rush to congratulate me. "There she is," Valeria says, slapping me on the back. "Now, do it again."

I do. Six more times, to be exact, landing us a 15–13 lead.

Still riding the high of the win, I return to my room. I start gathering my shower caddy and towel when my phone rings.

Plopping down onto a beanbag chair, I answer it. "Hey, Dad."

"Hi, sweetie. How are you?" He sounds as tired as I feel, and I realize it's Saturday. Our weekly call is on Sundays.

"I'm fine. What's going on?"

He clears his throat, his go-to stalling tactic. "Well, I'm hoping it's nothing, but I wanted to prepare you, just in case."

I sit up, my free hand grasping a section of the beanbag so tightly I can feel the individual beans through the fabric. Is he sick? Is it my mom? "Just say it, Dad."

"Sorry, sorry. Didn't mean to worry you. It's not life or death. I've just had a bit of trouble at the plant this year. Things never picked up after Christmas, and now one of your lenders is backing out."

The knot of panic in my chest loosens. "What does that mean?"

"Without the loan, we won't be able to cover your tuition for the term. I'll try to call around, figure something out. But you've got to make sure you keep up your end of the deal, okay? Don't let your GPA drop even a hundredth of a point."

"What happens if you can't find a new lender?" But I know the answer. If we can't get a new loan, the academy will kick me out. I'll have to finish the rest of high school at East Derry High, which is fine in theory. Except at Torrey-Wells, soccer starters have nearly a 70 percent chance at a college scholarship. East Derry's soccer team—their entire division—is ranked so low, I'll end up smaller than a blip on any university's radar.

It also means my days in the society may be numbered. If I'm going to find out what really happened to Polly, I'll have to hurry up.

"Let's just hope it doesn't come to that," my dad says.

When I reach the garden at my dormitory's entrance, dressed in Polly's sparkling silver V-neck dress, Polly's glittery mask from last year's ball tucked into my clutch, I think Gavin has stood me up. But I spot him ambling up the pathway, lampposts illuminating his lean figure.

"Miss Montgomery." His eyes widen and he staggers in exaggerated fashion, grasping the handrail that borders the garden. "You look simply stunning."

He doesn't look too bad either in his black tux, with his hair combed for once. "It's nice to see you changed out of your pajamas for the occasion." He tries to link an arm with mine, and I swat it away. "All right, spill. Tell me everything you know about Polly."

"I tried to tell you last night." Gavin shrugs, kicking a rock off the pathway. "Polly was doing great in the fall tournament. Moved up a couple ranks, and then one night, she missed a round of the games. We figured she was sick or something, only she never turned up."

"So there's nothing else? You people didn't bury her in a sarcophagus and forget about her?"

Gavin rolls his eyes.

"I just—I can't believe there isn't a connection between her leaving and the society. Polly seemed perfectly happy last year, and this year she befriends Annabelle, joins your twisted society, and then she's suddenly too distraught to continue on at the academy? I don't buy it."

We turn in front of Mills Pond, avoiding the aggressive geese that stand guard on its banks, and head up the slope leading to the old cathedral. The wind kicks at an oak tree off the path, flapping its leaves. "Well, if there's more to the story, you're in the right place to find it."

"Then you do think there's more to the story."

"No, that's not—" Gavin, apparently forgetting he actually styled his hair, drags his fingers through it, causing a brown tuft to stand on end. "I'm just saying *if*. I don't think there's more. But *if* your suspicions should prove founded, there's no better place to do some digging than from the inside."

"Which is the reason I put myself through that freaky initiation last night, if you'll remember."

"You just can't get caught. If Annabelle ever knew your heart wasn't really in the society…"

"What?" I say, hiking up my dress to avoid drenching it in a swampy section of path. "What would that Victorian Barbie do if she knew?"

"I don't know. But it wouldn't be good."

A sensation like a phantom breath rolls over my skin. For the first time since I've known him, Gavin sounds serious.

Several minutes of silence pass before I ask, "What station are you, Gavin?"

"Medi Supreme."

"So what happens when you become a Major?"

"*If* I become a Major—and it's a big *if*—I mean, you saw Gianna Guardiola. You can be anything. Have anything." I glance up from the mud to find his face lit with excitement. "The society makes dreams come true." His eyes glimmer with amusement now, and he starts humming the *Pinocchio* theme song.

But I don't laugh when I ask, "And what is it you want so much?"

The sparkle dims. "You wouldn't understand."

I start to argue, but Gavin pulls ahead, leading us around to the south side of the cathedral. He plays lookout while I push through the false door, crawling on hands and knees, trying not to tear Polly's expensive dress as the cement path converts to worn stone.

Once through, I stand up, brushing off the delicate fabric and making sure the V hangs in the right place. My linchpin pendant is fastened onto my bracelet, hidden among the other baubles I've received from my parents every year since I was eight—a rabbit from the year I was obsessed with bunny memorabilia, the panda from the year we went to the zoo, the heart from a year my parents didn't know what I was into, et cetera. Where is Gavin hiding his pendant? I examine his suit, his shiny black shoes, the coat. It's probably easier for guys, with all the pockets on their formal wear. The plunging V of my dress, on the other hand, leaves very little storage space.

I approach the trapdoor, and my heart sinks. The basket is there, and I'm all out of those rocks.

Gavin catches up with me, and before I can say anything, he grabs my hand. I start to wrench it away, but a series of cool, slick objects press into my palm. "*Peluio*," he says. "Translated *pebbles*, they represent the ones used in a common Greek game."

"And you just happen to carry a stash of these pebbles on you?"

"You were supposed to take a few last night on your way out. We recycle them." Sensing my frustration, he smiles, his eyes warm as he slips his hand onto my lower back. "You'll see," he says with a gentle nudge. "The society is really just about games. There's this huge tournament finale coming up next week. You're going to love it."

"I didn't come here to play games," I whisper, dropping my pebbles into the basket.

Down below, the lanterns are blazing again. This time, instead of hooded cloaks, the crypt is decked in sparkling formal attire. In place of silver chalices, bite-size hors d'oeuvres adorn the display.

The members are huddled off in dark corners, sipping from what I hope are non-poisoned glasses. Gavin grabs a shrimp and sidles over to chat up some guy.

Annabelle, draped in a red floor-length gown, her hair coiled on top of her head, blond wisps perfectly draping the front of her face, breaks away from her group to greet me. "Maren," she says, leaning in for a hug, "you look just divine."

"As do you," I return, trying out the posh-speak once more to no avail.

"We're just about to get started. This is one of my favorite society games. I can't wait for you to partake."

She squeezes my hand and drifts over to the display. There, she lifts a glass, clinking a knife against it. "May I have your attention, please? Our game is about to begin. The rules are simple. Once everyone is partnered up and given their first *illicit* task, we will head over to the ball. Each time you complete a task, you will receive a gold coin. The first team to obtain three gold coins wins. Take note: opening your envelope before entering the ball is expressly forbidden. Also, if you are caught by any of the teacher chaperones or the other students at the ball, you will be disqualified. Are you dying to hear the prize?" The room breaks into applause and howls as Annabelle keeps them in anticipation.

"The winning team will move up an entire station."

A collective gasp sounds, followed by another round of

applause. An entire station. Meaning I would become a Minor Supreme. Just like Polly. My mind floods with thoughts of my dad. The tired, worried edge to his voice on the phone earlier today. I know he's afraid of disappointing me.

What if he didn't have to be? If Minor Supreme means calling in a favor, would the society be able to pay off my loan? I look to Gavin to ask, but he's leaning against the opposite wall.

"When I call out your names," Annabelle says, reaching behind her for a stack of envelopes, "you will step forward. First up, Donella and Paul."

A blond girl wearing a fluttery black dress approaches Annabelle, followed by a tall guy with russet-brown curls and a sharp gray tux. They are handed a single envelope and dismissed to wait back by the trapdoor. Annabelle continues to announce the teams. When I hear Gavin's name, my heartbeat races in hope. Gavin might be tired of my questions, but at least I know him. And, if I'm honest, I have fun with Gavin. When he isn't annoying me. "And Larissa," Annabelle coos. My hope dies like an ant under a boot. Now who am I going to be partnered with? Up at the display, Gavin glances over his shoulder at me, his expression unreadable.

A new thought sneaks its way into my head, bolstering my spirits. Maybe Annabelle paired herself with me. She did seem rather *nice* when she greeted me. The more time we spend together, the better chance she'll spill what she knows about Polly. "Maren," Annabelle calls out, looking up to beam at me with brilliant white teeth. "And Remington." Excitement clashes with disappointment in me. "Best of luck to the neophytes."

On the one hand, I get to spend the evening with Remington Cruz. On the other hand, the society paired me with another newbie. Now we have no shot at winning. But I guess as long as the losers aren't forced to drink poison or spend the night in the catacombs, I don't really care. I just have to pretend to play, so I can get closer to these people. These people who will hopefully lead me to Polly.

I spot Remington across the tunnel, and together we make our way to the front to retrieve our task. He takes the envelope, and we meander to a clear space by a pillar.

"So, are you ready to smear cake in fancy hairdos?" he asks, waggling his brows.

"I thought we were going to pin tails on the backs of girls' dresses."

He laughs. "Speaking of dresses. Yours is nice."

"Better than the sweatpants, you think?"

"Not better," he says, tilting his head. "Just...different." In the winking lantern light, I try not to blush.

When the last members are paired and the tasks dealt, Anabelle clacks down the tunnel toward us. "One last thing," she adds, that wicked grin on her ruby red lips. "Thwarting your opponents is highly encouraged." All around, murmurs ripple through the room, the atmosphere sharpening. "Masks on, everyone. May the gods grant you favor tonight. *Victory or dust.*"

The mantra is repeated. As the teams begin clambering up the stairs, the words still hum in my ears.

EIGHT

The Masquerade Ball is held in the Grand Banquet Hall, like it is every year. Classical music rings through the air. Remington and I make it through the double doors, the elaborate rose and gold décor a flash in our periphery before he tears open the envelope.

The top half of Remington's face is covered in a villain-esque black mask with a long, thin crooked nose. It reminds me of "The Cask of Amontillado," a short story we had to read for World Lit, about a guy who eventually buries another guy in a vault. I try not to think about this as Remington reads, his voice barely audible above the shrill orchestral notes. *"Your task is to change the music to a tune of which the headmistress would never approve."*

My gaze floats around the room, skimming blush-colored globes of twine draped from the ceiling and white and gold flickering lanterns clumped on the refreshments table, before eventually landing on Dr. Hutchins, the ancient math teacher playing DJ on the expensive sound system. "How are we supposed to do that?"

Remington shrugs. "I should be able to figure out the system. The better question is how to get past Dr. Hutchins."

"I can try to distract her," I offer, taking the card from him and ripping it into shreds over a trash bin wrapped in gilt tulle. "I took Algebra II from her last year." Indicating the decimated pile in the trash, I add, "Just so none of the other teams can figure out our task."

"Good idea. Well, here goes nothing, I guess." Remington offers his arm, and my cheeks sizzle. Instead of refusing like I did Gavin's, I take Remington's arm, feeling his strong football player muscles through the coat sleeve. But guilt knots my stomach. Last year, Remington always had his girlfriend, Jane Blanchet, pasted to his side. I hope I'm not treading on her petite and probably perfect feet. Now that I think about it, though, I haven't seen them together in a while. Maybe they broke up. This is the thought I repeat to myself as I glide around the room, a queen on a king's arm.

We reach Dr. Hutchins, and I wish I'd spent the brief walk over here rehearsing my distraction speech rather than contemplating Remington Cruz's love life. "Dr. Hutchins." I smile, lifting my mask momentarily so she can recognize me. "How are you?"

"Maren," she says, matching my enthusiasm. Considering how quiet I was in her class, I'm relieved she remembered my name.

I station myself so that she's forced to turn away from the equipment. "I really miss your class," I lie, fiddling with my clutch. "I mean, don't get me wrong, Dr. Stravinsky is great too. You just had a way of getting those tough concepts across. Um...where did you go to school to learn how to teach?"

"Well," Dr. Hutchins says, her eyes gleaming with pride. I hit the exact right note. "I started at Columbia for my undergrad, followed by my teaching credential. This was back in"—her lips twist in thought—"1968, I believe. No, that's incorrect. 1969." She chuckles, like it's a big relief we got that straightened out. "Then I transferred to Yale for my MA and my PhD. Both in mathematics." Behind her, Remington is still squinting at the panels and the laptop that seems to control everything.

"Wow, that is impressive. No wonder you have such a gift." I shoot Remington a discreet *hurry-it-along* look, but he doesn't catch it.

"You're very sweet, my dear," Dr. Hutchins says, running her hands over the length of her velvet gown. The song is winding down, and I catch the distracted moment Dr. Hutchins realizes she needs to cue up the next one.

"Do you ever offer tutoring to students during your office hours?" I ask, attempting to reel her back in. "If they're not your current students, I mean." Remington finally has his fingers on the keyboard. Sweat beads on my forehead; this place is stifling.

Dr. Hutchins's head tilts in thought. "I can't say I've ever been asked before." Beyond her head of cotton curls, Remington slips away into the throngs of dancers. "I suppose, if the hours aren't occupied by—"

The last trilling violin note fades away. For an excruciating moment, I wait, certain another classical number is about to start playing. But the synthesizer starts in, followed by a lively drum beat as a pop number pulses through the speakers. Before Dr. Hutchins can bat an eye, the artist is making dirty innuendos. The room erupts with whooping as the choreographed waltz breaks into a frenzy of thrusting hips.

"Wha—did you see—" Dr. Hutchins begins, spinning around to grab for the laptop.

"No, sorry, ma'am. I wasn't paying attention. Do you need help?"

"No, it's—" She emits a guttural sound and presses one hand to her forehead, the other still toying with the controls. I sidle off into the manic crowd just as a bass note is replaced by the pluck of a harp.

The students moan and giggle as they reshape, the teacher chaperones shaking heads and waggling fingers at some particularly enthusiastic dancers. I find Remington toward the back of the room and tip my head in commendation. "Love the song choice," I say, high-fiving him discreetly. "So how are we supposed to get our next task?"

He turns his other hand over, revealing a brand-new card. "Some girl in a mask and fairy wings just handed it to me."

"Wow." I steal a peek over my shoulder. "That was fast."

"It's like they're watching us." His gaze floats to the ceiling, where cameras blink in every corner. He digs a hand into his jacket pocket, flashing me a hint of gold. "This coin was inside the second envelope."

A couple fumbling through the waltz bumps into me, apologizing profusely. Remington checks to make sure I'm all right, but my eyes fasten on to the back of the boy who nearly knocked me over. The one whose tuxedo jacket has a large red GS painted onto it.

I nudge Remington with an elbow, but a quick scan of the room turns up two—make it three—other vandalized jackets. "It must've been another team's task," I say.

"There are going to be some unhappy people in this room very soon."

"Then we should hurry. What does the card say?"

"'Your next task is to obtain an opponent's linchpin pendant,'" he reads. He rips up the card like I did the last round.

"Two problems," I say, fanning myself with my clutch and wishing we could afford to take a punch break. I force myself to ignore the allure of the table sparkling with orange and white frosted cakes and a crystal bowl of pink punch, raspberries floating on top like jewels. "One, I'd barely recognize most of our opponents, especially considering the masks. And two, no one is going to let us get that close. I could see if we were dancing, maybe, but none of our opponents are going to waste precious moments in this game to slow dance. Not for anything."

"They might. I know I'd be tempted to waste precious moments," he says, blushing, "if you were asking me to dance."

My already hot face scorches. The clutch halts in midair as my gaze drops to the polished wood floors. There is no way a guy like Remington Cruz is flirting with *Sweatpants Girl*. I already learned this lesson with the donuts. "Uh, right," I mumble. "But seriously, the only guy in the society I even know is Gavin Holt. And he'd never fall for me asking him to dance. We have sort of a hate-hate relationship."

"You mean that guy who helped you out of the cathedral last night?" Remington asks, forehead wrinkled. "He didn't look like he hated you. Not at all."

"Wha—" But I don't have time to play *what-the-hell-did-he-mean-by-that*? We've got a game to win, and the same competitive buzz that fuels me during every lacrosse match, basketball tournament, and soccer game runs through me now. "I'm not asking Gavin to dance. Next suggestion."

"I could be the distraction this time," he offers. "If it were you, what could I say or do to divert your attention long enough to allow someone to swipe your jewelry?" He peers down at me doubtfully, like he doesn't have a shot. Like he didn't have a gorgeous girlfriend the past two years. Up close, I notice the small scar left by a hard hit in football back in Form I. It runs through his right eyebrow, amplifying that ruggedly handsome appeal, and it's possible I spent way too much time staring at him when he wore a bandage over it in Professor Gross's class.

"Hmm," I say, trying to think past the obvious answer: *Pretty much anything.* "I missed that Intro to Pickpocketing seminar during Form I, but maybe we could stage something. Spill a cup of punch down the front of her dress, you know, 'accidentally.' Then start making a big deal of helping. Whip out your dad's checkbook, if need be."

"Right. The checkbook I keep on me for just such an emergency."

"Exactly."

Remington rests his chin on a fist for a moment. Then, his head of short, dark curls whips in the direction of the dancefloor. "That girl there." He points out a blond with a black dress. The girl I saw down in the crypt when Annabelle paired us up. Her feathered mask reminds me of a raven.

"Oh yeah. Diana or Dora or something."

"Donella," he says, and I feel a bizarre pinch in my gut that he remembered so easily. "Earlier I was trying to figure out what we're even supposed to do with these pendants—mine's in my front pocket, by the way. I don't imagine anyone successfully taking it. Yours, on the other hand..." He tips his head toward my bracelet, which I tuck behind my back in embarrassment. "Anyway, I started trying to figure out where our new friends were keeping theirs." I resist the urge to cut in and blurt that I was playing that very same game in the crypt. "I noticed Donella is wearing a silver chain around her neck that disappears beneath the neckline of her dress."

"And the pendant is probably tucked inside," I finish for him. "Hmm. You may be"—my cheeks burn—"easy on the eyes and everything...but if she recognizes you from the ceremony, she won't let you get close enough to swipe it."

"Except she might." His gaze sweeps the floor. "I happen to know she's had a crush on me since Form I."

"Oh." *Oh.* "That's pretty insidious, dude."

"Yeah, you're right." He facepalms. "Next idea."

I try to think, but the more I watch the dancers, the more my brain shifts to thoughts about Polly. Her in that collage photo, wearing a hot pink ball gown as we drank Sprite out of champagne flutes we bought at the dollar store downtown. There weren't any classes for Form IIs, since the entire grade was supposed to be on the trip, so we had free rein of the grounds. I was bent over the bubbling fountain behind her, dressed in her red gown and giggling hysterically as she tried to snap the photo before the bell tolled and the campus flooded.

Polly's jaw would be skimming the floor if she saw

me here with Remington. She and I always came to these events together. She should've been here tonight, keeping me company. Laughing about whom we'd ask to dance if we ever got the guts to ask someone.

If Remington and I don't win this thing, I may never get Annabelle to tell me the truth about Polly. "You know what, it's worth a shot. Donella will probably realize it's part of the game and slap you anyway."

"Exactly. Which is why you should work on a backup plan in the meantime. Like staging a task to divert from the task." He arches a brow coyly.

"Not bad." I nod to myself.

Remington turns to watch Donella, who is clearly plotting an attack of some sort with her partner. "She's definitely going to slap me." The ball has reached the point where Chopin is replaced by outdated yet halfway normal music. Waltzing transforms to slow dancing.

"Be so devastatingly charming that she doesn't."

"That's very helpful, thank you, Maren." He flashes a wry grin, and I can't help but like the sound of my name on his lips.

"Go get her," I say, giving him a shove. Because someone just cut the lights, which means another team just knocked off a task while we were standing around. Time is running out. If I'm going to stay in this society—hell, if I'm going to stay in this *school* and have a chance to find out what had my friend so spooked two weeks ago—I have to win.

NINE

THE DARK ROOM ERUPTS INTO GIGGLES. SOME KID STARTS hooting like an owl, sparking more laughter.

A warm hand grasps mine. "Here we go." Remington squeezes and releases my fingers.

A flutter runs through my stomach, but I bump into someone and completely lose track of Remington. I navigate through the masses in the dark, bodies pressing against me, chatter ringing in my ears.

When the lights flicker back on, I scan the room, finally spotting him on the edge of the dance floor. He's leaning close to Donella, whispering into her ear as her partner watches warily from a few feet away.

Remington holds up an index finger before her. *One dance.*

There's no way. She'll never fall for it. She wants to reach the next level in the society so she can gain twenty-four-seven access to wine and crypts and the Ivies.

But beneath the raven half mask, a pink glow washes over her cheeks, visible even at a distance.

That malicious, beautiful bastard.

He extends a hand, and Donella calls something back to her partner before placing hers in it. Remington pulls her closer.

The pair doesn't ease out onto the dance floor. Instead, Remington turns her, wrapping an arm around her waist and guiding her toward a shadowy corner of the room.

My stomach twists. Heat coils around my insides, my limbs. I don't have long to imagine what's going on back there, though, because Donella's partner is pacing and watching them closer than any teacher chaperone. Like he's seconds away from intervening.

I hurry my steps, unsure of exactly what I'm planning. When I reach the guy, russet-colored hair falling over a silver half mask, I smile up at him. "Want to dance?"

If only Polly could see me now.

Frowning slightly, he glances back in the direction Donella disappeared. He turns back to me, lips flat beneath the mask, and then shrugs.

A wave of surprise ripples through me. I'd asked in an attempt to buy a few seconds for Remington, not because I thought this guy would actually agree. He must not recognize me from the meeting because of the mask.

Either that or he's planning to perform some horrible task on me.

His arms move to my waist, and I loop mine loosely around his neck. "So, what's your name?" I ask, trying not to step on his toes. Polly and I only took part in the waltzes and the faster-paced numbers at these shindigs. Never the slow dances.

"Paul. Lowell."

"As in the Lowell Math and Science Building?"

Paul flushes. "Named after my grandfather, Theodore. But you didn't say your name."

"Mary," I lie, giving the nickname of endearment Polly always used to annoy me.

His eyes narrow within the slits of the mask, and my gut clenches. *He knows.*

But a dimple forms in his cheek. "Not sure how I've missed you around here. Maybe it's the mask. Could I—" He motions as if to lift my mask.

I tear my head back. "Now, what would be the fun in that? This is all very *Romeo and Juliet*, don't you think?"

"But how will I find you tomorrow?" A crooked smile plays over his lips. He presses closer to me, his arms tightening around my waist. Panicking, I let my arms fall from his neck, and my hand brushes his right coat pocket.

It rustles softly, a metallic swish.

Remington's words rush back. *Earlier I was trying to figure out what we're even supposed to do with these pendants—mine's in my front pocket, by the way.* But guys have many pockets. I push onto my tiptoes, our bodies crushing together as I whisper into his ear, "The hunt is part of the appeal." Like a prayer, I shut my eyes and slip my right hand into his jacket pocket as my left hand moves to the back of his neck.

His breath hitches, but he relaxes into me as I hunt through the pocket. My fingers dust his room key card, and my hope falters. I am beginning to remove my hand when my thumb snags on something cold and serpentine. The metallic object that made the swish.

Paul spins us, and the chain gets tossed from my finger, settling back into the depths of his jacket pocket.

He slows again, and in desperation, I nestle my cheek against his chest. Hooking the chain onto my index finger, I ease it out of the pocket. Then, wrapping my arm around his midsection, I snatch the entire thing up into my fist behind his back.

A finger taps my shoulder and I jump, wrenching myself away from Paul.

He noticed.

But his gaze floats to something over my shoulder, beyond me. I turn to find Remington, brow cocked. "May I cut in?"

Paul glares at him. "You weren't content with stealing my first partner?"

"*She*," he says, indicating me, "is my date."

"Get lost, man," Paul says, smoothing his lapel. "She's dancing with me now."

I swallow back the acidic taste rising up my throat. My fist is still balled around the chain I'm hoping with everything in me contains a linchpin pendant. "Sorry, Paul," I mumble. "I'll, um, see you around."

"But I don't even know what you look like."

"You will," I say, my head slumping. By the next society meeting, he'll realize exactly who I am and what I did. Moments ago, I was critical of Remington for playing with someone's emotions. But I'm no better than him.

Donella strides up to us now, smiling smugly. "Nice try, you two. Guess this means you're out."

"There's still time," Remington says unconvincingly. He hooks an arm around mine, and we amble away together.

"You failed?" I whisper.

He shrugs against my side.

"Good thing I got this, I guess." I unfold my fist, revealing the silver chain, its tiny pendant dangling off my palm. A linchpin.

Remington gapes at me and then breaks into a perfect smile. "That's my girl."

Whatever was smashed and battered inside me moments

ago buoys up weightlessly now. We push through the dancers, and I almost feel bold enough to ask him for a slow dance while we wait for the next task to appear.

But Dr. Sandoval, the world history teacher, stops right in front of us. His beady, dark eyes narrow at us from the slots of an ink-blue mask.

We're caught. He watched that whole charade, and now we're going down for thievery. "Good evening," he says, an unexpectedly pleasant lilt to his voice.

"Good evening, Dr. Sandoval," Remington says. "Lovely night."

"The Masquerade Ball is one of my favorite traditions." His catlike smile sends a squirmy sensation up my arms. "Traditions are what make this academy so special, don't you think?"

"Mmhmm," I say, shivering as the feeling reaches my neck. "Definitely."

"Enjoy yourselves." Dr. Sandoval salutes us before wandering off, shoes shuffling over the floor in a little jig.

"What was that about?" I ask Remington. But before he can respond, a girl in a mask and electric blue fairy wings thrusts a new envelope in front of us. I startle, then take it as she flutters off.

"Are these fairy girls members of the society or paid help?" I tear open the envelope, handing Remington the second coin. He pockets it as I read: "'Congratulations. Your final task is to spike the punch with the society's special brew.'"

Remington takes the card and squints at it. "How are we supposed to find this 'special brew'?" He flips the card over, like the answer will be scrawled on the back.

On the wall opposite the room, I spot the fairy girl, who gestures for me to follow her. "I think she might know." I tug on Remington's arm and we weave through the dancers after her.

Ben Davies—an enormously tall guy from the boys' basketball team—shimmies in front of me, laughing when he blocks my attempt at a left feint and a dive right to pass him. But he spots my fingers on Remington's arm, arches a brow, and lumbers back to his group.

I've lost sight of Fairy Girl. When we emerge on the other side of the room, she's gone. "How did she—?"

That's when I see it. A faint score mark along the wainscoting panel of the wall. "Be my lookout," I say, stealing over to examine it closer.

"You're clear," he whispers, so I give the panel a little nudge.

It moves. Hinging along the left side, it functions as a tiny door.

"She disappeared through the wall," I say. "The brew must be back here."

"I'll stand guard." Remington takes my clutch, stationing himself, his back to the wall beside what's likely a porthole to a magical realm. Before I can refuse to be the guinea pig, he whispers, "Okay, go."

I sigh and count to three. Crouching low, I push through the door and find myself in a dark space the size of a closet. Now I'm certain that if I push on one more wall, I'll be in Narnia. Because Fairy Girl didn't very well come back out the way she came. I press my fingers to the back of the wall, feeling around.

I can't see a thing. Remington has my phone, and this is going nowhere. I turn back to the entrance, tugging along the seam, but the wall nearly topples me as Remington eases into the room.

"What happened to playing lookout?" I whisper.

"Sorry, I wanted to see what was back here." Fabric rustles, and his phone light casts a glow about the room. The walls in front of us and to our right are bare. The wall to our left, however, contains two shelves stocked with bottles. The ones on the top are little apothecary vials that look like medicine, but the lower shelf contains a variety of wine, liquor, and cordials. Remington lifts his light as I squint at the labels.

"Special brew, special brew," I mutter, turning the bottles. "Here." This silver bottle is the smallest on the shelf. "Must be strong stuff." I grab it and pass it off to Remington.

He takes it, his fingers lingering on mine. His face is only inches above mine in this small space, his breath warm on my forehead. He smells like rich people—some mixture of cedar and leather, with a hint of orange peel. Normally, the scent makes my nose wrinkle, but right now all I want to do is drink it up.

And my hand is still clutched in his. His light flicks off, his jacket swishing as he returns the phone to his pocket. Though I can't see him, I know he's dangerously close.

"So, what happened out there with Donella?" I squeak out, my attempt at sounding casual failing miserably.

"She slapped me."

"Really?"

He laughs. "No, but she should've. We were slow dancing, and I thought I'd unclasped her necklace. So I yanked on it. Only it was still clasped."

"Ouch." I wince, rubbing my neck. Still, I can't help but feel a sweep of relief. He was slow dancing with Donella, not whatever it was I'd imagined happening in that dim corner.

"Mmhmm. You can say she figured out something was off at that point. See, I was right." His breath rustles my hair. "You were definitely the better distraction. It should've been you all along."

That effervescence is back, pushing my spirits higher. *It should've been you.* I can't help but wonder if he's referring to more than just our stupid linchpin-stealing plan. I shift, my back pressing into the wall, wondering if he'll move with me.

He does. His free hand runs along my shoulder, sending chills all the way down to my hips. I shut my eyes, trying not to tremble with nerves.

"Tonight's been fun," he says softly. "Couldn't have asked for a better partner." Maybe we should just crack open the bottle of society brew and stay in this closet, which is definitely, positively magical.

"Same," I say, stupidly, thoughts focused on what he's about to do next.

"So, funny story. But back in Form I..."

"Yeah?" I say because I might die if he doesn't spit it out.

He laughs. "Nothing. It's—we should probably hurry up and do this, before another team beats us to it."

"Mmhmm," I murmur before I realize "do this" means *spike the punch*, not whatever I'd been fantasizing. My hopes slide down, ending up somewhere beneath me on the floor. "Let's hope we can get out of here unseen."

He releases my hand to tuck the bottle inside his jacket, then peeks out through the seam. Straightening again, he runs his fingers through his curls. "There's no other way out?"

"None that I've found."

"Okay. Here goes nothing."

With a push, he slips out the door. I slouch against the right wall for support, my heart hammering in my chest. Someone had to have seen the football player walk out of the wall.

"All clear," he calls, knocking a fist against a stationary section of drywall.

Holding my breath, I squeeze through the opening, which flaps shut behind me.

I breathe again. Everyone is moving and bouncing to an upbeat song my parents probably loved in high school. Nobody is looking at us.

It's my turn to play lookout now as we make our way to the refreshments table. Fortunately, only a small group of Form II girls is gathered there. I sort of wish I had the bottle, so Remington could be the distraction. I have a feeling whatever charm was mystically bestowed upon me during the last task has been all used up. But Remington is the one with the coat. This task is up to me.

"Oh my gosh," I say, coming up alongside the girls. "Do you see that?" I point to Gavin, who happens to be tagging a corner of the banquet hall floor with a can of spray paint. "What is that guy doing?"

"Oh wow," pipes up a girl with an intricate braided updo. "That's like...vandalism, right? We should go tell someone." They scurry off, and guilt pricks at my gut for sacrificing Gavin.

"Still watching?" Remington rasps, handing me a cup of punch. Liquid sloshes as he starts to pour himself some of the untainted juice.

My back to him, I survey the room again. "Do it now." My hand shakes as I sip the punch, keeping an eye on passersby. A boy a few yards away makes a drinking gesture at his date, and they turn toward us. "Hurry up," I mutter into my cup. Then I crane my neck to watch him lean his elbow onto the table, letting his coat spread as he tips the contents of the bottle discreetly into the bowl. He gives it a quick stir with the ladle before tugging his jacket shut over the empty bottle.

"Done," he announces, joining me with a punch cup in hand. We allow the thirsty couple to pass us and wander over to rest against a wall.

"Did we just win this thing?" Excitement buzzes through my teeth.

"I guess we'll know if a game fairy awards us a third coin," he says nonchalantly. But a victorious grin pulls at his lips. And a fine set of lips they are.

My mind trips back to Gavin. What happened to him? I glance back to his graffitied corner, but an unnerving shriek cuts through the room, disrupting my focus. Over by the punch table, an inhuman howl continues over the music as several students gather around, forming a ring.

Some of them peer down at whatever's in the center— whatever's making that unnatural sound; others turn their heads away, faces distorted.

The howl turns into sounds of choking, retching, and a splattering of liquid. Gasps and cries erupt from the onlookers in turn. The rest of us flock to the scene, where a boy—no, *the boy* who just passed us on his way to the punch table—is crouched on the floor, face pale and eyes wide. "She only had one sip of the punch," he says in a hollow voice, almost to himself. "That was it. One sip."

Remington and I maneuver closer, until I can see the full form of the retching girl who is now convulsing on the floor. Red vomit paints the wood around her. I shudder as Annabelle's words from last night slither into my brain: *You'd be writhing and spasming on the floor. Your lungs would essentially be melting...*

With one horrendous heaving swell, the girl inhales a wheezing, groaning breath.

Then her spasms cease.

Dr. Sandoval pushes through the crowd to check the girl's pulse. He leans down, presses his ear to her chest. "She's not breathing. Somebody, call an ambulance," he snaps, waving a hand in the air. "And nobody touch a thing on the refreshments table." As he turns her over, ripping off her mask and trying to clear her mouth and throat to make room for air, I recognize her now from the catacombs earlier tonight.

I run my hands through my heat-tamed hair, my body wracked with a feverish chill. My legs suddenly numb, I back up, away from the crowd, away from the girl who isn't breathing. My hands—the ones that gave the bottle to Remington moments ago—feel like they're on fire. I keep backing up until I hit a chair, slumping into it. The room is a shifting blur of glittering fabrics and flickering lanterns. The cries turn to deafening silence as I watch teachers usher students from the building.

Overhead, the red lights on the cameras are still blinking.

TEN

THE MUSIC IS A HAUNTING ANTHEM OF CRIES AND SNIFFLES as ball-goers proceed out the doors in herd formation. I've lost Remington in the shuffle. My heart thrums like a battalion in my ears, competing with the buzz. My body is so heavy, like I've been superglued to this chair.

The cameras witnessed everything.

Soon, the administration will see Remington pour the mystery liquor into the punch bowl. They'll see the way I stood guard. The way I turned to watch him do it.

Sweat builds on my forehead. My body aches. Maybe I am coming down with something. Or maybe this is what it feels like to watch someone suffer—possibly even die—as a result of your actions.

But I didn't know the secret brew was poison. Did the society orchestrate the task that ended in this girl's demise? And not just any girl's demise—one of its own. We know the society isn't above using poison for the purposes of its games. But *why* do it?

An unsettling thought presses into the outskirts of my mind, one I try unsuccessfully to block: *And what did they do to Polly?*

Then there's Remington. My partner, who's now missing. He seemed just as clueless about the contents of the brew. But I barely know him. Did he know about the brew? Or could he have added something to the bottle when I was trying to get rid of that group of girls?

I scan the masses again for his tall frame, spotting his dark curls a few yards away. He looks around frantically until his eyes meet mine, wide and unblinking. His face is ashen.

I make my way toward him, and he pushes through the bodies until we face each other.

"What happened?" he whispers, a vein throbbing in his temple.

"I don't know, but we can't talk about it here."

"We certainly can't," comes a voice from behind us, smooth and composed in the midst of the cacophony. Annabelle's face is hidden behind a gilt Venetian mask as she slithers between us. But her red gown and perfect updo are dead giveaways. She tucks a gold coin into my hand. "Congratulations."

Is she serious? Before I can ask, her arms hook onto ours—Remington on one side and me on the other. I look past her at Remington, wanting to wrench my arm away. But he's busy glaring daggers at Annabelle. "What is going on?" he demands. "What did you do to that girl?"

"What did *I* do?" Anabelle flinches, like he slapped her. "I don't remember adding poison to the punch bowl. I guess it's a good thing the academy has security cameras. So that if I did poison that poor girl—and simply suffer from a case of amnesia—there will be proof." Flashing a wicked grin from him to me, she leads us through the doors, out into the cold night air.

"This is blackmail?" I ask. "You set us up. For what?"

"Blackmail?" she repeats with a laugh. "Oh Maren, you misunderstand. You've won tonight's game, and the only thing I want now is to award your prize."

Our prize. The next station. What Gavin described as the ability to call in a favor. "What are we going to do with your damn prize when they lock us up for murder?" I snap.

"I wouldn't worry about that," she says, withdrawing her arms to tuck a windblown strand of hair behind her ear and button her coat. "As long as you accept your winnings."

"We don't want any winnings," Remington says, his voice strained. "We want to know why you did this."

"That girl is society, Annabelle," I add. "You hurt one of your own."

"I guess Alicia shouldn't have gotten caught spilling society secrets."

"What are you talking about?"

She shrugs. "I may've overheard her trying to impress a Form II with tales of a meeting. We can't afford to let our members go around blabbing."

My head starts to spin. This is how they handle someone giving away information? Which is exactly what Polly seemed to be considering that day on the lawn. *I want to show you something.* Did Annabelle somehow figure it out before Polly made it to the fountain that night? Gavin is lucky Annabelle didn't overhear him telling me how to get an invitation.

Remington glances at me in horror. "We want you to tell Headmistress Koehler that we had nothing to do with this."

"And the police," I add, feeling sick as I picture Polly lying helpless, unable to breathe as blood fills her lungs.

"In that case," Annabelle says, pressing her lips together for a moment, "we might have an issue." Her heels clack along the cobblestone as she speeds her steps, voice trailing back with the wind. "You both really should reconsider."

Once her dark coat is out of view, I reach over and grip Remington's arm so hard my fingers hurt. "What are we going to do?" That girl was society. These people aren't even safe from each other.

He strokes the wool of my—no, Polly's—coat sleeve and peers down at me. "We'll go to the administration, together.

We'll tell them everything." The words sound noble and brave, but a tremor runs through his voice. Through my layers, I feel his fingers quiver.

"How will we explain the security footage?"

"I don't think there is any footage. I think Annabelle is just doing what she does best—playing with us." His hand moves down my arm until he's gripping my own frozen hand. "I just wish we hadn't torn up the task cards. That was the only evidence we had that the society was in control tonight."

"I still have the invitation to the initiation in my room," I say. "That could help. Do you have the bottle? Maybe the cops can test it for prints. Then they'll know we weren't the only ones handling it."

He nods, indicating his jacket. "It's in here."

In the distance, sirens blare and red lights ricochet off the brick buildings. The headmistress never attends the Masquerade Ball; she was probably woken up to attend to this nightmare.

"Let's go find the headmistress." I start back in the direction of the Grand Banquet Hall, and Remington follows. Though the faculty is still trying to drive everyone to their dormitories, clusters of distraught, gossiping students continue to ignore them. I feel like a fish swimming upstream, trying to get through. We reach the crowd camped around the ambulance, and I peer through to glimpse the stretcher carrying Alicia Jones.

Dr. Sandoval is shouting at everyone to move, and with a grumble, they drift away. Remington and I stay back with the stragglers, searching for the headmistress. "You two," Dr. Sandoval snaps, footsteps slapping the pavement as he nears us. "Are you listening? We need space for the ambulance to get out of here. A girl may die."

"Yes, we know, Dr. Sandoval," Remington says. "We need to talk to Headmistress Koehler about that."

"Well, you can't. Not tonight." He shoos us with a flick of his hand.

"You don't understand—"

"The headmistress is already in the ambulance," he says, pointing to the back of the vehicle, which has just rumbled off down the service road, lights flashing.

My stomach drops.

Remington's hand falls on my shoulder. "Okay, sir," he says, "then can we speak with you?"

"I've got to prevent this place from becoming a circus." His gaze darts to where a few guys in suits have wandered in the direction of the apple orchard. "And you two need to get to your dorms or you'll both be suspended for a week." Drops of spittle fly through the night air before he clomps off after the guys.

I turn to Remington, defeated. My legs feel weak. "Let's talk to Headmistress Koehler first thing in the morning. There's nothing we can do for Alicia now."

Remington nods. When he takes in my shaky hands and shallow breathing, his eyes narrow. "Let's get you to bed," he says, offering me an arm.

It's still dark when I wake. The sheets are drenched in sweat, and the curtains at my window billow as a cold draft seeps in.

I don't remember opening that window.

I get out of bed, wrapping my arms around myself as I flick the light on. Then I stride to the window to wrench it shut. My foot crinkles over something that isn't carpet, and I startle. Everything is fuzzy, the suddenly bright room still coming into focus. I step back and squint down at the floor.

It's another card, this time with no envelope. I bend down to retrieve it before glancing out the window. I'm on the fifth floor. How the hell did someone get up here? And did they open my window while I was sleeping? Shivering, I shuffle away from the wall to read.

CONGRATULATIONS. YOUR STATUS HAS BEEN ELEVATED TO MINOR SUPREME. PLEASE ENJOY.

My stomach performs a series of cartwheels, and I dry heave over the trash can. I guess there's nothing in there to throw up, considering I never actually partook of the society's appetizers or the ball's refreshments. Thankfully.

I collapse onto the bed, crumpling the card in my fist. Please *enjoy*. Enjoy what? The night sweats, the guilt writhing in my stomach like an alien entity, or the paralyzing fear that someone is about to come crashing through my door to read me my rights?

I never asked them for anything.

I grab my phone from the floor by my bed. 4:32 a.m. There's no way I'm going to fall back asleep, which means I have a mere four hours to sit here, sick with worry. I crawl back into bed, still too freaked out by the open window to turn off the light.

Maybe they were able to revive the girl. But the image of her body spasming on the banquet room floor creeps in, followed by her lying pale and still as Dr. Sandoval crouched beside her, desperately searching for a pulse.

If Remington and I get to Headmistress Koehler before the authorities start to investigate, she'll hear us out about Annabelle and her deranged society. We were playing a game, that's all. Annabelle is the one who took it too far. Once the headmistress and the authorities learn the truth, maybe everyone will finally realize that Polly isn't a runaway. That nausea pushes up in my throat again. I've played two games with the society, and both of them were deadly. It's not a coincidence that Polly joined and went missing shortly after.

Annabelle might know a lot more than just *where* Polly is.

––––––––

I flutter in and out of consciousness, trying so hard to sleep that I can't sleep, trying so hard to block out the memory of the convulsing girl that I think of nothing else. When I jolt up in bed with the sensation of missing my alarm clock, sunlight slants through the curtains.

I fumble for my phone. 7:25 a.m. I didn't oversleep. The headmistress only has office hours from 8 to 10 a.m. on Sundays before she heads to chapel. I have just enough time to try to look presentable before Remington and I plead our case to her.

After a quick shower, I pad back to my room, shower caddy in hand. I check the time on my phone again, finding a text from Remington.

Can you meet me downstairs in 15?

He sent it ten minutes ago, which means I've only got five left.

Down in a sec

I lift a pair of yoga pants from my chair but think better of it. A visit to the headmistress requires jeans, at the very least. After tugging on a hoodie and boots, I comb through my wet hair and dig inside my desk drawer for the Gamemaster's Society initiation card.

But dread pounds in my chest like galloping horse hooves. It's not here.

I rifle through and wrench things from the drawer, tossing

everything to the floor. Whoever came in here to leave my reward must've stolen the invitation.

Letting out a growl, I snatch that idiotic reward card from the bed and head down.

Below, Remington is pacing behind the garden bench. I greet him, startled by his appearance as he looks up at me. There are dark purple rims around his eyes, and his normally pressed tie and jacket are rumpled like they came straight from the dirty clothes hamper.

I glance down at my own attire, feel the weight dragging down my own tired lids, and for the first time, see exactly how intertwined our lives have become. "Ready to talk to Headmistress Koehler?" I ask, pulling my wet hair into a messy bun. "I hope you found your invitation, because someone—"

"Took yours?" he finishes for me.

"Yeah," I say, searching the grounds for spies as I near him. "Someone came into my room, left this *congratulations* note, and stole the invitation."

"Same here."

A tingle dances up my neck. "At least we have the notes and the bottle."

"Except," he says, gaze falling to a shrub, "they took the bottle too."

"Nooo." My head tips back.

"Look," Remington says, still not making eye contact, "I didn't ask you to meet me so we could talk to Headmistress

Koehler." His voice is rugged with anxiety or lack of sleep. "I asked you here to try to talk you out of it."

"What?" I swallow, like maybe it will unclog my ears, because he couldn't have said that.

A girl saunters out the double doors of my dormitory and down the path, eyeing the pair of us sharply, probably wondering what a guy like him is doing with Sweatpants Girl. Or possibly wondering what happened to my sweatpants. Remington shifts, putting his back to her. "Kids were already talking this morning. The girl, Alicia Jones, is still hanging on."

Relief swells in my chest. "That's great, but we still—"

"Apparently, she has a serious peanut allergy," he interrupts. "She wasn't paying attention, so she ate a cookie from the refreshment table that was labeled 'nuts,' and she didn't have her EpiPen on her."

"But that's not what happened," I say, my voice sounding strange and distant as I try to make sense of his words. "We know she drank the punch, right after we spiked it. That's what the guy she was with said."

"Well, apparently, he remembered wrong. I think if we lie low, this will all blow over."

"This will all blow over," I repeat, still getting the sensation that my words aren't coming from my own mouth.

"That's right. It's very tragic, but an accident. No one's fault."

"You don't really believe that."

"We weren't exactly paying attention to what Alicia did after we left that table. We jumped to conclusions because of all the society dramatics and the adrenaline. You should let this go."

"So you're just going to don a black cloak and keep attending these meetings? A girl almost died, Remington."

"And it's very sad. But it isn't the society's fault. And I can't turn on them now, especially not without proof. I need this, more than you know."

"Right." A bitter laugh escapes my lips. "You need your Ivy League connections and *Minor Supreme* status, whatever that is." I shake my head, tears stinging at my eyes. "I can't believe how wrong I was about you."

He's not just covering his own ass. By chickening out, Remington is keeping the truth about Polly and the society's role in her disappearance buried. I'm going to speak with the headmistress today, with or without Remington Cruz.

I mean, I put jeans on today, damn it.

ELEVEN

THE LAWRENCE ADMINISTRATION BUILDING STANDS HULKING in the center of a cluster of dormitories. On my way, gossip purrs along the pathways as students amble to breakfast. Most of it parrots that lie about a peanut allergy, but there's also the critical question of whether or not tomorrow's classes are canceled.

My stomach grumbles, but I press on in the opposite direction. Waving hello to Dr. Yamashiro, I reach the red brick steps, worry knotting my insides. There's a chance Headmistress Koehler won't be in her office. After all, she had a lot to handle last night, with a student nearly dying at a school function. She could be off comforting Alicia Jones's roommates or dealing with the girl's parents. I smooth my still-damp hair, take a deep breath, and head through the enormous, marble-floored lobby to approach the front desk.

The place is dead on a Sunday, causing my steps to sound like a jackhammer; still, the ancient woman at the desk ignores me. I pitter on the wood with my short fingernails until she peers up at me over tiny rectangular frames.

She scowls at the interruption like someone who hates teenagers and schools and would very much like to be doing anything but this job. "Can I help you?"

"Is the headmistress in? I need to speak with her."

"She's very busy this morning."

"It's extremely urgent." I push my shoulders back to try to seem important.

She folds her arms, considering me for several seconds with eyes half-obscured behind flaps of wrinkled skin. Finally, she turns her glare on the phone, lifting it. "I'll call and see if she has a minute. Name and subject of your visit."

"Oh, um, Maren Montgomery. And…" I don't want to admit to this judgy old lady that I know what happened to the almost dead girl.

But I came here to tell the truth. "This is about Alicia Jones. The one who…" I expect a nod so I don't have to finish the sentence, but she continues her blank gaze. "The girl who got sick last night at the ball."

The woman starts to lower the phone. "Well, if you need

to speak to someone, the counselor will be in tomorrow morning. The headmistress can't—"

"I don't need a counselor!" She flinches because, apparently, I raised my voice. I press my hands together in supplication. "I have information about what happened to Alicia that needs to be shared with the headmistress. Right now. Please."

Still looking bothered, she raises the phone to her ear. "I have Maren Montgomery here to speak with you, ma'am. Says it's urgent." A moment later, the woman, whose name placard I finally glimpse says 'Ms. Swishton,' sets down the phone in defeat. "She'll see you now."

Ms. Swishton is already back to ignoring me, so I stride through the palatial room lined with busts of former headmasters and headmistresses. Overhead, the ceiling is a fresco of naked gods and nymphs enacting some sort of feast.

I pass a large, glass display case containing the various accolades the academy has been awarded over the past century and a half. The shelf on the end is a memorial of sorts. Photos of teachers who passed away before my time. The administrator responsible for our world-class humanities program, whose photo also hangs in the entryway of said building. And there's another photo I recognize: Daniel King, a student whose tragic death a couple years before I arrived has become the cautionary tale for why you should never disobey the school's rules. Daniel and some friends decided to break curfew and go night swimming in a nearby lake while intoxicated, which didn't go so well for Daniel, who drowned. Every year at orientation, we have a moment of silence for him.

I take the staircase up to the second floor, where the offices are. Headmistress Koehler's door is the very last one at the end of a long hall.

My phone reads 8:10 a.m. It's quiet up here; the headmistress is the only administrator with Sunday hours. Every door is shut, including the one I'm headed toward. I was in this building last year on the third floor, finance. I had to sign a pledge to keep my grades up and to remain in at least two of my sports in order to qualify for my scholarship. But I think the last time I was on this particular floor was back before Form I, when my dad and I took a tour of the academy.

I creak down the tile floor, taking in the name placards that I never really registered the last time I was up here. Dr. Preston Harding, Dean of Admission; Dr. Isabella Marino, Dean of Students; Ms. Matilda Banks, Rector. The names continue, but when I am five steps away from knocking on the headmistress's door, the hallway lights shut off.

I freeze, waiting for them to turn on again. When they don't, I wave a hand in hopes of triggering the motion sensors. Instead, my phone dings in my pocket.

Startled, I press against the wall, tugging my phone out. I

squint back into the dark hall, but it tunnels into oblivion. I glance back down at the text, hoping it's Remington, apologizing for abandoning me and telling me to wait for him.

But it's not. It's from an unknown number. I click on it to find a video.

When I press play, a cold hollowness rolls through my gut. The video shows Remington. Leaning over the punch bowl, pouring his hidden bottle inside.

And behind him, I'm standing, watching it all.

The scene starts to play again. Mesmerized, I stare until something off-screen catches the phone's light. At my foot, an object gleams white on the tile floor.

Another envelope. I bend down to lift it, using my phone to illuminate the name scrawled over the front: Maren Montgomery.

I peel open the pebble-filled envelope and read the card:

Poor Alicia's too sick to keep her spot. No one has to find out what you did to her. All you have to do is replace her.
   Lure someone new into the society. As a bonus for your efforts, you'll get a clue to Polly's whereabouts. Bring your target to the next society meeting: 11 p.m. Tuesday, the old cathedral.

My heart performs a sickening flip. Annabelle *was* lying about Polly.

And now she's given me another task. Like last night's game never ended. The society isn't done with me yet. Not until I've trapped some other helpless soul. I take two quick steps in the opposite direction to find out if whoever left this envelope is still in the hall. But the lights power on again, just as Headmistress Koehler's door clicks open.

She stands in the doorway in a formfitting gray dress, brown hair slicked back into a bun. Flustered, I stuff the envelope into my back pocket, my heart thrumming in my chest.

"Maren," she says, eyebrows hoisted. "Did you get lost on your way up?"

"No, Headmistress Koehler," I squeak, scouring my brain for a way out of here. Remington was wrong about the cameras not working. Not only were they recording, but somebody is already using the footage to keep me quiet. Maybe blackmail is the way Annabelle and her friends get away with everything. "I had to stop by the ladies' room first."

I can't tell her the truth about the ball anymore. Not just because of the footage. I can't tell her because I was right about Polly. The Gamemaster's Society does know what happened to her. If I turn against them now, those secrets may stay buried forever.

"Well, why don't you come in? Ms. Swishton said it was urgent." She pushes the door back, motioning to a chair at her desk.

"Actually," I say, still without a clue as to what lie will

spill out next. "I wanted to ask about counseling for the students. You know, after what happened last night. There seem to be a lot of girls in my dorm who could use someone to help talk through what they saw."

Headmistress Koehler smiles softly, and my heart rate steadies.

After assuring me the academy will be hiring extra counselors for the next couple weeks, she sends me off to breakfast, which I desperately need.

And there's something else I need. To remain in the Gamemaster's good graces.

I need to keep winning.

The dining room smells of buttermilk pancakes, and my stomach cries out. But I push past the line to track down Remington. He's seated with a group of football players, and I have to talk myself into interrupting their boisterous conversation.

I tap him on the shoulder, and his cheeks bloom pink when he turns to find me. Here in the midst of hundreds of students, without the cover of our masks, he's ashamed to be seen with me. "Can I speak to you?"

The other guys laugh, waggling their brows as he excuses himself, leaving his tray there like he's about to bat me away. "Is everything okay?" I'm so over the nice guy routine. I saw

Remington Cruz's true colors this morning, when he chick-ened out.

But guilt writhes in my chest. Because I did the same thing, not twenty minutes ago, outside the headmistress's office.

I had to, though, didn't I? For Polly? Remington's motives were as shallow as they come. He wants to stay in this stupid society so he can keep gliding through life on the back of a diamond-encrusted falcon.

"No, everything isn't fine. I was blackmailed on the way to the headmistress's office."

"Blackmailed?" Remington pales.

"Yeah, that footage you thought didn't exist? The one that proves we *poisoned* a girl last night? Someone sent it to me. Do you really think someone would do that if they believed this was an accidental allergy situation?"

He stuffs his hands inside his pockets. "I hoped—I mean—" He shakes his head. "That didn't come out right. I guess I wanted to believe it wasn't because of me."

Sadness swells in my throat. For a moment, when he told me the peanut allergy rumor, I was desperate to believe it too. "Last night wasn't because of you." Jordan Park walks slowly past me, eyes narrowed as she takes in Remington and me talking, our expressions grave. I wave and then wait until she's out of range. "It was because of Annabelle Westerly and the rest of the society. Now they've trapped me into playing more of their games. If I don't play, they're going to leak the video."

I don't say *and I may lose my best friend forever*. Because it was all too easy for Remington to fall into the role of society acolyte this morning. For all I know, he's already agreed to something in exchange for his silence. I have to lure someone else into the club. Maybe he has to report any seditious behavior to Annabelle.

"What do you have to do?" He peers down at me, dark eyes concerned.

"I have to lure someone new into the club. Who knows what they'll do to this person? I have to ask you one last time." I pick at my fingernails. "Will you help me?" My hopes climb, despite my efforts to tame them. "Maybe if we get ahead of this by going to the headmistress or the cops *together*, the society won't be able to hold that footage over our heads."

"Maren," he says, biting his lower lip. "I can't. I wish I could explain, but—"

"I think I get it," I cut in. "You're one of them." I spin around, not sure if I'm ready for breakfast after all.

Remington reaches for my shoulder. "Maren, wait." He releases me, and that tiny hope rises again like a newborn sprout. "Look, the task you got? I got one too. But mine didn't just threaten me with the footage. They've offered me something too. Something I'd be a fool to refuse."

"Like a bribe?"

He shrugs, his foot tapping on the floor like he can't wait

to ditch me. Like he just needs to make sure I'm going to shut my mouth about the dance, so he can get back to his jock friends. The society probably offered to get him a perfect score on the SATs or to make him captain of the football team.

But another thought starts to form, painting the last one black.

Maybe the society offered to cover something else up. Who is Remington Cruz, really? Could he have done something he'd pay any price to keep hidden?

Then it hits me. Our *reward* for winning. All of this—nobody getting blamed for last night, the whole peanut allergy narrative—must be part of it. The society claimed to have their claws in every important avenue. Who's to say that doesn't apply to the academy itself? Being a Minor Supreme must be like…being untouchable.

No wonder everyone was so motivated to win the game last night. If you can get away with nearly murdering someone, you can get away with anything.

"I'm so confused," I whisper. "Why go through all this trouble to ensure we stay in the society? The task, the blackmail—they *poisoned* a girl, Remington." They must've known I'd try to get out. Because there's something seriously wrong with this club. And it looks like Polly might've been on the wrong end of their games.

"Maybe as insurance, so their secrets would stay safe."

"More secrets? We already know they're dangerous!"

But Remington's gaze shifts to the football players, who are now taking their trays to the dirty stack in clump formation. I've lost him to the society. Not that he was ever mine to lose. He's one of them now. I want to show him the card I found this morning in the administration building. The one that proves the society knows what happened to Polly. Maybe if he knew last night's poisoning wasn't the only nefarious act to come out of these so-called *games*, he'd realize it's not worth whatever he's after. Or whatever he wants buried.

The problem is, if I'm going to track down Polly, I have to be one of them too.

Which means I need to choose my target.

TWELVE

AFTER MY POST-LACROSSE SHOWER ON MONDAY, I FIND Jordan seated on a suede couch in our dormitory's common room. A heaviness presses behind my eyes. Polly and I used to spend countless hours in here, studying, listening to dorm gossip as the smell of burnt popcorn wafted in from the kitchenette. *Stolen Hearts* was usually playing in the background as studying turned to chatting.

Nothing plays on the TV as Jordan studies, shoulder-length hair damp around her face from her afternoon swim practice. Supposedly, she's a champion swimmer; I've never been to a meet. I've never even been inside the Arthur Aquatic Center. Or around a pool for that matter. Not since I was nine years old and my hair got trapped inside the drain of my grandparents' pool. Ever since that day, even the scent of chlorine makes me break out in a cold sweat. I wrote about the traumatic event and how it made me a stronger person or whatever in my Torrey-Wells admission essay.

Jordan understands. She doesn't get resentful that I don't watch her swim, like Polly used to when I missed her play rehearsals. Right now, Jordan looks at peace with her US history textbook. The sweet scent of freshly baked chocolate chip cookies replaces burnt popcorn, filling the space. I wrap my wet hair up into a bun, zip my hoodie, and sit down next to her. "Hey, Jordan. How's it going?"

Jordan looks up from her book, smiling. "Good," she says, then frowns. "Where are your books?"

"I'm not here to study. I was looking for you."

Jordan's cheeks blush pink. "Oh. Why?"

"Because we're friends," I say, like it's obvious. "I wanted to find out when you're going to the dining hall tonight."

Jordan glances at her phone. "It's only five. Maybe in an hour or so. I can text you—"

"Yeah, thanks." I force a smile, but my insides are at combat. I don't know why the Gamemaster's Society suddenly needs a new member. I thought they set up a series of challenges just to keep people out. Now, in order to save Polly—in order to save myself—I'm essentially sacrificing this poor girl to Annabelle. Gorgeous, graceful, sociopathic Annabelle. "Sorry I haven't been around much," I add.

Jordan shrugs. "Does it have something to do with

Remington Cruz? I saw you talking this morning. Are you two—" Her lips twist.

"Oh, that." I wave a hand like Remington and my speaking is not only no big deal but also yesterday's news. "No way. I haven't been around much," I say, lowering my voice conspiratorially, "because I've infiltrated the society."

"The secret one?" The book slides off her lap as she straightens. "Did they bury you?"

I laugh. "No. They play games. It's...fun." The lie sits heavy in the air, the sound of false laugher still ringing in my ears as Jordan gapes at me. "They even said I could invite a friend. A *worthy* friend. I thought of you."

"Me? Oh, I don't think so."

"It is a lot," I admit. "It's been taking up most of my free time. That's why I hoped you'd join. If you're not part of it, we probably won't get to hang out much."

Jordan's brown eyes flicker with something like hunger.

"I know having you there with me would make it even better. I'll tell you more about it at dinner," I say, getting up. I don't even need to stick around to know I've got her. She's starving for a friend, and some twisted part of my soul used it to betray her.

———

Having learned my lesson, I'm wearing jeans and sneakers Tuesday night. The creepy cloak I found on my bed earlier today is draped over the ensemble. By the time I get Jordan out of the dormitory after curfew, across campus to the condemned and forbidden cathedral, and through the hidden entrance, she has asked to go back approximately seventy-five times.

Clearly, Jordan Park is not Gamemaster's Society material. But my task didn't actually specify I had to lure a *worthy friend*; it just said *someone new*.

And each time I assure Jordan everything will be fine, that distorted part of my soul grows a new, gnarled, and knotted branch.

I can only hope Jordan will bow out of her initiation ceremony and be sworn to secrecy the way Double Espresso was. Then she and I can continue our friendship like none of this ever happened.

Ahead, Annabelle is manning the trapdoor, lantern in hand, black hood back to reveal polished blond waves. Beside her, a cloaked figure stands tall, ensuring each member pays the entrance fee. I toss my pebbles inside the basket and recite the mantra, nudging Jordan to do the same. I glance at the hooded figure's face and spot a russet-colored ringlet. Paul Lowell peers down at me, lips twisted in scorn. He recognizes me as the girl beneath the mask. In shame, I look away.

When I step onto the staircase, Annabelle stops me. "Let your friend go on ahead. I have something for you."

Panic flashes in Jordan's eyes. She's three seconds away from sprinting out of here.

"I'll take excellent care of her." Annabelle turns to nudge Jordan down toward the vault before another word can be uttered on the subject. "Here," she adds, handing me something small but heavy. Then she descends after Jordan, and I'm left alone with some sort of video recording device. "Your reward for a job well done."

The camera looks ancient, and I'm not sure what she expects me to do with it. The footage from the ball must be on here. Maybe she's giving me the evidence so I can destroy it. There seems to be a video queued up, so I press "play."

The recording starts, the camera zoomed in on a gray, stone wall. The time stamp is 5:00 p.m., November 23. *Today.* Just a few hours ago. When the film zooms back out, a girl with copper-toned curls is sitting on a bed. The room is small and unadorned, like a cell. The girl looks up, her stark blue irises on the camera, and my mouth goes dry.

The girl is Polly.

Her eyes are swollen, the whites woven with red. She looks thinner than I remember her. The terror in her face and the bleakness of the room don't fit the image imprinted on my mind: Polly snuggled in her rose-covered comforter, smiling down at the camera from her top bunk.

Suddenly, white block letters cut across the screen, covering Polly and the stone prison:

She's closer than you think.

The film cuts off. I try to swallow, to think of what to do. Someone in this club has to be trustworthy enough to help me with this video. But everyone is downstairs, guarded by Annabelle.

I scroll through the recorder's functions, searching for a way to send this video to myself. But it's so old, there's no internet capability. I dig my phone from my pocket and ready it for a video. I press play on the footage of Polly.

A creak sounds behind me, and I startle as the recorder is snatched from my grip. "That will suffice," Annabelle says, fiddling with the buttons. "There. Erased. That, my dear, was for your eyes only."

"What did you do to her?" I growl. But I already know. The stone. Polly is being held somewhere inside the catacombs.

I scramble away from Annabelle, toward the staircase. "I wouldn't," Annabelle warns in that irritatingly calm tone.

"You wouldn't *what*?" I snap. "You wouldn't try to save your best friend from an insidious beast?"

"Not when there's a more pressing situation at hand, no."

"What are you talking about?"

Annabelle sighs. "Polly is fine. She has food and water and plenty of air. Your friend Jordan on the other hand…"

A sensation like cold wire wraps around my heart, squeezing. I gasp, lurching toward the trapdoor. I only left her alone for a moment.

Annabelle laughs behind me. I spin on her, ready to wring her scrawny ballerina neck. "Only kidding." She rolls her eyes. "Jordan is downstairs, mingling. I promise you, tonight is going to be fun."

"You think I want to have fun?" I say, still pretty sure I'm going to choke her or at the very least, shove her down the trapdoor opening. "When I know Polly is being held prisoner down there?"

"We're not savages, Maren. I told you, Polly is being looked after."

"But why are you keeping her? I'm in the society now! I demand some answers!"

"You haven't quite risen to that station, though, have you? Perhaps after tonight, if all goes well."

"This is unbelievable. What's to stop me from waking up the headmistress right now?"

"I deleted the video. It's my word against yours, and frankly, one of my words holds more weight than your entire vocabulary." That devious smirk slides onto her lips now. "But I don't think you'll tell the headmistress, or anyone for that matter. I think you'll stay here with us, Maren. Because I think you want Polly to stay alive and well."

"You would—" Despite fighting with every fiber of my being, a sob escapes. Tears are leaking. My nose is running.

Annabelle is winning.

"Just keep playing the games, and she'll stay fine." Laughter trickles up from below, and I grab my head in my hands. No one in this society understands what she's doing.

And if I tell, she's threatened to hurt Polly. I sniffle, then fix my face into a sharp glare. But Annabelle is unfazed. "Keep winning, and I'll be able to share everything with you."

She descends, and I'm left standing in the drafty ruins of the old cathedral, trying to stop my tears. Behind me, wood groans, and I turn to find Remington. His black cloak dusts the floor as he crawls through the society's entrance. "Maren?" He rushes over, and I wipe my eyes to hide the fact that I've been crying. "What happened?" His strong arms envelop me as he looks down.

"Like you care," I spit, even though my body has essentially melted into him. "Go back to your perfect SAT scores and your Ivy-painted future."

"Tell me what happened," he insists.

I look up at his dark, concerned eyes, knowing I can't trust him. Knowing he might turn around and tell Annabelle everything.

"Nothing." I pry myself from his embrace and clumsily lower down into the vault.

"Maren!" Remington is still calling after me when my feet touch the stone floor. In the dim light, the faces blur together. I search for Jordan, desperate to make sure she's okay. But I find another face. A face that forces another strangled sob to rise up in my throat.

Gavin pales when he sees me. He makes his way to me across the tunnel, and it's the fastest I've ever seen him move.

"What's wrong?" he asks, holding back, his fingers slipping around my wrists. So different—so much gentler, so much more reserved—than the way Remington met me moments earlier. I lean forward, pressing my cheek to his shoulder, an act that makes him flinch. But his frame relaxes as he takes a breath, his hand moving to my back. That sweet, smoked candy scent starts to calm me.

"I can't say much here. But it's Polly. I think she's down in these tunnels somewhere."

He wrenches his head back to look at me, eyes wide. "Maren, that's...you can't let Annabelle get to you. She's practically a professional mind gamer."

"She's not playing with me," I hiss. "She showed me proof."

He doesn't look convinced as his gaze swings to where Annabelle chats serenely with Donella. "Stick with me tonight." His voice is rough but soothing. We turn to face the front of the chamber, where as usual, there's an elaborate display of wine and bite-size snacks. To our right, Remington slumps against a pillar, his eyes on us.

My skin heats, but I wrench my gaze from his; for someone so strong, Remington is weaker than I ever imagined. And right now, I need strength to beat Annabelle. It's going to take every ounce of my strength to get Polly back.

Gavin's fingers remain on my wrist, sliding down to my hand as I take a calming breath. His warm touch on my skin might be the only thing keeping me together right now.

Ahead, I spot Jordan in the glow of the lanterns. The gown I'd dressed her in earlier—one of Polly's—is now covered by a white muslin shroud. Her black iron-curled hair has been gathered up high, soft tendrils left loose to frame her face. A gilt crown adorns her head. "Why is Jordan dressed like a virgin sacrifice?" I hiss at Gavin, clutching his hand so tightly my short fingernails dig into his palm.

"I—I don't know," he whispers back, twisting his hand, either to pry it from mine or to calm me.

"Welcome, everyone." Annabelle's voice slices through the low murmurs. "Tonight, we have a special game for you, called Rescue the Princess." Applause rattles the chamber. "Jordan here has accepted the role of princess, which means it's up to the rest of us to save her."

Two of Annabelle's minions—a guy with inky black coils and a girl with a crisp brown bob—take Jordan's arms. They turn her, and the three begin pacing farther into the dark tunnel leading to the next chamber.

"We'd better hurry," Annabelle calls out, Jordan's white train still cast in lantern light. "Before she's lost to the dragon forever."

A muffled shriek resounds from where Jordan's front half has disappeared. White fabric ripples; sounds of struggle ensue. But just as quickly as it started, the tussle is contained.

The three figures, the white muslin train—the darkness swallows it all.

THIRTEEN

I RELEASE GAVIN'S ARM, CHARGING THROUGH THE SMALL crowd to get to Jordan. What did Annabelle mean by *dragon*? Some minion blocks my way, so I shout past him, "Where are they taking her?"

Annabelle makes a calming gesture. "The princess is being hidden somewhere in the catacombs. I assure everyone, she is fine"—she licks her lips—"for now. It does tend to be rather tight inside a sarcophagus, so we'd best get on with the rules, hadn't we?"

My heart pitches into my ribs, but Annabelle lets out a small laugh. Gavin's words bounce back at me: *She's practically a professional mind gamer.* Suddenly, I have no clue if Jordan really is in danger.

"You valiant knights will head out on a quest in search of the fair princess. Each of you will carry a token of gold—for everyone knows a dragon cannot resist gold. In order to release the princess, you will need to have at least two tokens. Knights will also have two duel cards, used to challenge fellow knights as they choose. The winner of the duel will take a coin from the loser. If, at any point, you end up without a single coin, you are eliminated from the game."

"But there's a twist." Annabelle raises an index finger. "Our dragon likes to take on human form to deceive those around him. One of your fellow knights is actually the dragon in disguise. Challenge him, and he will take all of your coins and your game is over."

"The first two knights to find the lair, pay the dragon, and rescue the princess from the sarcophagus win the game. And the prize for the most valiant and cunning knights of all? They shall be promoted to the next station of the Gamemaster's Society."

Applause rumbles throughout the chamber. A couple guys roll their shoulders and drill fists into palms, trying to get amped up. Annabelle shushes everyone. "Oh, I almost forgot. We're down a member after what happened to poor Alicia. So, if Jordan makes it through the game, she'll become one of us."

If Jordan makes it through the game. "What does that mean?" I shout, trying again to push through the minions, but meeting resistance. This time, I slam my knuckles into a guy's lower back.

"Hey!" He spins around to glare at me.

"Get out of my way," I growl, raising my sore fist again.

He starts hissing some retort, but I drive through, lunging at Annabelle. "What does that mean, *if* Jordan makes it through the game?" I stop just short of grabbing her by the throat. Would Annabelle let Jordan run out of air?

But I know she would. She has Polly imprisoned somewhere down here. She poisoned Alicia Jones. My heavy head falls forward and I lean with my palms on my thighs. I made a mistake coming here. I thought I was helping Polly, but now Jordan is in danger, all because of me.

Annabelle lays a cold hand on my back, attempting to pull me up. "I meant if she doesn't get claustrophobic and quit, of course. What did you think I meant?"

I straighten, knocking her hand off me and looking her in the eyes. But those blue irises are as devoid of any authentic emotion as her smiling lips.

"So, if she freaks, you'll pull her out?"

"Of course. I'm not a monster. But everyone goes through an initiation here. She can't very well become a member simply because she's your friend. We have to test her, to see if she has the mental endurance to become one of us."

A hand falls onto my arm. Gavin is behind me, his glare matching my own as he pushes past me to reach our lovely leader. "But we chose to participate in those ceremonies, Annabelle," he says.

"As did Jordan. I didn't force her into the costume. Give her a chance, both of you. She may stomp all over your expectations. And if not, the guards who watch over her will release her from the sarcophagus."

The guards. She must be referring to the guy with the black coils and the bob-haired girl. Relief washes over me like a warm bath. She has people with her. They must've instructed Jordan to pretend she was being captured for show.

"What happens to the dragon?" Donella asks haughtily, touching up her lipstick in a hand mirror. "Why should anyone want to play the dragon if it doesn't come with an opportunity for promotion?"

"Of course," Annabelle says, lightly palming her forehead. "The dragon could well win the game. If every knight is eliminated, or if the princess is not recovered by sunrise, the dragon is champion."

Sunrise. Jordan could well be out of air by then.

"She'll be fine," Gavin whispers into my ear. "My friend Dallis was with her. He's not going to let anything happen."

Of course. It's just a game.

"And," Annabelle adds, her cerulean eyes glimmering in the firelight, "if the dragon wins, he or she will not only be promoted, but will receive an advantage at the next meeting's game."

A girl to my left gasps, and the room bursts into cheers. I try to clear my head, to get into competition mode the way I would before a lacrosse game. Annabelle promised to confide more about Polly if I reached a higher station.

I just have to be the best.

Annabelle begins doling out gold coins and envelopes—the duels. Each one is sealed with a wax linchpin. Annabelle tells us that we may not refuse a duel, the one exception being if our challenger's envelope has been previously opened.

Lastly, she passes out our roles. I cup my hands around mine, shielding the word from wandering eyes. My heart races. Maybe the role of the dragon comes with the princess's location. That way, I could check on Jordan throughout the game. But I read my role, and the idea slips and flops like a dying fish.

Knight

Guess I'll have to find her the Gamemaster's way.

Now, for dramatic flair, Annabelle walks the perimeter of the chamber, blowing out each lantern until we're cast in utter darkness.

"Victory or dust," she says, drawing the words out ghoulishly.

And we're off, bungling and bumping through the chamber and into the dimly lit corridor to the next room. Already, this is the deepest I've traveled into the catacombs since joining the society. The stonework, the pillars, the linchpin carving—it's all the same as the previous chamber. Only there are two doorways in here. The one at the back of the room, leading to the next corridor, and another on the right, containing a narrow, winding staircase.

My fellow society members break off, some headed straight while others take the stairs. "Come on," Remington says, motioning for me to join him down the steps. "Let's be allies."

"Allies?" I ask, confused but following him anyway, because I'm also in favor of the stairs, which means the alternative is slowing down.

"There are two winners. If we do this together, we can both win."

"How do I know you're not going to challenge me to a duel and take my coin?"

"I'd have to be an idiot to challenge the dragon," he says.

"Ha ha."

"You're still mad at me."

"Imagine that." Remington's legs are so long, he's taking the stone steps two at a time. "Probably not used to anyone being immune to your charm and good looks."

"So, then, you think I'm good-looking."

My cheeks scorch. "Shut up."

There are no lanterns in the stairwell, so it takes every effort not to tumble the rest of the way down. By the time we make it to the bottom where the stairs end in an arched doorway, my thighs are burning.

I attempt to pass through, but Remington sidesteps in

front of me, forcing me to face him. "Look, Maren, I have my reasons for not going to the headmistress."

"You said." Steps pound above us, and Remington ushers me out of the way right before Donella barrels us over. "Though you didn't actually say what they are."

"I see you followed through on your task," Remington says, ignoring my remark. "Doesn't that make you just as bad as me?"

"No," I say, though it takes some effort to push past the guilt coagulating in my throat. "Because I'm not here for glory or status or perfect SAT scores."

"That's what you think?" Firelight dances on the stairwell, its tendrils illuminating Remington's face, which jerks back now. "Maren, that's not what this is. Remember when I said the society offered me something?"

"Something you'd be a fool to refuse," I finish.

He nods. Here it comes. Whatever vile act he committed that the Gamemaster's Society has agreed to erase. His eyes don't meet mine as he runs a hand through his dark curls. "Last year," he starts, lowering his voice when more movement rumbles through the stairwell.

"I'm listening," I press.

But a shadow covers him now and blots out the flickering firelight. "You," comes a voice from the bottom step. The shadow transforms, becoming Gavin. He thrusts something forward and nearly hits Remington in the face. "I challenge you to whatever's in this envelope."

FOURTEEN

"You're an idiot," Remington says, irritation carving lines over his forehead.

Gavin *is* an idiot. At least, if the duel is a battle of strength or athleticism.

If it's a battle of the mind, however, it could be anyone's game.

"Maybe I am." Gavin slouches against a pillar, fanning his face with the envelope, even though it's freezing down here.

Remington sighs loudly. "You only have one coin. If I beat you—and I assure you, I will beat you—you're out."

"It had to be done," Gavin says simply. "You were bothering Maren."

"I wasn't—"

"Shh." Gavin smirks, knowing he's riled Remington up. "We're wasting my search time with talking. I have to eliminate you so you'll stop slowing my ally down."

"*Your* ally?" Remington throws me a wide-eyed look.

"I mean, technically," I say, "I didn't agree to be anyone's ally. Maybe you two *should* fight it out. Victory or dust and all."

Remington seethes in a way that makes my insides flutter.

Gavin smiles proudly. "So we're agreed." He makes to rip open the envelope, and I grab his hand.

"Wait!" I shout. "Maybe we should hold off on the duel." Remington's eyes are stuck to my hand on Gavin's, but he lifts them to join Gavin in staring incredulously at me. "The three of us could align ourselves until the very end. I think with both of your...very *different* skill sets, the three of us will get to Jordan a lot faster than any two of us. Then, once we've located her, the two of you can duel it out." They've barely blinked since I started my appeal. "You don't want to sit out the whole game, do you? This way, at least you both get to play."

The slap of a shoe against stone sounds in the stairwell again, and Gavin jumps to attention. "I'm in if he's in."

The footsteps are closer now. Remington slips an arm around my back, and the three of us press beneath the archway and into the next, lantern-lined chamber. I stride to the far wall, where another sunken arch leads to an alcove. A massive stone sarcophagus sits in the center, and I have to duck to make it beneath the recessed ceiling.

Elaborate carvings adorn the stonework of the sarcoph-agus, and I kneel, shining my phone's light over it to get a better look. I make out a horse-drawn chariot, its rider baring sharp teeth as his steed tramples a bleeding charioteer on the ground. I frown up at Gavin. "There would be guards with Jordan, right? If we were at the right sarcophagus, I mean."

He turns around, heading back into the chamber. "The only thing I know is she wouldn't be this easy to find. The Gamemaster wants to challenge us. We're looking for a locked vault or a hidden chamber you don't see unless you happen to hum the right tune as you pass by it. Something like that."

"So, something straight out of a fairytale, basically."

"Yes."

"Well," Remington says, brushing the dust off his pants, "on the off chance that Annabelle stuck Jordan right in front of us so she could sit and laugh about it for the rest of the year, help me move this lid."

Gavin spins, annoyance pinching his lips. But he concedes, probably because that sounds exactly like something Annabelle would do.

Together, the three of us lift and push the massive stone lid enough to reveal its contents. The already-musty scent of the tomb ripens. "Jordan," I whisper into the box.

"She's not in here," Remington says, his hand falling onto my shoulder.

"No, but…" *Something is.* "What's in it?"

"I don't know," Gavin says, "but we don't really have time—"

Remington and I are already situated with our fingers beneath the lid. We grunt and heft until the lid moves another six inches.

My breath hitches. Inside the box, dressed in ancient, tattered clothing, lies a skeleton.

"Whoa," Gavin whispers, reaching into the sarcophagus.

"What are you doing?" I snatch his hand back.

"Some archaeological work," he says, shaking his hand like I've injured him. "When's the last time you were in a *real* crypt with *real* bodies?"

"Apparently, two nights ago," I deadpan. "And the night before that too. You're telling me you didn't know this was an actual crypt?" Annabelle said this place was built for the society, before the academy was even erected. I figured they liked the secrecy below grounds, not that they'd actually buried people down here.

"I knew." Gavin leans over the dust-ridden box. "But I never opened one of these things before."

"Who do you think this guy was?" Remington asks, as enthralled as Gavin.

"We need to find Jordan," I say, abandoning the coffin. "For all we know, this poor dead guy was simply playing princess for a former Annabelle."

The guys follow me back inside the open chamber, where two wooden doors with brass knobs stand.

"Left or right?" Remington asks.

"Right, obviously." Gavin strides toward it before turning, head down in the exact opposite direction. "I meant left, of course."

"Maybe we should split up," Remington says uncertainly.

"Excellent idea." Gavin nods, looping his arm through mine. "We will definitely meet up with you later, and definitely include you when we find the princess. Victory or dust to you, sir."

"No." Remington blocks the left door. "I meant, Maren and *I* will go through the right side, and you'll go through the left. We have our phones, so we can text each other once we find Jordan."

"Likely story," Gavin says, leaning an elbow onto a low stone wall.

"Even if you two could trust each other," I add, holding up my phone, "there's no cell reception on this level. Either we stick together, or the alliance is off."

"Maren," Remington pleads through his teeth, "this guy is only slowing us down. Cut off the dead limb."

Gavin's smirk sinks slightly as he watches me.

"He's not a dead limb," I say. "Just an absentminded, somewhat pyromaniacal limb. And he may come in handy, you know, if the only way to get through a door is to devise a bomb out of materials you find in a tomb."

Gavin's eyes light up, his shoulders straightening. He twists the knob on the right and pulls, and the three of us make our way into another dark chamber. On the far wall, lanterns are mounted in small niches. Beneath them, a large cutaway holds another sarcophagus.

We race toward it, but a door off to the left swings open, nearly knocking Gavin over.

In struts Donella.

We spin, our backs to the coffin as she marches over, whipping a card in front of my face. "I challenge you," she snarls, and I wish more than anything I were the dragon so I could laugh in her face and take her gold.

My fists ball. "See if Jordan's in there," I whisper into Remington's ear, tipping my head toward the sarcophagus.

He nods, and I turn to face Donella, who's already tearing open the envelope. "What's the duel?"

"'First knight to complete the challenge wins,'" she reads. Then she holds her hand out to me, sliding one of two cards as well as a miniature fountain pen into mine. Before I comprehend what's going on, Donella dives to the floor by the wall where the lantern light shines brightest and begins scribbling furiously.

It's almost impossible to see in the chamber, so I fumble in my pocket for my phone and turn on the light, examining the card.

It's a labyrinth.

The maze is intricate, the walls formed of mythological creatures baring fangs and talons. My first attempt ends in one of the many heads of some beast, so I reroute, ignoring Donella's frantic scribbling and the grating sounds of Gavin and Remington searching the sarcophagus.

A warm light hovers over me now, illuminating the card. One of the guys must've grabbed a lantern from the wall by Donella to aid my efforts.

Beside me, she lets out a growl and scrambles to find more light. Hand blazing, my pen tip winds past Medusa's snakes, through the fires of Hades, and under a harpy's wing. It lands on the peak of Mount Olympus, otherwise known as the finish line.

"Done!" I yell.

Donella flings her card to the floor. "You three cheated."

"There weren't any rules against helping or hindering fellow knights," I say, turning to find Remington returning the lantern to its niche. "You should've made allies." I stuff the card into my back pocket and hold out my hand, waiting as Donella, jaw clenched, digs through her shoulder-slung purse for her coin. She drops it into my palm and spins off, probably to tattle.

"Nothing in there?" I ask the guys, but they're already motioning for me to follow them out the door.

The next section of vault is narrow, with a sunken ceiling and no lanterns. Suddenly, a thought hits me like a bolt of lightning: a door could be hidden along these walls and we would never know it. Still hurrying, I dust my fingertips along the rough stone, checking for any grooves or variations in the surface.

Polly's cell is down in these catacombs, yet Annabelle is holding a game of hide-and-seek here. She must be pretty confident we're not going to stumble upon the wrong prisoner. A horrible sensation wriggles through my veins.

Just how far do these catacombs go?

My fingers hit air again, and one of the guys takes hold of my wrist, tugging me around a pillar and into the next chamber. There are no lanterns inside. I move along the walls, not wanting to miss any sign that Polly or Jordan could be in this room.

A door slams, jolting me. "What was that?" I ask, my hands out in front of me, feeling for Gavin and Remington.

"I don't know." Remington's voice. I activate my phone's light and find the two of us alone in the chamber.

"Where's Gavin?" I ask, whipping my phone around.

"Must've ditched us."

I sigh. Typical Gavin. Just when I thought he was being so chivalrous.

I step past Remington, his cedar-barreled lemon scent punching through the dankness of the vault.

"Wait." Remington's hand moves to my shoulder, spinning me to face him. My phone drops at my side, and its light spills onto the floor. "I never got to tell you why I stayed in the society."

His hand lingers on my shoulder, the only thing ground-ing me in this black void. "No, you didn't." The darkness, the scent, his close proximity—it all reminds me of that moment in the hidden liquor closet. The moment I wondered if Remington Cruz's lips might meet mine.

"And you never told me why you stayed."

"I didn't." But I want to. With everything in me. If only I could be certain he hasn't made a deal with Annabelle. If word gets back to her that I'm doing anything other than playing her game, she could make good on her threat to hurt Polly.

If I tell Remington, though, maybe we can search for Polly together. I thought Gavin was on my side, but he ditched me.

Then again, what if Remington doesn't believe me? It is only my word against Annabelle's that the video proof of Polly even exists.

"You can trust me," he says, his voice warm in the damp, frigid air. "How about we swap reasons?"

I consider this, letting his hand trail slowly down my arm. My ability to think clearly melts away as tingles course to my fingertips. I breathe in, tucking a loose strand of hair behind my ear. *Think, think, think.* If he tells me whatever dirt the society has on him—whatever they're covering up—it would be insurance. He wouldn't be able to double-cross me.

His index finger draws a trail back up my bicep, and I shut my eyes, even though the only light in this room is shining on my feet. Somehow, this is easier in utter darkness. "Fine," I say. "Tell me your reason, and I promise to tell you mine."

He takes both of my hands in his now. "I believe you." Though we're technically far beneath the cathedral, within these antiquated stone walls our exchanged words feel like a vow.

"Over the summer," he starts, "my girlfriend Jane and I broke up. It was completely amicable. We'd grown apart. But afterward, I noticed her hanging out with Annabelle." I feel his body shift uneasily. "This past February, I found out she'd opted to study abroad in Switzerland for the remainder of the semester. I was happy for her, but when I texted her as much, she didn't text me back. So I tried email, and same thing. No answer."

My head spins. I've barely been breathing, afraid of missing even one of his words. I inhale, my hands unmoving in Remington's.

"When I contacted Jane's parents, they told me to stop worrying. That Jane had been emailing them from Switzerland, and I needed to let go, to let her live her life. So I did. But then a couple weeks ago, I discovered one of Jane's handbags in with my banquet attire—one I must've missed when we broke up." His fingers trace over my palms. "Inside, she had this." He lets go of my hands, rustles through a pocket, and presses something cold into my palm.

I don't need my light to recognize the object; it's a silver linchpin pendant.

"I did enough digging to figure out that it's the society's symbol, and then I tracked down Annabelle, ready to join if I had to in order to find Jane."

"So," I say, pausing to clear my throat, "your dad was never a member."

He gives a subtle headshake. "He was a student here, back in the nineties, but never a member." He flushes. "I'm sorry, Maren. I didn't know you. I had to come up with a reason for knowing the society existed."

"And that thing Annabelle offered you—it was Jane?"

"Only information about her," he corrects. "But now that I have it, it seems pretty clear she's in trouble."

He must've received a video, like I did. "But if you say anything to anyone," I mutter, "Annabelle will hurt Jane."

Remington doesn't answer, so I flick my phone light up at his face. His brown eyes watch me warily. "I know because I'm here for the same reason—not for Jane. For my best friend, Polly. At least, she *was* my best friend before she traded me for the society." My voice cracks. Remington wraps his arms around me, and I nearly unravel as I sink into him. I draw in a breath, forcing brimming tears back down. "After I brought Jordan," I continue with my cheek pressed to his chest, "Annabelle showed me proof that Polly's alive. I think she's somewhere in the catacombs, but I won't get more information unless I keep playing the games."

Remington lets out a sharp sigh, his breath rustling my hair. "We're going to find them, Maren. Both of them."

"But how? This whole time we've been searching for Jordan, I've been searching for Polly too. I keep checking the walls for a hidden door, something like the one in the Grand Banquet Hall. So far, there's nothing."

"If I win," Remington says, his voice husky, "Annabelle promised me another clue about Jane's whereabouts."

"She promised me the same thing. But in order to win, we still have to find Jordan." My head tips back in frustration. "You don't even have your second coin."

A sharp knock on the door sounds, followed by a series of thumps, each one rattling my nerves. "It could be another knight," Remington whispers. "I can win a coin."

"Be careful. We don't know the dragon's identity." But a thought pushes my spirits up. Maybe the knocking is Gavin. Maybe he got lost in the dark and finally found us. I nearly laugh out loud; that would be *so* Gavin. I reach for the knocker, tugging a few times, but it's stuck. "How could it be locked?"

My heart thrums at the thought of being locked down here overnight with the skeletons.

Remington brushes past me, giving one hard yank. It creaks open. I'm about to joke that I loosened it for him, but a figure stumbles into the chamber. When I raise my still-lit phone to illuminate his features, my blood chills.

It's Gavin's friend, Dallis—the guy with the black coils who escorted Jordan to her hiding place.

The one Annabelle promised would be watching over Jordan right now.

And there's something on the floor by his feet. A piece of fabric, white and trimmed with lace, like the shroud Jordan was wearing before she was taken away. The edges are rough, like they've been torn.

And it's doused in blood.

FIFTEEN

"You." DALLIS LIFTS A LANTERN IN THE DOORWAY AND frowns, assessing Remington like he might catch a flash of dragon scales.

"I challenge you," Remington spits, wrenching an envelope from his pocket.

"Wait a minute." I throw myself between them. "What is that?" I rush to the piece of fabric, crouching to pick it up by a clean corner.

Cold drips down my spine as I stand, holding up the bloody muslin and staring at Dallis. "What did you do to Jordan?"

He scoffs. "*I* didn't do anything to her. But we'd better find her fast."

"We?" The room starts to narrow. "You're supposed to be guarding her. What are you doing here?"

Dallis flashes an irritated glance at me. "Annabelle relieved me of my duties so I could participate in the game."

"And the girl who was with you?"

"Playing the game."

"No, no, no, no." I grab my head in both hands, spinning until my shoulder hits the wall. "You left Jordan alone with *Annabelle*?"

"I follow commands, same as you." He turns to Remington. "Now let's duel."

"Reming—"

"Go," he says. "I'll catch up with you afterward. You have your coins. Go find her."

Torn, I grip the doorway so hard the jagged stone digs into my palms. The last thing I want to do is navigate this creepy lair alone. But too much time has passed. I glance at my phone. 1:05 a.m. Best-case scenario, Jordan is out of her mind with panic.

Worst-case scenario…

My legs liquify beneath me. Pushing the thought aside, I turn on my heels and dive back into the dark corridor. This time, I wave my phone ahead of me like a flashlight, searching for a new chamber. Did I even check the last one for a second door? I don't remember, and everything is starting to look the same.

This place is a maze.

At that, a thought lights up, as if charged. The duel. I dig the card from my back pocket, squinting at it in the wispy light. *It can't be.*

But the staircase we took is at the bottom of the card. I trace my finger through two suspiciously familiar rooms. I start to move again, glancing down at the card, which shows a chamber guarded by a hydra on the left, followed by a corridor looping off to the right.

I look up, and sure enough, I pass the chamber on my left. While there's no creature standing guard, there is a passage-way up ahead. And it veers right. My pulse quickens.

The labyrinth on the card is a replica of the catacombs.

And Mount Olympus?

That could be where Annabelle is keeping Jordan.

Ahead, light pours into the dark corridor. If it's a door, it could lead to the passageway guarded by the cyclops on my map. I pick up my steps, turning toward the light.

I'm nearly there when something hits me like a brick to the stomach. I bounce backward, stumbling into a wall. The thing I ran into—a person—slips a hand around my waist to steady me. I catch my breath and squint up into a pair of glasses. "Maren? Are you okay?"

"Gavin," I mutter through a cough. "Can you do anything right?"

"Why would I want to do right," he says, a grin forming,

"when messing up got me here?" His gaze flicks to his hand still on my waist.

My cheeks burn, and I shove him off me. "I didn't just mean knocking into me like a wild boar. You ditched me back there."

"Ditched you?" His smirk falls. "That wasn't me. Your pal, Remington, gave me the slip. He stole my phone so I couldn't see, and I had no way of finding you. I've mostly been wandering these corridors—I nearly killed myself stepping onto a staircase that I thought was a new chamber. I mean, I get it. I would find me pretty intimidating too. Remington must've been too afraid to duel me. But"—he waggles his brows—"the good news is that Tony, may he rest in metaphorical peace, challenged me to a duel, and I won. So now our purses are full, and we shall save the princess."

"This isn't a joke, Gavin." I push past him into the passage, relief bubbling up inside me when I see that it matches the one on the map. This is the way.

"What do you mean?" he asks, chasing after me.

"Your *friend*, Dallis, the one you promised was trustworthy, abandoned Jordan." Lantern light spills down the dark corridor and onto the arched doorway at the end. "She could already be running out of air, and we both know Annabelle wouldn't lift a perfect finger to help her." When we reach the doorway, sure enough, the next passage opens in both directions. According to the map, the right side is guarded by the cyclops; we have to go left to find Mount Olympus.

"Okay," Gavin says, huffing to keep up with me. "So then, hurry up already. Let's find her. Also, what are you looking at?"

"The maze. The one from my duel. It's a map of the catacombs. I think if we follow it to Mount Olympus, avoiding the mythological creatures, Jordan will be there."

"Why did you get a map and no one else?"

"Technically, Donella got the map. Anyone could've won it off her." I fly through the next passage, barely slowing when I enter a wider chamber with its own alcove. There's likely a sarcophagus inside, but I have to trust my instincts about the map. It's my best shot at finding Jordan alive. "Maybe everyone has a clue and they don't know it. What was your duel?"

"One of those brainteaser puzzle things where you have to be the first to say how many rectangles there are, counting the rectangles outside and excluding the colored rectangle inside, but *adding* your great-aunt's second cousin on your dad's side." I roll my eyes even though he's behind me. "As soon as I got Tony's coin, I crumpled the puzzle up."

"Could the rectangles have represented chambers?"

"Well, I mean…"

"And the colored chamber? What do you think that was?"

Gavin's growl echoes through the corridor. "So, what is this Mount Olympus, then?"

"We came down a staircase at the very beginning of the game. We have to get back up to that level, but on a different set of stairs at the far end of the catacombs." I reach the doorway, pausing to double-check my map. Voices float through the upcoming passageway, and I spin around, pressing an index finger to my lips. I grab Gavin by the bicep and drag him behind a pillar opposite the alcove. Together, we duck down as the voices near the chamber.

Gavin's breathing is ragged beside me. The footsteps in the doorway compete with my heart pumping in my ears. A shadow crosses the threshold, and the lanterns cast a glow over the approaching face: Remington's.

Gavin jerks forward, but I dig my stubby fingernails into his arm. He turns to object, and I clamp my hand over his mouth.

Because Remington isn't alone.

A girl trails after him. The one with the sleek brown bob—Jordan's other "guard." So what is she doing with Remington? A hot sensation rolls through my stomach.

Gavin wrenches his arm from my grasp. "Call my phone," he whispers into my ear, each word punctuated with fire.

But I can't afford another duel. I already have my two coins. All I need is to get out of here and reach Jordan. If Bob Girl notices us—if the sound of the phone draws attention from other knights—it could be disastrous. "Forget your phone," I say, and across the vault, Remington's head snaps in our direction, eyes wary for a moment. But then his attention shifts back to the girl.

"Probably no signal anyway," I whisper, my lips pressed close to his ear. "We'll get it back after we win."

Gavin looks ready to leap to his feet, and at this point, all I can do is shut my eyes and hope he doesn't do something moronic.

"I think you're headed the right way," Remington says to Bob Girl. "See if that passage goes through. I'll check this sarcophagus and catch up with you."

Bob Girl nods and scurries through the archway. The moment Remington disappears into the alcove, Gavin and I stand, tiptoeing past the pillars.

"Guys," Remington hisses, and my heart seizes. I consider making a break for the doorway, but his hulking figure is on us in seconds.

I spin to face him. "Hey!" I force a note of surprise into my voice. "You won your duel."

"Yeah," he says, drawing the word out. "And now I've caught up with you, to find Jordan. So…" He casts a sharp glance at Gavin. "What's he doing here?"

"Call my phone, Maren," Gavin says, crossing his arms.

I press my fingers into my temples until it hurts. "Seeing as how Remington made a new *friend*," I say, incapable of keeping the venom off my tongue, "we have to stay quiet."

"You're really going to take him with us when he tried to sabotage me?"

"Sabotage you?" Remington asks, looking at me for

answers before turning on Gavin. "You abandoned *us*, and you're really going to claim I tried to sabotage you? Which would be a complete waste of energy, by the way, seeing as how you're a natural screwup."

"Maren," Gavin starts, but I hold a hand up.

"I don't care. You're forgetting that Jordan is trapped in a sarcophagus somewhere. She's all alone, and you two idiots are still fighting over this game."

"Sorry," Gavin mumbles.

"I apologize," Remington says, head lowering. "Let's go find Jordan."

I lead the way, past the mother of all sarcophagi tucked within an alcove the size of a chamber. But I'm not tempted to check the space. I have my map; I have to trust that it's leading me to Jordan. "What about your new *friend*?" Gavin asks Remington wryly. "Surely, you weren't intending to abandon her?"

"Yes," Remington blurts. "I mean...she found me, and I had to align myself with her for a while, only until I could find you again. Maren, you know how important it is that I win this."

I shush him, because we've reached the staircase on the map. The one that leads to Mount Olympus. My chest inflates so big it could carry me to the top, if not for these bickering boys. Instead, I have to force my leaden legs one stair at a time until, huffing, I make it.

Candlelight flickers at the top of the stairs, illuminating a passageway that continues in either direction. But something straight ahead captures my attention. A cutout in the wall containing an enormous fresco: two eyeballs overlooking a mountain as a bloody battle plays out below.

I shudder. Tucked beneath the image is a display table filled with wine chalices and loaves of bread, just like in the antechamber. With one major difference.

This table has been crafted with human bones. Lengthy limb bones make up the legs and the bumpy tabletop, while a skull's hollow sockets stare from each corner.

Cringing, I glance to the left, where a wooden door with a brass knocker looms, and release a heavy breath.

We made it.

I hurry over and reach for the knocker, fumbling for the coins in my left pocket. But I pause, turning back to the guys.

"Go ahead," Remington assures me, touching my shoulder lightly. "You have your coins. We'll sort the rest. You go in and get Jordan."

I inhale, wanting to agree but fearful of what I might find beyond this closed door.

And fearful of something else. Behind Remington, Gavin stands, fist in palm, ready for battle. "Gavin," I say, taking two quick steps toward him.

"What is it?" He places a protective hand on my wrist, peering suspiciously past me at Remington.

"You have to let him win."

Gavin's head wrenches back. "What?"

"I can't explain, not here." I keep my voice low, remembering the cameras during the last game, remembering the way we felt watched every step of the way. "But Remington needs this. It's a matter of life and death."

Gavin stares at me, his ever-present smirk contorting. "But I—"

"Please." Wincing, I turn back to the door.

I lick my dry lips and knock once. Twice. Three times. It bangs, brass against brass. The door remains shut. My palms are damp, but I try to yank on the knocker, to open it myself.

Suddenly, the door groans as it cracks open, and the breath flees my lungs.

I wander into the room, passing Annabelle, who smiles smugly at me. I search for the sarcophagus, listening— hoping Jordan still has enough life in her to call and scream and bang on the lid.

And I almost miss it, because it's not a sarcophagus at all.

Perched on a stone ledge, candlelight turning her dark waves a radiant Bordeaux, is Jordan. She's still draped in stark white, like a dove on a windowsill.

She bounces on the ledge when she spots me, her hands clapping together in delight. "Maren, you've won!" There's a small bandage wrapped around her index finger, and the hem of her dress has been torn; other than that, no signs of bodily damage or whatever I saw on that scrap of fabric earlier.

Have I won? I stagger, feeling for the wall to hold me up. I have my coins. I've located the princess. Found her alive and well.

But winning feels a lot like being played.

SIXTEEN

"MAREN, ARE YOU OKAY? MAREN." THE VOICE RINGS IN MY ear, distant and foreign. I don't want to get closer to it, so I shut my eyes and cover my ears with both hands.

"Maren!" Fingers tug on me now, removing my hands and shaking me. I blink the darkness away until the girl comes into focus, an angel in this inferno.

"Jordan." Even my own voice sounds like it's coming from a boat, far out at sea. "I thought they'd drained your blood and then trapped you inside a coffin."

"What? No!" Jordan tucks a strand of my wild hair behind my ear and helps steady me. "Annabelle said all the initiates have to give blood, which was kind of gross, but I decided to be brave like you. She and I have just been chatting. And," she says, leaning closer conspiratorially, "drinking something we're not supposed to have at school."

Panic blares in my head like an alarm. "She gave you wine?"

A laugh, light and airy, echoes through the chamber. "Oh Maren, you really missed your calling, didn't you? There's still time to get you up on the stage before graduation."

"It's not like you haven't poisoned someone in the last week."

Annabelle glares sharply at me. A warning. Speak up any more, and Polly could end up worse off than Alicia Jones.

"Just give me my next clue," I say, exhaustion creeping into my head, my muscles, my everything. I'm tired of playing Annabelle's games.

"Oh, but we're still waiting on our male victor," Annabelle says vibrantly.

I want to be carried to my bed, so I can sleep until next week. But voices trickle in from the passageway, and I duck out to check on the commotion.

Leaning against a wall beside the table of bones, Gavin is wadding something up in his fist.

Opposite him, Remington stands with his eyes shut, his chest rolling in a set of long breaths. Then, passing me a quick nod, he presses on into the room.

I near Gavin, who stares down at the floor, unwilling to meet my gaze. "I did it for you, not for *him*. And if Annabelle ever finds out I threw a game, she'll probably drop me a station, or worse." I swallow, my head spinning with visions of Polly trapped in that cell. "It was a brain game, just so you know." His voice is calm and low; I'd rather have him blow up at me. "If the card had asked us to wrestle until the other guy cried mercy, at least that would've been believable. I had to wait forever for that idiot to figure it out."

He shoves the card into my hand. BORN OF BATTLE AND SHROUDED IN CLOUD. TWELVE SETS OF EYES WATCH FROM ON HIGH. NAME THAT LOCATION.

I glance at the fresco before me, an uneasy feeling shifting in my stomach, like insects crawling over my intestines. Mount Olympus. The home of the gods.

"Gavin!" I call out, but he's already headed down the corridor.

"Just get my phone back," he says, his figure already fading to black.

My legs are too weak to chase after him. "Thank you," I whisper to no one but the skulls.

I wander back into the room, where Remington is checking on Jordan in the center of the room.

"I'm really fine, I promise," she says, blushing.

"Well then," Annabelle says, sitting on the sill where I found Jordan, sipping wine from a chalice. "Jordan, if you'll see your way to the entrance, I need to speak with the champions in private."

"Oh." Jordan glances out the door, paling. "I'm not sure I know the way. What if I just—"

"Don't be silly. Take that corridor all the way down and make a right at the end."

"We'll catch up with you in a sec," I assure her, still so relieved she's alive but also wanting to keep her that way.

Jordan tiptoes out, brandishing her phone before her like a weapon. I turn to Annabelle. "Where's Polly? I did what you asked. I won the game. Now give me back my friend."

"*My* friend, if I remember correctly. Or at least she was, until I locked her up." Annabelle shrugs, staring down at the bloodred liquid in her cup.

"Quit stalling, Annabelle," says Remington.

"You always were so impatient, weren't you?" She sets her chalice down on the ledge and glides toward Remington, her long dress train swishing across the stone floor as she looks him over.

"You promised information," he says.

"And I make good on my promises." She runs a hand over his bicep in a familiar way that makes my insides clench. "Show me the map."

I flinch. How could she know I have the map?

As if reading my mind, Annabelle rolls her eyes. "I gave it to Donella, who was eliminated by you. Without the map, it would've been another hour before anyone stumbled upon this back staircase. Now, give it to me."

I study her another moment, then tug the map from my back pocket and hand it over. This must mean she's going to point out Polly's location. Jane's even.

Annabelle holds the drawing of the catacombs out on her palm, her other index finger doodling through the air above it. Her finger flicks up in dramatic fashion, slowly lowering with its sharp ruby-colored fingernail. But her finger swipes take a jagged turn, trailing off the page. "The location of your friends isn't on the map."

Bile rises in my throat. I stagger backward.

Remington catches me, letting me rest against his sturdy frame. "That's not a clue, Annabelle."

"It is. I've just eliminated every chamber on this map."

"And added literally every other place on the face of the earth," I mutter, snatching it back from her.

"Funny, Maren. Your friends are in the catacombs. But I can't give away every one of my secrets. So, I left my favorite location off the map."

"What do you want from us?" Remington asks, ensuring I'm steady before stepping toward her. "How do you think this is going to end?"

"How do *you* think this is going to end?" Her gaze snaps to mine.

"I don't know." My head falls into my hands. "I don't even understand why you have Polly and Jane."

"Maybe they asked too many questions," she says, meandering back to her chalice. "Maybe Jane and Polly are doing penance for crimes committed against the society."

"But how come no one's come looking for them? How

could Jane's parents believe she's studying abroad when she's really trapped down here?"

"Jane wants to stay alive. She tells her parents whatever I want her to tell them."

"And Polly? You forced her to write that note, didn't you?" Annabelle's shrug suffices as a response.

"What about Alicia?" Remington asks. "How could the academy convince authorities—doctors even—she suffered from a peanut allergy after you poisoned her?"

A drop of red wine sits on the rim of Annabelle's glass, and slowly, she licks it off. "I think you'll find the society's reach is further than you can imagine."

"What does that mean?" She doesn't answer, and I don't really care. I just want my friend back. "How long do you expect us to keep playing these games? When are you going to release them?"

"Release them?" Annabelle's brows draw together. "Is that what you think is going to happen?" She giggles, the sound sending chills up the base of my skull. "*I'm* not going to release them." She sobers suddenly. "*You* are."

Remington and I exchange a glance. "But how?"

"Keep playing. You'll soon receive another task. Something that will narrow down all that blank space around your map."

"No way," Remington says. "We're going to the cops tonight."

"Do that, and you and your friends will end up worse off than Alicia Jones. I'd barely have to snap my fingers to make that happen." Annabelle crosses the stretch of cell before him and heads out the door. "Now let's announce our champions to the others. I can't wait for you both to see what's in store for Medi Supremes."

"If it's anything like Minor Supreme," I mumble to Remington, "it'll be blackmail and the feeling that I'm a mouse being dragged around by its tail." We follow her through the narrow corridor, and my gaze travels back up to the fresco of the enormous eyes, watching the battle below from the clouds. As if some inoperative part of my brain has been suddenly switched on, Gloucester's next line from *King Lear* wriggles into my brain.

As flies to wanton boys are we to the gods;
they kill us for their sport.

A shudder wracks my body, and Remington removes his coat, placing it over my shoulders. I thank him and carefully skirt the creepy bone table. But the chill isn't from the cold.

Following Annabelle, who struts with her lantern held high to light the way, you would never know this place is a tangled monstrosity. "You were right," Remington says, his voice low. "We should've told someone. I don't like waiting around, letting her have all the power. Maybe a teacher would listen."

I think of Dr. Yamashiro and nod. Annabelle threatened

the lives of our friends, but maybe Dr. Yamashiro would know what to do. As long as Annabelle doesn't hear about it. I pull his coat tighter around me, noting the weight tugging one side lower than the other. I slip my hand inside the pocket, finding a phone.

Gavin's accusation ricochets back. I have to erase it, once and for all.

I tug my own phone out of my jeans, and as suspected, there's no signal. I keep checking, glancing down at the screen every few seconds. When we reach the final corridor before the antechamber, the weakest little bar appears at the top of my screen, and I call Gavin.

The phone in Remington's coat pocket rings, startling me. Annabelle stops, glancing sharply back at us.

"Sorry," I mutter, fumbling through the coat pocket. Beside me, Remington's eyes widen in the dim light.

Still shaken, I grasp the phone and silence it, picturing only Montresor from "The Cask of Amontillado" with his black mask, deviously plotting down in the tomb.

Annabelle turns to keep walking. "Gavin was right," I whisper to Remington. "You stole his phone and ditched him."

Remington's steps halt. "That isn't what happened," he says, scrambling to catch up now. "He asked me to hold his phone for extra light while he checked some inscription on the wall. But by the time I got the light turned on, he'd vanished."

I can't look up, because his warm brown eyes will turn my willpower to putty and my mind to mush. "Right."

"Maren," Remington says, reaching for me.

"I'm too tired for this." I shrug off his coat and toss it at his chest.

Moments later, we reach the antechamber, where we're greeted by rumbling applause and a banquet not even my brain can digest.

I leave Remington beneath the archway, stride to the display, and take a swig of wine.

Then, spinning to face what I now see is a tide of envious glares, I search for the only person I can trust in the society.

SEVENTEEN

IN THE MORNING, MY EYES OPEN, DRINKING IN THE SUNLIGHT seconds before panic hits me like a lacrosse ball to the face.

What time is it? I scramble for my phone on the floor, dread wrenching me out of bed. *9:30 a.m..* I slept through not only breakfast, but through half of chemistry. Which means I'm missing a test.

I vaguely remember thinking about setting my phone alarm last night—or early this morning, whenever I stumbled into bed, half-conscious—but I must've fallen asleep before getting to it. I throw on a sweatshirt, grab my backpack, and start for the door, almost making it into the hallway in my pajama pants. But some stubborn part of me can't give Gavin the satisfaction, so I waste precious seconds wiggling out of them and tugging on sweatpants.

Then I race across campus to the Lowell Math and Science Building.

By the time I arrive, the bell rings for the end of class. I peer through the glass cutout in the door to watch my classmates pack up, turning in their tests to Dr. Yamashiro on their way out. My head tips back, and I shut my eyes against the coming tears. I cannot believe I did this. After my dad told me I couldn't afford to mess up. After he told me my financial situation was dangling on a nonexistent limb. What's he going to think of me now?

I didn't need Gavin and his explosions to screw up my chemistry grade. I did it all on my own. Even if the best possible outcome magically occurred and I walked up to Dr. Yamashiro and got him to give me a makeup test, I would probably fail. I've spent so much time playing these Gamemaster's Society games, I let my studies fall completely through the cracks.

"Hey, Maren." There's a tap on my shoulder, and I open my eyes to see Gavin looking at me strangely. "Are you okay?"

I take a slow breath. I don't want to cry in front of him. "I guess all these late nights finally caught up with me. I fell asleep without setting my alarm."

Gavin winces, glancing back through the open door. When he turns to me, he's staring at the floor. With a stab, I remember the way we left things only hours ago. I returned his phone and thanked him for throwing his duel. He walked me back to my dorm, broody the whole way; I'd refused to share the reason I needed Remington to win so badly. "Maybe Dr. Yamashiro will let you make it up."

"There's no way. He hates athletes. And what excuse could I possibly give? Sorry, I overslept because I was up late breaking countless school rules, not the least of which are breaking curfew, breaking and entering, and underage alcohol consumption."

"Sounds like a winning case to me." I slap him on the wrist, and he grins. "You have to try."

"Yeah," I say as the final stragglers pass through the door. Minutes remain before Dr. Yamashiro's next class will start filing in.

"I know this is…" he starts, lips twisting in thought, "a bit manipulative. But use Polly. As an excuse. It's the truth, isn't it? You missed class because you're investigating a secret society you believe will lead you to her." He shrugs. "Only leave basically all of that out. The teachers at this school are very understanding."

I nod, like I'm considering it. In reality, Gavin's idea just stirred up Remington's words from last night. *I don't like waiting around, letting her have all the power. Maybe a teacher would listen.* This could be my opportunity. Remington might've lied about Gavin's phone, but he's right about this: we can't keep letting Annabelle have all the control. We've been playing her games for days, and all this time, Polly has been suffering in a frigid cell.

Maybe with Dr. Yamashiro's help, we can keep Annabelle somewhere she can't hurt Polly or Jane while authorities search the catacombs.

Does Dr. Yamashiro even know about the catacombs? Our story sounds incredible, even without the whole ancient subterranean burial ground aspect. I look at Gavin, someone familiar with the inner workings of the society—someone who could vouch for everything I've said. Maybe he'd come in there with me. "Gavin," I say, but a sudden fear clamps my mouth shut again.

He was in the society before me. He joined it *willingly*. As much as I've grown to trust him, he could try to talk me out of confiding in Dr. Yamashiro.

Or worse. He could report my actions to Annabelle.

"Yeah?" He asks, leaning in close enough for me to smell the spice meets eucalyptus scent of his shampoo.

"Nothing." I smile. "I should get in there and accept my fate."

"Good luck." He reaches for my hand and squeezes it. When he lets go, his fingertips trail lightly up the length of my arm.

My stomach flips. I back up, and the door jabs my spine as Gavin ambles down the hall, tucking a stack of books beneath his arm, unaware of the effect he just had on me.

A decidedly weird effect.

I start to turn around when some papers slip from his

stack, landing on the floor. "Hey, Gavin," I call, scampering after him. "You dropped—" I stoop down to pick up the stapled stack, which a quick glance reveals to be facts about a drug called Zipromyacin.

"What is this about?" I ask as he reaches for the pages.

"It's nothing," he says quickly, tucking them into a notebook. "Some research for chemistry."

"You mean the class we have together?" I ask, a strange, heavy coating settling over my lungs. He just lied to my face.

Gavin inhales, biting his lip as he stands in front of me, silent for a too-long stretch of time. He reaches into the back pocket of his khaki pants to retrieve his wallet.

"Wait a minute," I say, suddenly certain he's going to try to pay me to keep quiet about his "research."

But it isn't money he hands me a second later. It's a photo of a little girl. She has the same honey-strewn shade of hair as Gavin's, only a touch lighter. Same green eyes. She's sitting in a wheelchair, unsmiling.

"My sister, Gabriella," Gavin says. "She's ten. A few years back, she started having health problems. Lots of them. Trouble breathing, moving, even speaking. Doctors ran millions of tests, but they never figured out what's wrong with her."

"That's terrible," I say, staring at the photo.

"Whatever it is, it's progressive, and it seems to be moving quickly. I don't know how much time Gabby has left. The papers you saw are trials for various medications that always seem promising, but never end up working."

"Is that why you joined the society? To try to pay for your sister's medical expenses?"

Gavin shakes his head. "This is about more than money. I'm in the society because I'm my sister's only hope." He lowers his voice, glancing over his shoulder. "At first it was a financial thing. I thought maybe if I could get high enough in the society, one day I'd have the resources to help her, or at the very least keep her comfortable. But now, since reaching Medi Supreme, these medications—these trials—I don't even know where they're coming from. Some doctor who is in the society sends me the results and moves on to the next drug. These people are doing things no amount of money can buy. Things that aren't exactly...aboveboard."

"You're letting them experiment on your sister?" I hiss.

"What else am I going to do? Let her die?"

"Gavin, these people are not good. I know it seems like it, but they *took* Polly."

Gavin's gaze drifts away from mine. "The more I think about it, the more I think Annabelle's playing with you. Like she did with Jordan. You were pretty worried about her too. It's what the Gamemaster does."

My stomach drops from under me. "No, Gavin. You don't understand."

"I don't need to understand," he says, green eyes

shimmering. "I need to win the games." He takes the photo back from me, returning it to his wallet with great care.

I remember the pained way he looked at me when I asked him to let Remington win. He might've given up progress with his sister's treatment because of me. "I'm sorry."

"You didn't know." He tightens his grip on his books and plods off, leaving me to face Dr. Yamashiro. Passing periods between classes at Torrey-Wells are fifteen minutes, which is necessary considering your next class could be a twelve-minute walk across campus. I've already spent half of these minutes with Gavin.

Inside, Dr. Yamashiro is sweeping his room for trash and possibly notes my class left for the next one about the test.

"Hi, Dr. Yamashiro," I say, cowering near the door.

"Maren." He meanders back to his desk. "I was so sorry to hear of your illness."

"My illness?"

He nods, sifting through the stack of tests. "Yes, but the take-home examination worked out perfectly. Ah, here it is." He lifts an exam and waves it before me. "I had time to grade it while your classmates were testing."

"The take-home exam," I repeat, licking my lips.

"Yes, one of your friends turned it in for you. Should you be walking around in your condition?"

"Dr. Yamashiro," I say, taking the exam from him. "I think you were misinformed."

But sure enough, my name is scribbled in the top right-hand corner.

Along with a big, red letter A. *Ninety-nine percent.*

A dagger of shock pierces my spine, up and out through my skull. When I attempt to speak, my mouth feels cottony.

One of your friends.

That's it. I'm telling him. Not just my suspicions concerning the test. All of it. Polly and the Gamemaster's Society. Alicia and the blackmail video. The proof Anabelle showed that Polly is being held in the catacombs.

"Dr. Yamashiro," I start, setting the test back down on the desk, "I have to tell you something."

"What is it, Maren? Are you sure you're okay?" He places his hands palm-down on the desk, peering at me through the frames of his glasses.

"Look, this is going to sound ridiculous." My gaze dives to the floor, searching for some way to explain the absurdity of the past few days to my completely rational and logical teacher. I glance up at the desk, where his hands still lie beside the fraudulent test, and a gleam from his coat sleeve snags my eye. A shiny, round, silver cufflink. Not any cufflink.

It's a linchpin.

My heart flops. I might be sick. *I think you'll find the society's reach is further than you can imagine.*

My vision narrows and darkens like the corridors of the catacombs. A pinprick of light flickers at the end, and I blink it into focus, finding only Dr. Yamashiro's smiling face. "What's going to sound ridiculous?"

Staggering back, I press a hand to my forehead. "I have a fever of 102." I giggle hysterically. "You're right. I shouldn't be walking around. I'm dizzy and I might be contagious. But I was so worried about the test."

"Nothing to worry about," he assures me. "I only wish all of my students were half as responsible as you. But you do need to get to bed. I'll send the campus physician to your room."

"No!" I say too forcefully. "I just need some sleep and tea. I'm sure my friends can manage. Thank you, sir."

"Okay," Dr. Yamashiro calls after me. "But get some rest."

Out in the hall, the immaculate tiles spin as I hurry over them, not even conscious of where I'm headed. This is what Annabelle meant. We're untouchable now.

Minor Supreme means elaborate cover-ups. Medi Supreme means getting bogus grades. Then there's whatever path Gavin's headed down, toward Major Supreme and its shady dealings. Lastly, there's Annabelle. The Gamemaster. And if Alicia, Polly, and Jane are any indication, being Gamemaster means playing with people's lives, even to the point of death.

It means becoming a god.

I hop on the escalator down to the lobby when my backpack starts ringing. I wrangle it off me and dig through the little pocket to find my phone.

Remington.

I don't want to hear about how he didn't try to sabotage Gavin last night. My finger moves to the "ignore" button but drifts over to "answer" instead.

"Maren." The name sweeps out with relief.

"Listen, Remington. I only answered to warn you. You can't tell anyone about *you know what*." I reach the lobby, where a solar-powered fountain towers up through the cylindrical building beneath a glass ceiling, and check my surroundings. "I spoke to Dr. Yamashiro—I didn't tell him anything. But it was bizarre. I missed a test this morning and he said it was fine because I'd already taken it. Then he waved a test at me, and the thing is, it was already graded. He'd given it an *A*."

"Do you think he made a mistake?"

"No, he didn't make a *mistake*," I practically spit. Students are still flooding through the glass front doors, so I slip between them and out into the gardens. "At first I thought maybe I was dreaming or that Annabelle had given me some sort of hallucinogen last night. But then I noticed his cufflink. And Remington"—I lower my voice—"it was a linchpin."

I wait for Remington to ask another frustrating question or to assure me I imagined it all; instead, he says, "Something similar just happened to me."

"What?"

"With Dr. Sandoval. Last night, my world history project

was on my desk, all ready to be turned in. When I woke up this morning, it was gone. I went to Dr. Sandoval to try and explain, but he told me to go back to my room and get some rest. He said he was giving me an *A* on the project. No explanation."

"Wow," I whisper, pausing on the bank of Mills Pond. Overhead, the blooms of a magnolia tree flutter in the breeze. "You didn't say anything about the society?"

"No, I got out of there as fast as I could. I didn't see a linchpin, but he's involved. Definitely part of it. Like Gianna."

I nod, even though he can't see me. I thought it was strange at the ball that Dr. Sandoval was right there after I stole Paul's linchpin pendant, yet he said nothing. Maybe he covered up the true cause of Alicia's illness as well. He was the first faculty to reach her when she got ill. Maybe he's still covering things up. "Dr. Yamashiro too." I shiver. "The fact that he already had this whole story by the time I made it to class…it felt even worse than being watched. It felt like someone knew what I was going to do before I did."

"But how could someone know you'd oversleep?"

I consider this. "Someone has been in my room at least twice. Maybe whoever it was snuck in last night and turned off my phone alarm. And took your project too."

"Why would they do that?"

"A demonstration? To show what's possible when you rise in the society's ranks?"

"Or to warn us," Remington says gravely. "Maybe

someone overheard us talking about confiding in a teacher. And now Annabelle is making sure we know it's not an option."

"Well, consider me duly warned." I back up, the scent of the magnolias itching my nose as I take the cobblestone path. "And duly creeped out, for that matter."

"Jane and Polly are still trapped somewhere beneath us," Remington says, his voice strained. "What are we going to do?"

"Right now? I'm going to sprint to the humanities building. I'm not giving another teacher a reason to hand me a freaky pardon. Not today, at least. Let's talk at lunch."

"Okay, but Maren? I need you to know that I didn't do what Gavin said. The guy has a crush on you, and—"

"*What?* Gavin? No." Suddenly, it's stifling beneath this sweater.

"Trust me on this. I think he felt threatened by me or something."

I frown at my phone. "Why would he feel threatened by you?"

A long beat of silence passes. "I guess because I—I don't know what he thought. He has issues."

Well, that's obvious. But it's also something only I'm allowed to say about Gavin.

"Whatever. I'll see you at lunch." Maybe an hour of American Lit will be enough time for me to decide what to say to him at lunch. Because a plan is already stitching together in my head.

I'm just not sure if it's something I can share with Remington.

EIGHTEEN

WHEN I REACH AMERICAN LIT, SWEAT DOTTING MY FOREHEAD after running the entire way, an envelope addressed to *Maren Montgomery* sits on top of my desk.

A prickling sense of dread settles over me. Annabelle's next task. "Did you see who left this?" I ask the girl who sits to my right.

"Sorry, no." She shakes her head.

I start to ask the guy behind me, but at the front of the room, Dr. Wallace clears her throat. "Good morning, everyone."

I spin around in my seat, hiding the envelope beneath the desk. I should stuff it into my backpack and forget about it until after class.

But I have to know what she wants me to do next.

I peel open the envelope, coughing to cover the sound. Then, checking that Dr. Wallace is turned to the whiteboard, I slide the card out.

PREVENT REMINGTON CRUZ FROM ATTENDING THE NEXT MEETING.

My teeth clench as I fold the card up. Wonderful. As if Remington and I don't already have enough trust issues. If I do something this diabolical, it will end us. Whatever *us* there is.

For a second, on the phone, it seemed like Remington might've thought there was an *us*. But it was all in my head. He must still be hung up on Jane. Why else was he checking up on her, making sure she really was studying abroad in the first place?

All I really know is that I can't go through with this task. Annabelle said the way to find our friends was to play the games. If Remington misses a meeting, he'll lose out on another clue. I can't do that to him.

But the significance of this decision needles at me. If I refuse the task, I won't get any closer to releasing Polly.

An hour later, this thought is still weighing on me as I plod through the barbeque chicken line in the dining hall. I pile food onto my plate and grab a glass of water. Astonishingly, I find Remington sitting in a corner, alone.

He smiles when I set my tray down across from him. "Thanks for meeting me. Sitting around is making me anxious."

I stuff a bite of chicken into my mouth, buying some time

as I debate showing him my task. There's no reason not to show him, is there? I mean, since I've put it out of my mind. Since I'm not considering going through with it.

Which I'm not, at all.

I swallow. "I think we have to sneak back into the catacombs and find the girls ourselves."

Remington's fork full of rotini halts in midair. "You do?"

"Yes. And we have to do it tonight, before the society throws another meeting at us." Saying these words is physically painful. I haven't had a decent night's sleep in days. The last thing I want to do is stay up all night searching the forbidden tunnels of bones.

Remington's fork lowers back onto his plate. "So you and I are going to spend the night in the catacombs."

I bristle at the phrase *spend the night*. "Don't bother bringing a pillow."

"I'm in," he says without a second thought. "Let's do this." His gaze travels, fastening on something behind me. "Your friend is watching us."

"What friend?" I spin around to scan the room.

"Who else?"

I turn back to side-eye Remington, but he's busy waving archly at Gavin. "Don't tease him," I say, not sure why I'm so protective of Gavin today.

Remington leans forward, chin resting on a palm as he grins at me. But his expression softens. "You like him, don't you?"

"Gavin?" Short of covering my scorching face with my sweater, all I can think to do is shovel more chicken into my mouth. But I forgot to deny the accusation, so I mumble through my full mouth, super-attractively, "Of course not." After swallowing, I add, "He's just been there for me since Polly..." I want to say *vanished*, but the truth is that Gavin has been one of my only friends since Polly ditched me for Annabelle.

"Maren," Remington says, eyes narrowed. "You can talk to me too, you know. We're going through the same thing."

A harsh breath escapes my mouth. "Right." How is an ex he's hung up on the same thing as a best friend?

Though technically, Polly became an ex-best friend.

"How did you know Jane was missing and not"—I wave my hand—"done talking to you?"

"That's not her. Being with Jane always felt like being with my best friend, and in the end, we realized that best friends was exactly what we were. Just not the kind who kiss." His lips curve shyly. "She would've told me she was headed overseas for a semester."

So it's exactly the same thing. We both lost our closest friends to this sick society.

"We're going to get them back," I say.

He nods, laying one hand out, palm up on the table. An invitation. A treaty.

Shoving all thoughts of Gavin aside, I place mine in it.

Then as a show of good faith, I pretend to wipe my mouth with a napkin as I whisper, "I got a task."

His eyes widen.

The group at the table beside ours starts chanting, "Do it, do it!" I peek to find a series of milk glasses lined up as a short kid chugs one of them. I lean in closer to whisper over the racket, "During American Lit. I'm supposed to prevent you from attending the next society meeting."

"What, like by maiming me or something?"

"It left the execution to my discretion."

Remington's expression darkens, his attention sliding off somewhere I can't follow. I half-expected him to admit to getting the same task. Then again, he didn't have to lure someone into the club when I did. So maybe our tasks are always different.

A few tables away, I spot Jordan nibbling a salad at Annabelle's table. She looks radiant and happier than I've seen her; still, guilt stabs at me. She could've been hurt because of me. "When I had to lure Jordan into the club," I say, wrenching my gaze from the back of her head, "what did you have to do?"

Remington hesitates, running a hand over the back of his neck. "Something I'm not proud of."

My jaw clenches. "I'm not proud of what I did to Jordan. She's lucky Annabelle didn't actually stuff her in a sarcophagus."

"Look, my task was pretty small compared to what she made you do. No one is or was in danger because of it."

"Okay," I say, because I don't know this person well enough to force him to confide in me. But irritation rubs at me like a grass burn on soft flesh. He said I could trust him. "I confessed my task, though."

He reaches out, placing a hand over mine. "Hey, it's not even worth talking about. Seriously." He smiles, and I feel my insides playing tug of war over whether to feel angry or to melt under the blazing heat of his touch. "I've gotta get to the weight room. But we'll talk later, okay?" He squeezes my hand, gets up, and speeds off to join his friends by the exit.

The anger wins, smashing that bubbly feeling. I told him my task. I ruined my chance to get another clue.

And he hasn't told me a single thing.

Maybe he did receive the same task. And he's planning to use it to sabotage me before the next meeting.

NINETEEN

WHEN I GET TO MY DORM ROOM AFTER LACROSSE PRACTICE,
I nearly step on another envelope stuffed beneath the door.
My heart sinks. Flopping onto my bed, I tear it open.

Dear Maren,

*You are cordially invited to attend tonight's
meeting of the Gamemaster's Society, located in the
old cathedral. Please arrive promptly at 11 p.m.*
Victory or Dust.

Sincerely,
The Gamemaster

Another meeting. How can anyone survive on the society's grueling, sleepless schedule?

After a shower, I try to sneak in a nap. But my conversation with Remington gnaws at me, keeping me wide awake.

He must've received his invitation by now. If he was tasked to keep me from the meeting, what would he plan? Seducing me, like he did Donella, and then telling me to meet him somewhere, only to ditch me?

He wouldn't resort to more dangerous means. He's in this whole mess for the same reason I am: to help someone.

Still, I can't keep my doubts at bay. Like the image of me walking to the meeting beneath a starless sky, only to have him throw a bag over my head and lock me up somewhere.

I grab my phone and dial Gavin. "Hey, Maren," he says, tone aloof.

"Gavin, hi. I need an escort to the meeting tonight." He starts to laugh and I blurt, "Not whatever kind of escort you're thinking! I just…I think Remington might be involved with this whole Polly thing." A necessary lie. "And I need to make sure he stays away from me, at least until the meeting starts."

"Oh, thank God you finally see it," Gavin says, his reserved tone cracking apart. "I tried to tell you."

"Yeah, well, he told me you asked him to hold his phone."

"Asked him to—why would I hand over my only connection to the outside world, my only source of light in that serpentine dungeon, to someone I don't trust?"

"I don't know."

"Are you going to tell me now why you made me throw the game?"

I chew my lip, torn. "Do you remember a girl named Jane Blanchet? She would've been in the society last year."

"Yeah, Remington's ex."

"Right. Well…" I'm still battling myself over how much of his secret I can reveal when another call comes through.

Remington.

"You know what," I say, "I have to call you back."

"Okay, but—"

I hang up and answer Remington's call, bracing myself for his attempt to keep me from tonight's meeting. "Hey."

"Maren," he says, "did you get the invitation?"

"Yep."

"So then, our plan is wrecked. We can't search the catacombs tonight while a meeting is going on."

"Nope."

"Look, Annabelle wants me to prevent you from attending—I just found my next task in my dorm room." I sit up straighter on the bed, shock bursting like a rocket through my limbs. "I'm not going to do it, though. I just wanted you to know. I'll tell her at the meeting that she has to give me a different task. I want to save Jane, but not at the expense of keeping Polly locked up down there."

Relief trickles down and eases my extremities. Suddenly,

I need to see him. He didn't sacrifice me and Polly for Jane. Guilt clogs my throat as I push out, "Can you meet me downstairs?"

"I'm already here."

I end the call, rushing out the door and down the stairs. Outside, he's leaning against the pathway railing. He tips his head for me to follow him, and that uneasy feeling that made me call Gavin in the first place seeps back in as he ducks behind my dormitory, half-obscured by foliage. My steps slow, and I toss a look behind me. This was a mistake. He's plotting something. I begin to pivot, but his hand darts out from the shrubbery to grasp my arm and pull me toward him.

I shake him off, backing up until my elbow hits brick.

"Hey, what's wrong?" he asks, showing his hands and shuffling backward.

"Nothing, I—why the bushes?"

"I didn't want Annabelle to see us together." His fingers lower to fiddle with the hem of his shirt. "She seems to want to pit us against each other, and I'm not sure why."

The tightness in my stomach loosens. "Maybe the rest of the society is upset that we keep winning everything."

"No one has quite the motivating factor we do."

"I'm going to refuse the task too," I say. "We can defy Annabelle together."

"Do you think she'll do something to Polly and Jane if we refuse?"

"I hope not. She only threatened to hurt them if we told anyone. Refusing a task should only result in losing out on the next clue." Still, I can't help but worry what sadistic Annabelle will do when she learns we disregarded her task. "Hey," I say, an idea forming. "What if we make her *think* we completed the task? I mean, one of us. You could show up, claim your clue, and meanwhile, I'm already hiding in the catacombs. After the meeting, you can find me, and if we're lucky, your clue will lead us to both of them."

"So you want to try to trick Annabelle," he says, the words sinking with doubt. He stuffs his hands into his pockets. "That could fail miserably."

"What choice do we have? If we refuse the task, best-case scenario, we lose a day or two. Which means Polly and Jane have to spend more time locked away in a cell. Worst-case, Annabelle does something horrible to them. If we can pull this off, we might be able to find the girls tonight."

He nods, still frowning. "And you'll be okay down there? It could be hours before the game ends. Where will you hide?"

"Hopefully, somewhere bigger than a sarcophagus. As long as tonight's game isn't hide-and-seek, I should be fine. Maybe I'll even have a chance to do some searching while you play."

"You'd have to be so careful," he says, reaching out but then pulling back. "If anyone spots you..."

"I know." I take a breath and grab his hand, pressing it between both of mine. "What will you tell Annabelle?"

He stares at our hands for a long beat. "Would she believe I seduced you and tied you up somewhere?" He laughs uncomfortably.

"The first part, yes." I trace small circles with my thumb over his palm, letting one of my hands fall away.

Another silent moment. "Tell her you seduced me, and then told me it was a task. And I was too upset with you and Annabelle to show up tonight."

His eyes dart up to mine, something like fear flickering in them. But he shrugs, and I wonder if I imagined it. "You'd never fall for that."

I glance back down at his hand, which he has maneuvered so that our fingers are interlaced. "Of course not," I say, even as he steps closer.

"I'll refuse to disclose my methods." His free hand moves to my hip, and in a swoop of momentum, my back presses firmly into the brick wall as his body becomes flush with mine.

My breath catches. His eyes latch on to mine, so fiercely I have to shut mine as he drops my hand, placing his palm on the wall above my shoulder.

My arms dangle stupidly at my sides. He's waiting, breath hot on my cheek. Waiting for a sign.

I reach for the back of his neck, and as soon as I touch warm skin, his lips are on mine. I try to push out the thoughts, the questions of whether or not I'm doing this right, and kiss him back. His lips are soft, his hand on my hip gentle as it drifts around to the small of my back, pulling my hips closer to his.

I move my fingers up into his hair, and his palm lowers from the wall to my neck, sending tingles down my spine.

When we part, I try to catch my breath, try to remember what we were even talking about moments before.

He smiles shyly down at me, touching the base of his neck where my fingers were. "That wasn't a task, I promise."

I roll my eyes. "Maybe not for you." His upturned expression falters, and I snatch his hand, which feels rough, warm, and amazing in mine. "A joke," I assure him as I thread our fingers together again.

"You know," he says, gaze skimming our feet. "I totally had a crush on you back in Form I."

I'm too shocked to reply. The donut incident. It wasn't all in my head. My lips are parted in awe, and by some miracle, my phone pings in my back pocket, rescuing me. I let go of Remington's hand to read a text from Gavin.

What happened? Are you okay? Did he do something?

Remington runs a knuckle over his scarred brow. "Gavin, I presume? What does he want?"

"Nothing. I'll get rid of him."

Don't need an escort after all. Thanks though!

I see the rippling dots and silence my phone. He'll be fine. The more Gavin worries about me not showing up tonight— the more he accuses Remington of being involved—the more convincing our plan will be.

TWENTY

AFTER DINNER, I'M SLOUCHING IN A BEANBAG CHAIR, TRYING to focus on my English homework but really just staring at Polly's empty bed and the rose-print sheets no one ever bothered to remove. I can't stop wondering what exactly Polly wanted to show me that night at the fountain. What did she find that had her so worried about the society? What would cause her and Jane to do something risky enough to get punished?

Polly had asked to meet. Whatever she wanted to show me, she couldn't do it in our room. Was that because she didn't feel safe inside? With a chill, I think of the open window in the dead of night, of the cloak left sprawled on my bed earlier this week. That could've easily been it.

But another possibility teases my consciousness. That she wanted to meet at the fountain because the thing she wanted to show me was *there*.

Before I can talk myself out of it, I'm tossing my homework to the floor. Then I'm on my feet and out the door, making the trek downstairs and out to the garden in front of the Lowell Math and Science Building. In the distance, the sun dips behind the new cathedral, casting the campus in twilight. I stop beside the white iron bench, situated perfectly for viewing the splashing merman fountain and the shrubs trimmed into his sea creature friends—the one Polly and I considered *our* fountain. We always speculated about the significance of the ocean theme, usually arriving at the same consensus: that Lowell guy must've been a real nut.

Now that I'm looking at the fountain and not cracking jokes, the figure on display is no ordinary merman. He's Poseidon, the Greek god of the sea. One of the twelve gods that lived and ruled from Mount Olympus. Suddenly, I get a flash of the fresco from the catacombs, the one of the eyes watching as the bloody battle rages on below. I remember the copy of *The Iliad* stashed among Polly's belongings. I'd assumed she had to read it for a class, but Polly and I have always had our Language Arts classes together. Dr. Hernandez read selections with us back in Form II, which he photocopied and handed out in class. We were never required to purchase our own copies of the epic poem.

What is it with these people and the Greek gods? I press closer to the fountain, my gaze skipping over the stonework.

I continue searching, hoping for a clue engraved somewhere, a note from Polly tucked away between the stones. But I make it full circle, fountain water misting my sweater, without a single clue. I know a little about Poseidon and the other Olympians from class; I know nothing about this Pelops guy, other than what Gianna mentioned down in the catacombs. I sit back down on the bench, opening up my phone's browser.

I type *Pelops* into the search engine and skim the articles that pop into the results. Despite variations in the story, most of them echo the one Gianna told down in the catacombs. When I run through the suggestions at the bottom of the results (*Pelops Curse, Pelops Son, Pelops and Tantalus*), my eyes hitch on the last topic.

Pelops Cult.

Instinctively, I look up from my phone to scan the courtyard. I click on the topic, finding only a Wikipedia article and another article on something called *chthonic cults*. "Derived from a word meaning 'subterranean,' *chthonic* in English describes deities of the underworld, especially as pertaining to Greek mythology."

A group of students ambles past me in the direction of the library, reminding me of the stacks and stacks of homework awaiting me in my room. My eyes skip down to *Pelops*, who was apparently celebrated in the form of hero cult worship at Olympia dating back to the Archaic period. "Though part god, being a grandson of Zeus, Pelops was considered of the earth after death, and as thus was worshipped by means of offering libations and animal sacrifices into a pit belowground. Though scholars have theorized that sacrifices were burnt in their entirety, others believe the sacrifices were simply slain and lowered beneath the earth."

After finishing the article, I scroll through the remaining hits. There isn't much, other than a purchase link to a book about Greek and Roman hero worship and some scholarly journal articles. I click on the first article, which looks promising but requires a subscription to an online database. The next article was published back in 1812 and requires a subscription as well.

Though I can't access the full article, there's a snippet at the top that sends a red-hot rush of terror through me. "Remnants of Pelops's shrine indicate there may have been radical subcults that offered human sacrifices every four years, possibly in synchronization with the tradition of the Games that originated in his honor, in hopes of achieving a similar heroic, godlike status."

Nausea rises in my empty stomach.

Human sacrifices.

There's no way the Gamemaster's Society could possibly

be related to this archaic cult that participates in human sacrifice.

And yet it's a society that claims to honor Pelops. It exists underground, complete with shrines and burial places.

This year, the sacrifice could be Polly or Jane.

I force myself to breathe slowly, typing in *Torrey-Wells Catacombs* next, but nothing comes up. *New Hampshire Catacombs* is also a bust. It's as if those miles and miles of stonework beneath me don't even exist. When I try to get to my feet, they seem to have gone numb.

———————

Remington meets me at the hidden entrance to the old cathedral at 10 p.m. He holds the door open, and I push my bag full of supplies through before crawling in after it, my heart racing. We're pressed for time, but the words from my research reverberate in my ears. Before he can push ahead to the trapdoor, I take his arm and pull him with me, so we're both leaning against the dusty stone wall. I proceed to fill him in on my findings.

"Human sacrifice?" In the moonlight pouring in through the broken tower window, Remington pales.

"This"—I toss a hand in the air, scrounging for a word to describe a cult within a cult—"*Ultra*-radical sect believed that the occasional human sacrifice would be looked upon more favorably. The more I think about it, the more it could fit.

The underground chambers, the glorification of the Games. Maybe I'm wrong and they're not planning to kill anyone. But after what she's put the girls through, do you really think Annabelle's going to let us all waltz out of the catacombs together?"

"So, that would mean Polly and Jane are being kept alive down there to become sacrifices. How could the society get away with that?"

"I don't know. The article mentioned aligning the ritual with the Olympic Games, every four years." My mind cartwheels to the Lawrence Administration Building—to the memorial photographs in the glass display. "It's been exactly four years since Daniel King's death was ruled an accident."

Remington's eyes grow. "Back in the seventies, a kid died when the old cathedral burned down." He starts twisting the fabric on his cloak. "The guys in my dorm talk about this kid who overdosed in our hall about a decade back. His name is carved into the wall in his old room. Every few years, a student dies, and it always ends up looking like an accident."

"Or like nothing happened at all," I say. "Everyone believes that Polly ran away and Jane is studying abroad. And Gavin says the society has doctors. Doctors who do shady things. Maybe they're faking medical reports, like the one that was obviously faked for Alicia Jones. Who knows how many other deaths have slipped through the cracks over the years?"

Remington stops twisting the fabric, letting it drop. "My

father," he says in a hollow voice. "When he was a student here, his friend, William McKinley, was this star athlete and stellar student. Only William never graduated. Tragic ski club accident." His fingertips move to his temples, clawing at the skin. "It wasn't an accident, was it?"

I reach out to console him. "Probably not," I say, running my fingers down his arm.

Remington leans into my touch. I'm close enough to feel the rise and fall of his chest. "And we have no idea when this sacrifice is supposed to happen?"

I shake my head. "But Gavin did say something about a big tournament finale here at the school this week. Maybe that's when they..." My throat tightens, the words dying down there.

"Then we'd better find them tonight." He turns toward what's possibly our biggest hurdle a few feet ahead: the trapdoor.

Neither of us has witnessed Annabelle secure the door. If the locking mechanism is too involved, our plan is DOA. I sprint ahead over the rubble-strewn stone to peel back the dusty red rug. Beneath it, a handle is fitted neatly inside a hollow notch in the wooden door.

Remington's footsteps sound behind me as I lift the handle from its hollow and pull.

The door sticks. I yank again with all my might. But it's locked. Remington shines a flashlight over the area, and I inspect the handle. There's no padlock—too obvious beneath the rug. "I don't get it," I say, making room for Remington, who crouches beside me. "It's not locked."

His light flits over the edges and ricochets back to the spot beside the handle. "Just old," he says, digging into his coat pocket to withdraw a Swiss Army knife. "The wood is so warped that it's stuck." With a click, the shiny metal blade flashes, and I startle. He goes to work jamming it into the groove, working his way around until, finally, he grasps the handle and tugs.

It works. The door lifts and Remington eases it all the way back to the ground. I reach for my pack, hefting it on over my shoulder, my jaw clenched in determination.

"Hey." Remington touches my arm. "Let me do it. I can go down there and you can stay and play the game. You have a much better shot at winning whatever challenge Annabelle has planned anyway."

I shake my head, even though my brain is screaming at me to accept his offer. This is stupid. Going down there. No cell signal—Remington can't warn me if something goes drastically wrong. And that's if I can trust him one hundred percent, which is still doubtful. He says he likes me, that he has since Form I. But he was with Jane for a very long time. Would he really help me at her expense?

And even though I came up with this plan, it technically ends with *him* winning the next clue. What if my gamble doesn't pay off? What if Annabelle shows him the way to Jane, but Polly isn't there?

If we switched places, *I* could win the clue. I would get to ensure that Polly is found and not sacrificed for this sick society. Remington would have to make the gamble.

Despite my brain's pleas, though, I decline his offer. Going down there means I get to search for Polly. "I want to do this. You stay and be charming and cunning and strong. I'm going to investigate, and if all else fails, I'll roll into a tiny ball and hide until the coast is clear."

He opens his mouth to object, but I press a finger to his lips. "Just promise me you'll come. No matter how late things go."

Without warning, he removes my hand from his and kisses it. "If all else fails, meet me beneath the trapdoor at 2 a.m." Then he leans in, still holding my hand. "I promise. I'll find you, and we'll save Polly and Jane."

He passes me his flashlight, which I tuck under my arm before lowering down into the crypt. When my foot lands on the last rung, Remington shuts the trapdoor. The darkness congeals around me like molasses.

I click on the flashlight, light scribbling over the stone walls until it finds a lantern perched in a niche. I fumble through my pack for the lighter Remington insisted I carry and ignite the wick. Double-fisting my light sources now, I continue through the corridor.

The labyrinth from the last game is tucked inside my back pocket, but I've basically memorized it. I have to avoid every place I touched last night. Because if Annabelle was telling the truth, Polly is somewhere beyond the reaches of the map.

Our meeting time is 2 a.m. Nearly four hours away.

I really hope I'm not alone down here that long.

Ahead, a staircase leads deeper into the catacombs. I went that way last time, and though I could've missed a hidden room or passageway, I opt for the door instead.

When it seems like I've traveled a mile of endless stone corridors, I reach an arched doorway marked by an unlit, standing torch on each side. Instead of a door, a wrought-iron lattice gate barricades the entryway. But it isn't locked, and with a small push, the gate hinges open with an eerie creak. Setting down my lantern, I slide my map from my pocket and hold the flashlight to it. I've passed the siren in the lower left-hand corner.

I'm off the map. Somewhere beyond this point, Polly and Jane are being held prisoner.

I grab my lantern and enter a gallery with sunken ceilings. At the far end is a vaulted alcove where a stone altar draped in red cloth stands as the centerpiece to some sort of shrine. All around the wall, unlit candles fill tiny nooks. I don't even want to know what this place is used for.

I turn to the left, where a dark hole in the wall catches my eyes. It's the only way out other than the gate I came through, so I duck my head inside what seems to be a pitch-black tunnel. Pushing the lantern ahead of me, I get down on my hands and knees and crawl, my backpack scraping the ceiling, the stone roughing up my knees.

My heart thunders in my ears. This is the part in the movies where any moment now, I shove my lantern a little farther to illuminate the face of the lunatic who's been living down in this tunnel for decades, feasting on rats. Though I'm not sure how a lunatic would even be able to live down here. It's frigid. My teeth are chattering, and I get the feeling that if I stopped moving, hypothermia would come on within the hour.

My thoughts swim to Polly. *Poor Polly.* The chambers aren't as freezing as this tunnel, but they're still cold. And she's been down here for weeks. Her health must be in serious jeopardy. I scramble a little faster, trying to shimmy through the stones without dislodging any of them. The mortar is crumbling in places, trickling down to coat my hair; one wrong move and I could be trapped forever.

The farther I make it, the more a disquieting thought weighs on me like bricks coming down one layer at a time: this could very well be the only way back. If I continue on, I'll have to do this again. But there isn't enough room to turn around in here, and besides, I'm nearly to the end.

Ahead, my lantern light flashes on another corridor, this one with standing room. I get up, brush myself off, and pull out my phone. No reception, of course. There's no way Remington is going to find me. If something happens down here, no one will find me.

Like no one's found Polly or Jane.

I've made it this far, though. Against my better judgment, I press on, through the corridor, turning right into the largest gallery I've come across. Some sort of chapel. Pillars line both sides of an aisle, and another stone altar, larger this time, sits atop a platform. The same stone from the rest of the catacombs lines the floor, with one exception: colored tiles are interspersed to form an image. I don't see any sarcophagi in this room, just more unlit candles and dusty jars. I make my way beneath the arch over the platform, which looks like the kind of place that could hide an entry to the hidden prison. I run my fingers over the rough stones, one at a time. Maybe one of these pushes or pulls and the entire wall swings open.

But nothing works. I swing around, lifting my lantern high. And that's when the hairs on the back of my neck prickle up.

The colored tiles on the floor—red, I see now, like blood. They form a linchpin.

Gavin claims the society is all about fun and games, but these catacombs were clearly designed for more. This chamber could be the place where they perform the sacrifices.

Jostling my pack higher on my spine, I head back out the way I came, turning right when I reach the corridor, toward the next level of this inferno.

When it feels like I've traveled in a complete circle, I reach a doorway. Like the one earlier, it's marked by a standing torch on each side, the same latticed iron gate blocking it.

Only this one is locked. I squint at the lock in the dim lantern light, yanking on it. There are only two reasons to lock a gate: keeping people out, and keeping people in.

"Polly!" I yell, lacing my fingers through the bars to shake the gate. "Jane?"

No answer. I set my lantern down and shine my flashlight through the bars, making out stone walls on each side. It looks like the room from the video, but there's no bed pushed against the wall. Instead, there's a small desk and a chair with a red coat slung onto the back of it. A shiver dances up my neck. Is Annabelle down here?

A laptop sits open on the desk, the screen timed out. This could be her lair. Whatever's on that computer may hold valuable information about the society—about Polly and Jane.

I have to get inside. Dropping down onto the cold ground, I dig through my backpack for something to pick the lock. How come girls in the movies always have bobby pins on them? Suddenly, I resent my messy lacrosse ponytail and its flyaways with everything in me. All I have are water and snacks and basically everything Remington forced upon me.

But hope lights up in my chest. When he gets here, he'll have that Swiss Army knife. It must have some sort of lock picking mechanism. For now, I'll have to use my time searching for the girls.

I stuff everything back inside the pack and stand, giving the locked room one last glance. But a flash of white snags my eye as the lantern light passes over it. There's something on the ground, a few feet from the gate. An envelope. Larger than the ones containing our invitations.

I might be able to reach it. Crouching down, I maneuver my hand to make it fit, scraping my skin as I slide it through the bars. Then, I lean into the gate and push all the way to my armpit.

But I'm a few inches short.

Growling, I pull my arm back through, iron rubbing against tender flesh, and rack my brain for a way to reach the envelope. I'm so close.

I get up and scan my surroundings, noting the torches again. I examine them and find that each stand contains a base and a torch. Neither end would fit through the bars. Except, I realize with a metaphorical facepalm, these standing torches weren't actually made in the medieval times. They come apart like anything in the Amazon era, meant for shipping. The torch slides right out of the stand, and so does the base.

Leaving me with a post perfect for sticking through the bars.

A few grunts, twists, and yanks later, I've removed the torch. I drag the stand, base and all, over to the gate, sliding the narrow end through the bars. When it catches on the envelope, I draw it toward me. Right beneath the gate.

I let the torch stand fall to the ground with a clatter and slump down against the wall. Despite the cold, my palms are sweaty as I open the envelope. What is so important and classified that Annabelle kept it down in this dungeon?

The contents tumble out into my lap. A bunch of photographs. My heart hammers in my chest. If these photos contain Polly or Jane, I can take them straight to the cops. I thrust one into the lantern light, letting my flashlight illuminate the details. Blond hair, a long, lean leg crossing the bottom corner of the frame. Slender fingers tangled up in a head full of dark curls.

Not Polly or Jane. The girl in the photo is Annabelle Westerly.

And she's kissing Remington Cruz.

TWENTY-ONE

MY STOMACH FLIPS. I DROP THE FLASHLIGHT AND TURN aside to dry heave.

Still hunched and weak, I force myself to look at the other photos. They're all the same. Annabelle and Remington in compromising positions. My thoughts tumble and collide. I can't make sense of it. Was he always a part of this? He and Annabelle? Did he do something to Jane? To Polly?

One thought continues to surface, separating from the others: Remington is a liar. While he was kissing me—while he was telling me I could trust him—he was keeping this from me.

Of course Annabelle is trying to pit Remington and me against each other. He means something to her. It's obvious from these photos. And I have no idea who he really is or what he wants.

Or what he'll do to me to get it.

I check my phone: 1:18 a.m. The meeting's been going on for two hours already.

I have to get out of here. I gather my things and turn back the way I came, but I stop. What about Polly and Jane? I cast a look the opposite way, where a corridor leads to the unknown.

I'll bring the authorities here. Tonight. Before Annabelle even knows what happened.

Nausea suddenly replaced by a spark of adrenaline, I stuff the photos back into the envelope. I slip it inside my backpack before haphazardly reassembling the torch stand to cover any trace of my existence here. Then I rush to tuck the lantern into a corner to make the return trip through the tunnel a little lighter. My flashlight will have to suffice.

I shrug on my pack and head in the direction of the tunnel, crouching to duck into the opening.

When I get a few yards in, a scratching noise makes its way through the hollow space, and my blood freezes. The sound gets closer, claws or teeth against stone. I attempt to turn around, but my pack gets jammed. The space is too small for me to reach back and push it down. I can't even contort my body enough to remove it.

This is it.

A horde of rats is headed straight for me.

My lantern bathes the stones before me in a yellow glow. But as the noise approaches, a large shadow smothers the light. Despite my efforts to brace myself, I shriek. I punch and kick and whack at the shape with my flashlight.

"Hey, hey!" booms a deep voice as the flashlight is ripped from my grasp. My throat constricts.

Remington.

"Maren? Are you trying to break my arm?"

"Maybe," I growl, instantly regretting it. I can't let on that I know about his deception. Especially since he's currently blocking my escape route. "You did just attack me in a dark tunnel."

"I didn't attack you. I *found* you, like I said I would. Remember?"

"Well, there's been a change of plans. So if you could figure out how to turn around and head right back out the way you came, that would be great."

"What? I thought we were going to search for Polly and Jane. Everyone else is gone. We have all night to find them."

It's too convenient. How did he find me? This place is enormous, sinuous, and convoluted. The only way I got this far was by using my map to eliminate sections.

"Remington, we're going back. This is the wrong way." He can't call my bluff without giving himself away as a traitor.

"No, it's not. We're almost there."

I spider-crawl back a few inches. "How do you know that?"

"Because Annabelle gave me a new map for winning

tonight's game, and it led me here. Just let me—" He reaches toward me, and I jerk back, a tiny squeal escaping my lips.

"Maren? Are you okay?" He tries for my hand this time, and it takes everything in me not to wrench it away. "You're like ice. Let's get out of here, so I can take off my coat."

"Stop pretending you care if I die!" I snap. *Oops*. How did I beat Annabelle at Texas Hold'em with zero poker face or poker voice or poker anything? The lack of oxygen is getting to me. I can't catch my breath. I crawl backward the remaining few yards until I'm out in the corridor, where I scramble to my feet, using the wall to steady myself.

My flashlight is still on, but everything is black. I inhale. Exhale. It's no better. I fall forward, resting my hands on my knees until finally, I slump to the ground.

I can't believe I let Remington play me again. I knew he couldn't be trusted—I had Gavin on the phone and I declined his help.

Remington emerges, rushing to me, reaching for me. I cringe, remembering the last time his hands were on me. When I wanted them on me. When I wanted his lips on mine.

But his heart was Annabelle's the whole time.

He drapes his coat over my shoulders and pushes a water at me, holding it there until I take it. Hustling away, he drags one of the torches back across the stone to place it beside us. He lights it, crouches down again, and rubs my hands as he presses his rough cheek against mine. And I hate myself, because he's strong and warm, and some sick part of me wants to unravel in his arms.

"Stop," I say, my teeth chattering, from fear or from the cold—I don't know anymore.

His head draws back. "Maren, do you need—"

"Just stop." I jostle my arms and scoot back until I hit the wall.

"Look, I'm sorry I took so long, but—"

A clomp resounds at the mouth of the tunnel. In the flickering light, a shadow unfolds over the wall to tower over both of us. Footsteps now. They pound the stone as the shadow moves to envelop us.

"She said *stop*." At the voice, my muscles relax, and I squint up to find Gavin standing in the corridor.

"You—" Remington's features distort as he pushes to his feet. "You followed me?"

"Of course I followed you. You really thought I'd forget about Maren, after she warned me you were after her?"

Remington's shoulder sink, and slowly, he turns to me, eyes soft and glossy. "Is that true, Maren? You thought I was after you?"

"No—I mean, *yes*, I was worried about our task. I thought you might try to sabotage me. But after we spoke behind my dorm..." After we did other things behind my dorm. "I trusted you. I was wrong, though. To trust you."

I rifle through my pack, tossing the envelope at Remington's feet. He lowers to the ground, removing the photos beneath the torch light. Gavin brushes past him to check on me.

"What were you thinking coming down here by yourself?" he says, his voice rough with concern as he settles down next to me. He reaches beneath the coat for my hand, trying to rub some warmth back into it.

"I wanted to search for Polly. And Jane," I add, resting my head against Gavin's shoulder, "even though I'm not sure Jane exists anymore."

Remington tosses the photos to the ground, stomping them. "She exists. And she's down here somewhere. These are—" He motions to the images scattering the stone floor. "When you asked what my task was the night you had to lure Jordan into the society? I didn't answer because I didn't want you to know about this. Because it was *meaningless*. She tasked me to kiss her. I didn't know why she wanted me to do it. And I didn't know someone was taking photos." He grabs both temples. "I didn't think I was hurting anyone. I never thought that you and I would..."

That he and I would *what*? Would kiss behind my dormitory? Would develop feelings for each other? Would become entangled in this game of cross and double-cross over and over again until we both ended up broken?

"Even if that's all true," I say, "you should've told me. I deserved to know about you and Annabelle."

"There is no *me and Annabelle*! Don't you see?" He looks up, biting his bottom lip. "There never was. There's only you and me."

At my side, Gavin bristles. His hand releases mine, and my heart sinks; he's repulsed by me. But I turn to check, and it's something else. He looks like someone just threw his favorite box of explosive devices into one of the academy ponds.

"She must've planned this the second she saw us getting close," Remington continues. "You know she has this twisted desire to separate us." He moves nearer, and Gavin stands, pushing himself between us.

Remington cranes his neck to look at me. "Please, can we talk about this without *him* listening in?"

"Absolutely not." I shake my head. "Gavin stays."

Remington sighs, running a hand through his curls. "Annabelle's getting exactly what she wants."

"She didn't slide the photographs under my door, Remington. I found them myself."

"And when's the last time you truly made a choice on your own—one Annabelle didn't plan out for you in advance?"

"That's absurd," I whisper, tugging his coat up higher. "She didn't know I'd come down here."

"Didn't she? Did she not tell you that Polly was being kept somewhere off the map? Did she not leave this envelope dangling in front of you?"

"But I—*how*?"

"Shh," Gavin says without looking at me. "Don't listen to him."

"And who should I listen to?" I ask, turning on him. "You? You're a part of this society that"—I brush a loose strand of hair out of my eyes—"will do *anything* to get what they want. The way Pelops did."

His gaze snaps to mine.

"Did you know what they were planning to do with Polly and Jane?"

"I told you," he says, frustration curling the words, "this is the Gamemaster messing with you. There's no one down here."

And suddenly, I see it. *He doesn't know.* Gavin and who knows how many society minions actually think they're playing a bunch of games, when in reality, they're helping the Gamemaster plan a murder. "It's a cult, Gavin. They worship Pelops. And I think they're planning a human sacrifice."

Gavin's head wrenches back. "Human sacrifice? No." He shakes his head. "Pelops is a figurehead. Like a Batman-themed birthday party. It's a story they tell at every initiation, meant to rile up the masses and get them pumped up for the Games."

"Look around you," Remington spits. "The décor's a little much for a birthday party, don't you think?"

"It's an old society," Gavin says with a shrug. But his eyes are unfocused in the bleary wash of torchlight.

"It's a cult, Gavin," I say, witnessing the new mix of

horror and grief in his expression. He really believed he was close to discovering a cure for his sister. A path that trampled over ethical boundaries, true. But nothing like murder.

"The question isn't whether or not Annabelle has Polly and Jane," I add. "It's whether or not they're even down here."

Remington shrugs. "According to her newest clue, we're only a few corridors away."

"I still don't get why she's trying to turn us against each other."

"Because if we're isolated, we may never be able to rescue the girls. I'm so sorry, Maren. I should've told you everything when you asked about my task. I...was worried you'd hate me."

"I do hate you. Stay away from me tonight."

"So then," Gavin says, slouching against a pillar, "we're staying down here? To search for Polly and Jane?"

"We've come this far. We have to try."

Remington nods, body sinking in relief. He removes the torch from its post, studies me for a moment, and resignedly starts checking the corridor ahead.

"Can you even get up, Maren?" Gavin offers me a hand, but his posture is rigid and withdrawn.

"I'm fine," I say, taking it. "I just got freaked out by my encounter with a two-hundred-pound rat."

"I deserved that," Remington calls back. Beside me, Gavin doesn't even crack a smile. He does take my pack, though, hefting it onto his spine.

"Hey," I whisper once Remington has disappeared behind the next corner. "Thanks for coming after me. I was really scared until you showed up."

"That's what friends are for," he says, but the word *friends* carries a sardonic bite.

I tug on his coat sleeve until he stops walking. "It was stupid. To hang up on you. To leave you out of the loop."

"Well, it sounds like you had better things to do." Gavin's gaze is glued to his boots.

My cheeks heat. "What does that mean?"

"I can read between the lines. You kissed him."

"Yes, but it was only because—"

"You don't have to explain it to me."

"I'm sorry, Gavin."

He nods, but his head is still slack. There's nothing left to say. To him, I'm ruined. I grab the lantern I abandoned earlier, handing Gavin my flashlight.

We follow the haze of Remington's torch until the passageway swings left. The cold is nearly an entity in its own right, a frosty presence coating the walls and the air in front of me. The silence is more unnerving than an actual walking skeleton at this point. "So, how did he manage to win again?"

Gavin and I pass beneath an arch leading to a dank corridor that smells of sewage. I gag into Remington's coat, which I'm still wearing because I'm not going to kill myself in an attempt to be dignified.

"Hope it's not a fresh body," Gavin mumbles through a hand.

I swat him, like I always do in chemistry. And I swear he's smiling beneath that hand.

"The game was *pankration*," Gavin says, when we finally make it past the horrible stench. "An oldie-but-goodie combining boxing with wrestling. A challenge of brute strength, perfect for your *boyfriend*."

I release a hard breath that rustles the wisps of hair around my face. "Why are you making me feel worse about this?" I snap, frustrated with myself, but also frustrated with him. Why can't Gavin just stay my goofy, accident-prone lab partner?

He keeps striding along, ignoring the question, so I hit him again. Except this time, as my arm falls away, Gavin twists around, snatching my wrist with his free hand. Stunned, I don't try to wrench it away. Instead, I let him move until his face hovers inches over mine, the lantern light crackling in his eyes. My heart is racing and jumping and smacking into things. Biting my lip, I wait as he looks at me like he's attempting to read my thoughts.

Gavin's jaw is steadier than I've ever seen it as his wrist loosens and his thumb moves lightly over my skin. He lets my arm fall, moving his fingers up to lightly brush my cheek. "Because I wish you'd deny it," he says finally. "All of it. Any of it." He removes his hand. "But you don't."

I glance down, the feverish wish that he'd touch my cheek

again spiraling through my brain. "You want me to say he's not my boyfriend? He's not my boyfriend, okay? Better?"

"No," he says softly, pressing closer. "Say you didn't kiss him." I let him walk me back, and when my spine grazes the wall, he stops. "Say you didn't call me for help only to turn around and kiss *him*." His breath is hot against my cheek.

"I'm not going to lie to you."

"Then say I wasn't imagining everything. That I wasn't delusional to think you and I make a pretty great team." His chest lifts, like he's holding his breath.

I don't answer.

His chest falls again. "When you called, I guess I thought—I just thought..." He shrugs. "Doesn't matter." A weak laugh escapes. "You were thinking something else."

The words, the laugh—they're like a sledgehammer to my chest. Because I had the same thought about him, and I ignored it. "You're not delusional," I say. "You're negligent, cocky, and a poor dresser, generally speaking. What I'm trying to say is that you have a lot of negative qualities." At this, the corner of Gavin's mouth quirks. "But delusional isn't one of them. And you and I do make a pretty great team. I've been spending a lot of time with Remington, I think because Annabelle wanted us to. And now I don't know what she wants anymore."

"Forget about what Annabelle wants," he says. "Forget about Remington, too, for that matter. I did try to warn you about him."

"I know." Shame heats my neck, Remington's coat almost stifling as Gavin's eyes trace over it. I want to throw it to the ground, to show Gavin I don't need Remington in any way, shape, or form.

But I don't get the chance. Because Remington calls my name, his voice rattling every pillar as it snakes through the corridor, followed by a piercing scream.

A female scream.

TWENTY-TWO

I REACH REMINGTON FIRST, FINDING HIM BENT OVER WHAT looks like a sarcophagus, face ashen. "What happened?" My lantern swings as I rush toward him. Beneath my feet, the ground is coated in a fine layer of dust and rubble, like a massive stone rolled through here, decimating this place *Raiders of the Lost Ark*–style. "Is it Polly?"

"No," Remington says, putting a hand out to stop me from looking any closer.

"What is it? She's not—is she—?"

"Polly isn't in here. It's a recording." The same ancient camcorder Annabelle gave me a couple days ago is tucked against his chest.

"Give it to me." I climb the few steps up the platform to

reach him. Behind me, Gavin's footsteps skid over the debris-ridden stone.

"Maren." My light traces over Remington's pallid skin. "It's difficult to watch."

That sick feeling is back now. "I have to."

Hesitantly, Remington hands over the recorder. I slump down onto the step and press play, feeling Gavin's palm on my shoulder as he looks on.

The recording begins with a shot of black. Slowly, white letters trickle onto the screen to form a message:

You failed your tasks. Now Polly and Jane must pay the price.

A girl appears in the frame now, Jane Blanchet. Straggly strands of her once-pristine caramel-brown hair dangle over one eye. She cowers, attempting to scramble back but hitting the wall as the unknown figure holding the recorder nears her. Then the camera cuts to the bare stone, and Jane's terrified screams morph into tortured howls.

Up on the platform, Remington's eyes are shut.

I cover my face with my hands, but the recording isn't over. I have to watch. It could hold a clue to finding the girls.

The same stone lines the walls in the next shot, only the girl isn't Jane. It's Polly. My stomach clenches as the camera nears her, shaky in the filmmaker's grip. *Please, please, no.*

Over the last two years, I've heard an endless variety of Polly screams: her playful scream, her spider-in-the-bathroom screech, her stage scream, her I-jammed-my-toe-on-the-bedpost yelp.

This sound is unlike any of those. This scream rattles the chamber, fraying every nerve in my body.

The camera trails away, focusing now on a single section of stone floor, which appears dirty at first. But the shot zooms in, and it's not dirt at all. It's blood.

Blood that continues to drip onto the stone until it becomes so thick that it splashes and runs into the cracks.

A new message appears on the screen now:

Remington's attempt to share the clue will result in a restart. You'll have one last chance to redeem yourself and save your friend. A duel: Maren vs. Remington.

Only one girl can be saved. Await further instructions here.

"That's—" I breathe. Disoriented, I stand, missing a step and falling smack into Gavin. He catches me, but more importantly, he grabs the recorder before it shatters over the stone.

"Maren," Remington says as if in a daze. He finally pushes himself upright and marches down the steps toward us.

"Stop," I command, wheezing in the dusty air. I don't

know what Annabelle's planning, but it seems pretty clear we can't work together anymore.

He jerks back, as if struck. "Maren, you don't honestly think I'm going to play this game." His voice is grave. It's too dark for me to make out his eyes.

"Won't you? Jane could die. The girl you would do anything for, including lying. I've never fully trusted you, not since the start. And I definitely don't plan to trust you now." Remembering his coat, I wrestle it off, tossing it at him.

He catches it by a sleeve. "*Trust* is the only way all of us make it out of here. We can find Polly and Jane if we—all three of us—work together."

"Are they even here anymore? We all know she managed to waltz down here and plant this video. She said the clue is void, that we're restarting. I think that means she moved them."

"She's not superhuman," he counters. "If she really snuck down here, it would've been in the last few minutes. Which means we might be able to catch her."

"But *how* did she get down here?" Gavin asks, waving a hand.

"There must be another access point," Remington says. Now that he mentions it, I have a hard time envisioning Annabelle crawling through that rat tunnel.

As much as I'd like to stand around and argue with Remington some more, if his theory stands, we would have to move now. And quickly.

I nod, my legs already moving toward the exit when Gavin grabs my shoulder. "Maren? Are you sure you want to disobey? She asked you to stay here. The last time you two broke her rules, she took it out on the girls."

"Follow her rules so we can save *one* girl? That's what you think I should do?"

Gavin's hands fidget at his sides. "There are so many ways this can go wrong if we stick with him. An hour ago, I saw what he could do with his bare hands. Let's say we go rogue. As soon as you turn a dark corner—which will be very, very soon in this place—he is going to grab you and play *pankration* on your neck until it snaps."

"I know," I say, cringing. I'm an idiot. For ignoring Gavin's advice, yet again. "But you saw the video. I've done all of this to save Polly. If I give up now, she could die."

Gavin rubs at his temple, clearly incapable of handling my stupidity. "Fine," he mutters. "Let's run Annabelle down and try not to get pankrated."

"Getting pankrated is the worst. Especially when it's your neck."

In the doorway, Remington hovers, holding his torch. When he spots us coming, he slips out into the dark passage to lead the way.

A few yards down, we hit a *T*. "Should we split up?" Remington asks, lifting his torch to glance in either direction.

"No," Gavin says before turning to me. "See? He's trying to go off on his own so he can win."

"We don't even know the game, Gavin."

"Still. He can't be left alone. And you can't go with him, for obvious reasons."

"Well," I say, my throat drying up, "*you* could go with him."

Gavin's mouth opens, but he only blinks and clutches his neck. "Have you listened to a word I've said?"

"He's not playing against *you*."

Beside us, Remington taps his foot in irritation. "Any day now would be great." He starts pacing. "And I'm not playing *against anyone*. Except maybe Annabelle."

"Who's getting away," I say, bouncing on the balls of my feet.

Gavin growls, swinging his flashlight to the left. "Fine. But take one last look at this neck. Because in a few minutes it's not going to be this perfectly straight."

Begrudgingly, he marches off after Remington, and I turn down the corridor to the right, awkwardly dangling my lantern handle as I race. A few paces in, it becomes clear that this corridor isn't like the rest. Unlike the bare stone walls elsewhere in the catacombs, my weak light zigzags over a series of frescoes. A very unsettling series.

To my right, a finely dressed young woman sits down to a feast. But as the next image unfolds, the food set before her is made up of the faces of living people, while the guests seated

at her table are decomposing corpses. Another scene plays on
the left, but I barely glance at it before a flash of light plays
over the tunnel up ahead.

It isn't my light.

I pick up my steps, my lantern clanging against my thigh.
"Polly!" I scream, diving after the bounding glow.

"Maren!"

My heart catapults into my throat. It's really her.

"Help!" she shrieks.

My feet slap against the stone, backpack jostling over my spine
as the light is lost behind a corner. Polly's screams fade as if sucked
into an abyss. "Polly!" I call again, panic shredding my voice.

A roar sounds, like stone scraping stone. I fly to the end
of the passageway, my lungs burning. The sound stops before
I can decipher where it's coming from, and I nearly stumble
over a still-lit torch abandoned on the ground.

Firelight dances over the cracks and grooves as I scan the
corridor. Annabelle must've escaped through the wall. But I
can't tell where.

I move on to where the passageway swerves to the left,
and that's when I see it.

Another room, its gate still knocking against the frame.

I take one step inside and then back up immediately. This
could be a trick. Annabelle could be waiting back there, ready
to lock me inside.

Besides, I've seen enough. This is the room from Polly's

videos. Her blue sneakers peek out from beneath the dirty mattress, and that square stone is a few feet away, covered with dark matter that pools into the cracks.

She was just here. I choke out a sob and sag against the doorframe. Annabelle must've forced her out of here and through some secret passageway so suddenly, Polly didn't even have time to put on her shoes.

Footsteps pound the floor as I struggle to breathe through the sobbing. "Maren?" Remington baseball-slides down to inspect me.

"I'm fine," I say, sniffling. "But we missed them. I heard Polly. She called for me, and I couldn't catch her." I failed her.

"They couldn't have gotten far," Gavin says, inspecting a plate of half-eaten crackers on a stool.

"No, but they pulled a disappearing act back in the corridor. Unless we can figure out which wall they walked through, they might as well be one hundred miles away." I wipe my tears haphazardly. "It was our only chance to save them. And we blew it."

"Maybe not." Gavin strides past me back into the corridor, flashlight in hand.

"Where are—" But his figure is swallowed by the darkness.

At the far end of the room, Remington crouches on the ground, torch in one hand, feeling beneath the bed with the other. He pushes onto his knees, rocking slightly, head bent low. "Maren, you said you heard Polly's voice. Was there…"

"Another voice?" I ask, unable to meet his eyes. "I didn't hear one. But that doesn't mean Jane wasn't with her."

"If I could find a clue, one small trace that she was in here…" He tears the ratty sheet from the bed.

I force myself up on wobbly legs to help him search, lifting my lantern. "We don't know they were in the same room. If Annabelle only managed to move Polly, maybe Jane is still back here somewhere."

He nods, pulling himself up by the rusty bedframe. From somewhere out in the passageway, a low grunt sounds, followed by a thud. "What was that?"

"That," coos a new voice an instant before the gate slams, "was Gavin being knocked unconscious by Dallis and Paul." Annabelle places a brass skeleton key into the lock and, though Remington lunges at her, turns it with a click.

Through the bars, she smiles at us. "There. Now you'll see that the only way to save anyone is the Gamemaster's way."

TWENTY-THREE

"What will you do to Gavin?" I rush to the gate, lashing at her, fingers knocking iron. She steps back, just enough to avoid my clawing.

"I'm not sure yet," she says, swinging the key by the ring to taunt us. "Might have to interrogate him until his true loyalty surfaces. Or..." She shrugs. "Make an example out of him."

The image of Alicia Jones writhing on the ground slices all other thoughts in half, and I lean against the gate for support.

"We could always add him to the winnings," she muses, twirling a strand of hair around her finger. "Up the ante, so to speak. If you play the game and stop wasting everyone's time, I'll release him too. How's that for a prize?"

Remington shakes the bars hard enough to make Annabelle flinch. "We know you're planning to kill one of the girls in some sick ritual. We know this isn't just a game and that the society isn't simply one big, rich, happy family."

She stares at him, like she didn't comprehend his words.

"So why go to all this trouble to choose?"

"You haven't figured that out?" She squints at him, and then her gaze flicks up to the ceiling above her. "The Games are the society's greatest source of entertainment. Each one leads up to the tournament's finale tomorrow night." She tosses her hair back behind a shoulder. "Think of it as our Superbowl."

"Except no one gets sacrificed to a pagan god at the end of the Superbowl," I snap.

"Why are you doing this, Annabelle?" Remington asks. "You don't have to go along with these monsters."

Her gaze tracing over him, and I can't tell if it's with desire or disgust. I shut my eyes, still picturing the two of them, lips pressed together, limbs entwined. I rub my arms, trying to wipe off a sensation like ants crawling over me.

The Remington who now glares at Annabelle through the bars certainly doesn't look like the one in the photos.

Annabelle sighs. "I've never known anything but the society. The Games are my life. The society is my family. And when my father became embroiled in *less-than-reputable* business dealings, it saved his career." For a moment, her smug expression falters. "The society rescued him—rescued all of us." So that's it. Annabelle mentioned that her father had been a student at Torrey-Wells. He must've joined the society, and Annabelle is simply carrying on the legacy. "Now, are you going to listen to the rules?"

"We're not doing this," I spit.

"That's up to you. But it would be an odd decision, considering what happens to whomever you can't save." She buttons her coat up higher and pulls on her hood, as if suddenly noting the chill down here. "The game is simple. Somewhere in this cell is a key to unlock the gate." She digs into her coat pocket, removing a long, red ribbon that she ties onto a standing lantern out in the corridor. "Once you're out, be the first to grab this ribbon. Whoever presents it tomorrow night receives an advantage in the tournament, where one girl will be freed, and one will become part of the conclusion ceremony."

"You expect us to believe you're going to let us walk away from all of this?"

"Walk away from all of this?" Annabelle frowns. "After the ceremony—after you *see*, the idea will never cross your mind again." She glances past me, her pupils large and devilish.

She spins on her heel, and I grip the bars so tightly the iron digs into my palms. "Annabelle, wait!"

When the sound of her heels clacking over the stone fades away, I'm suddenly aware that Remington's pocketknife is

in his grip, blade extended. I jerk away, and the backs of my
thighs hit the bed.

"Oh, come on, Maren," Remington says sharply. "This
whole thing where you equate one kiss with Annabelle to
me trying to sabotage you? It's getting old." He kicks a dirty
mug, which shatters on contact with the wall. "I told you. I
didn't want to kiss her. But I did want to kiss you. That"—he
shakes his head—"wasn't an act."

"Give me a little more credit," I retort. "You've been
shady since I met you. You have a never-ending supply of
secrets."

"I was trying to find Jane."

I fiddle with the hem of the mangy bed linens. "Well, what
are you doing with that?" I indicate his Swiss Army knife.

"Thought we might be able to pick the lock with it."

"You don't think there's really a key?"

"No chance," he says, moving to inspect the lock. "We
lost whatever trust she had in us by sneaking you down here.
Now that we know her plans, she'll never release us from this
cell."

A cold rush of terror hits me. He's right. I check my
phone for a signal, but of course, there's nothing. And to
make matters worse, my battery is on its last leg. The time
is 2:48 a.m. I reexamine the room, noting an empty water
bottle beneath the bed and a tattered blanket balled up on the
floor. A chess set lies in one corner, its pieces scattered about

the board. Did Polly play this game alone? Or was Jane in here with her?

"The knife won't be of any use," Remington says finally, and I move closer. "We need something malleable. Don't you have a bobby pin on you?"

I resist the urge to scream. "No, I don't have a bobby pin on me. Last time I checked, I wasn't a Pretty Little Liar."

"You are pretty," he says, that half-grin returning.

I roll my eyes and turn to face the rest of the room, throwing my hands up. "Can we use the knife to remove the stones?"

"If we had a lot more than twenty-four hours."

My teeth are chattering, so I jog in place. "It's freezing. How did Polly survive down here?" Near the end of soccer season, she used to leave my games at halftime because she couldn't hack the cold. She preferred my basketball games inside the gym.

Remington begins to remove his coat, but I wave him off. "I'll use this nasty blanket," I say, lifting it between two fingertips and coughing as dust swarms the air.

"Don't be so hardheaded." He strides across the room, and before I can sidestep him, his arms envelop me. I stiffen, but he rubs my back, jostling me a bit until my blood seems to thaw and I barely even remember that the idea of us working together is senseless. Because only one of our friends can be saved. "Better?" he asks, running his hands up and down my arms, head pulling back to look at me.

"Mmhmm," I mumble.

"Put this on." He shrugs his coat off and stuffs me into it, one arm at a time. "You're useless to our grand escape plan shivering like a drowning cat." His fingers graze my wrist as he peers down at me.

"I'm good now. Besides, my plan is working. I'll keep stealing layers of your clothes until you catch hypothermia. Then I'll be able to search for the key by myself, thus winning this elusive advantage."

The torch light illuminates Remington's smirk before I realize what I've said. "Take what you want."

My cheeks heat. "That's not what—"

"Kidding, Maren." He spins back to the gate. "Now help."

"You said there was no key."

"On the off chance that there is a key and Annabelle lets us waltz out of this place, one of us should be looking."

I get down onto the cold stone to search under the bed, which is filled with dust and cobwebs. I move onto my knees, wiggling my nose to stifle a sneeze. There isn't anything down here but crumbs.

After checking every rusted and rotted inch of the bed, my stomach grumbles. I dig the two granola bars Remington forced upon me from my backpack. I open one, nibbling at it before pushing the other at him. He accepts it without looking, his eyes trained on the gate. "What is it?"

"I've been focused on the lock." Absentmindedly, he unwraps the bar and takes a bite.

"Yeah…"

Remington blinks suddenly, flicking his head to the corner of the room. Confused, I follow. When he spins me so that my back is pressed against the wall, panic tornados through my head. He whips out the pocketknife, and I squirm in his grasp. "What are you—"

"Shh," he says, leaning to whisper into my ear. "I couldn't tell you before. Don't look, but there's a camera beneath the stool. It doesn't have much of a view, but it's listening."

My heart pounds. The lines from *King Lear* echo back. The fresco of the eyes. The Gamemaster is always watching. Plotting.

She's playing with us.

TWENTY-FOUR

"This is what Annabelle meant by the Games being the society's biggest source of entertainment," I hiss. "They're watching us."

"Yep."

"We're screwed."

"No, we're not. The gate hinges are. Screwed on, I mean."

I inhale a morsel of granola, choking. Remington pulls me from the wall to knock me on the back.

I cough and flick my chin toward Remington's hand around the knife. "I'm hoping what you're trying to tell me," I whisper, "is that your knife contains a screwdriver."

He's close enough that I feel him nod. "You reposition the stool to take away the camera's view of the gate. All

conversation from here on out will have to be about searching for the key or..."

"How much we hate each other."

"How much we *despise* each other." His fingers trail over
the back of my neck beneath my ponytail. "We're going to
get out of here."

He steps to the side, and I wander in front of the camera,
pretending to search the room. "There's some sort of shelf up
here." I point before dragging the stool over to the wall, aiming
the camera at a blank stone backdrop. Then I stand on it for
good measure, watching Remington work away. Torch stowed
inside a wall mount above him, he removes a screw, tucking it
inside his pocket and moving on to the next one. "Nothing up
here," I say, dropping down to the ground. "Why are you just
sitting there, Remington? You're completely useless."

Remington's focus halts as he slings me a look of feigned
irritation. "I'm thinking. Which is impossible to do in here
with your constant prattle."

"Did you say *prattle*? No wonder you're so slow. You're
a few hundred years old. Go ahead, keep thinking. Polly and
Jane are really going to appreciate all those thoughts when
they're dead."

"Maybe they won't have to die if we just use you for the
sacrifice."

At this, I whack my shin against the iron bed frame,
releasing a noise somewhere between a cry and a delirious

laugh. In an attempt to cover it, I cough, which is timely, since Remington has removed the entire first hinge. The gate groans, and I fake a full-on coughing attack to cover the sound. "It's so dusty in here."

Remington proceeds to the top hinge, and I settle onto the bed. "Don't bother getting up to help a choking girl," I groan. "Keep searching for your damned key."

"That is the game, isn't it?" The first screw is out.

"Gavin was right about you." The words sizzle with a heat I tell myself is good acting. Remington's hand pauses momentarily, but he returns to tediously twisting the knife. A thread of guilt knots in my stomach—and I don't even know if it's for Remington or for Gavin, who's locked up and injured for trying to help me. Gavin, who earlier tonight sent a flood of convoluted emotions through me.

A *ting* echoes in the room as the final screw falls to the ground. The gate clanks as one side sinks. Remington moves to catch it, and I rush to help. Together, we lift and pull to keep the iron from grating over the stone. But it's too heavy.

It screeches like a beast in the night. We've created just enough space to escape, though. Remington turns to grab the torch, and I sling my backpack on, cursing myself for giving Gavin the flashlight as I grasp the lantern handle.

I ease through the bars first, followed by Remington. But as soon as we're in the dank corridor, he rushes for the lantern, tugging on the end of the red ribbon until it unravels.

He stuffs it in the pocket of his pants as I stop to stare in awestruck horror. Then he starts to run, motioning for me to hurry like it never happened.

And I have to pretend like it didn't, because our friends' lives depend on what I do now. I follow him at a sprint toward the only certain exit—beneath the old cathedral.

Once we're out of earshot of the camera, I yell back to him, "When we get out, we have to call the cops. We have the video of Polly and Jane. They'll have to take us seriously."

"If we tell, Annabelle will kill them." Remington's voice bounces off the dank tunnel walls. "We should go after Annabelle ourselves. Tie her up and force her to tell us where the girls are."

It's a thought. Speaking to the police would be a huge risk.

But I have to believe that there's a way to save the girls and Gavin—one that doesn't involve becoming Annabelle. "We need some insurance," I say, almost believing it as we pass the gallery where we found the camcorder. "When we get to the old cathedral, we'll copy the video. That way if everything goes wrong, we can threaten to send it to the cops—hell, to the media even—if she lays a hand on anyone."

I don't remember the rat tunnel until I've nearly crashed into it, but this time with adrenaline so high, I fly through it like my limbs have evolved into a sewer creature's. Out in the corridors, my body hums with a heightened sense of direction. I don't even need the map as I lead us through each bend, never stopping to contemplate until we've reached the antechamber.

Remington passes me his torch and bulls up the stepladder, barreling through the trapdoor. Once the door is secured above, he hurries back down to help me snuff the torches.

Abandoning both the torch and lantern below, I click my phone light on to navigate the rest of the way up and through the old cathedral. Remington reaches the exit through the secret door, and I grab him by the coat. "Wait," I whisper, already sliding my backpack off. "The recording." I fall to my knees, rummaging through the pack until I find the camera. My phone blinks its near-death warning, but I check that we finally have reception and ready it to record. With a shaky finger, I play the video of Polly and Jane, my stomach souring at what's to come.

When it ends, I email the video to myself, Remington, Gavin, and Polly. I can't afford to let it spread any wider until I'm certain the girls are safe. "Okay," I say, tucking the camera back inside the pack. I glance down at my phone, ready to dial 911, but the screen goes black.

"Damnit," I growl, shaking it. "Where's your phone?"

Remington searches through his pocket and pulls his out. He stares up at me.

"What is it?"

"It's dead."

My stomach drops. We can't call the cops. Even if we scaled the school gate, we wouldn't be able to call an Uber to take us to the station. "Then what do we do?"

"We could find a security guard."

I shake my head. "Night after night, the society members sneak out, and no one is ever caught. I don't trust security."

"We'll have to try the headmistress. She can call."

I start to nod, but the memory of my bizarre experience in Dr. Yamashiro's classroom slithers into my head. The linchpin cufflink. "What if she's in on it?"

He considers this, his dark eyes shifting to graze the ancient stonework beneath us. "When Annabelle first showed me evidence that Jane was being held in the catacombs, she warned me not to go to the headmistress."

"She gave me the same warning."

"Once we tell Headmistress Koehler about the video stream and how many people are already watching it, she'll have to help us."

"But who's watching it, Remington? Not Gavin. Not Polly."

"The headmistress doesn't have to know that."

Out in the windy night air, the hazy light of the lampposts guides us past the Lowell Math and Science Building, standing dark and beastly over the grounds. Soon, the sweet scent of apple blooms fills the air as we weave through the branches, the moon our only source of light. Ahead lies faculty housing, a series of cottages scattered around the orchards and streams.

We keep going. Headmistress Koehler doesn't board near the other staff; she has her own cottage on the far side of Woodbriar Pond.

She lives alone, other than the wild geese that flock to her yard in search of food. At this time of night, though, the coast is clear as we slink through her pristinely maintained garden and up the path to her unlit porch.

Remington pounds on the door, which might not be the best strategy. "She's going to call security," I hiss.

"What else can we do?" He knocks again, just as hard, and I cover my eyes like this is all a scary scene from a movie. "Headmistress Koehler?" he calls, still thumping on the door.

A white flash races through my periphery. The curtains. Inside the cottage, a light flicks on.

"Headmistress Koehler?" I try this time, hopefully less suspiciously than Remington.

"Who is it?" comes a muffled voice. "I've already called security."

My heart sinks, and I punch Remington in the arm. "It's Maren Montgomery, ma'am. From the other day at your office?" Remington opens his mouth, but I silence him with a look. "And Remington Cruz. Please, may we come in?"

"It's four in the morning."

"We know. It's an emergency. Someone—two people will die if we don't speak to you."

No response. Sweat beads on my forehead. "I'm waiting for security."

"We don't have time, Headmistress," Remington calls. "It's about Annabelle Westerly. We have proof that she and her secret society are keeping Polly St. James and Jane Blanchet prisoner. They're hurt, and the society has threatened to kill them in a matter of hours."

"If this is a prank, you're making a grave mistake. Annabelle Westerly is one of Torrey-Well's finest students."

Remington growls under his breath. "And she locked us up in the dungeon beneath the school! We can show you the proof—proof that we've already emailed to everyone we know." His voice is strained. "But you have to open the door."

The seconds tick by, my palms stickier with each one. Our headmistress—the person whose entire life is supposedly wrapped up in her school and her students—isn't going to listen to us. But finally, there's a click and a turn of the knob, and the door pushes open. "Show me," she says, extending a pale, open palm.

Frantically, I dig through my pack to produce the camera. I give it to her, and the door shuts in our faces, the bolt sounding again.

I close my eyes and inhale the pine scent of the forest bordering the cottage. When I open my eyes again, Remington is sitting on the porch, head in his hands. I lower beside him, timidly touching his back.

"It's too incredible," he says without looking up.

"It is," I agree. "But it's the truth. She can't ignore the time-stamped video. And even if she does, we have a backup plan. We'll show the authorities."

"Thank you," he says, "for being in this with me. Despite everything Annabelle's done to drive a wedge between us."

I shrug. "Thank *you*, for having a screwdriver back there."

He laughs weakly. I rest my tired head on his shoulder, and after a moment, he straightens, wrapping an arm around me. It's a small comfort that does little to stop my mind from spinning with worry. The headmistress has had plenty of time to watch the video. What's taking so long?

Before I can repeat the question aloud, the bolt clicks behind us, followed by the creak of the door.

"Come in," Headmistress Koehler says. "I—I…" I turn to find her ashen face staring through the doorframe. She steps back, and we follow her inside, where she looks us over. She reaches out, taking my hand in hers and wincing. "You're like ice." She motions to a floral couch. "I'll get some blankets and tea. I canceled my call for campus security and contacted the proper channels instead. They'll be here momentarily to take your statements. And they'll be bringing Annabelle down to the station for questioning."

"She has Gavin Holt too, ma'am," I say. "He was taken somewhere else when she locked us up."

"How can one girl do all of this?" Headmistress Koehler asks, looking timid and frail, so unlike the confident woman who sits at her administrative desk during the day.

"She has the society under her control," Remington answers. "Teachers too. They all do her bidding."

Headmistress Koehler takes a deep, silent breath and wanders to the hearth. "Does this have something to do with your coming to my office the other day, Maren?" She strikes a match and bends to light the fireplace.

"Yes, ma'am, I was going to tell you that Annabelle was responsible for Alicia Jones. But then the society threatened to pin Alicia's illness on me. I panicked. I'm sorry."

The flames roar to life, and the headmistress stands, turning to face us. "We're going to make this right," she says, nodding to herself. "Here, warm yourselves until the tea is ready."

She exits the room in a zomebielike state, and Remington and I waste no time moving to crouch by the fireplace.

"It's going to be okay," Remington says, rubbing my hands. For the first time in days, some tightly coiled part of me loosens.

She's going to help get the others back.

"I'm going to find the bathroom," I say, squeezing his hand. They don't exactly have functioning toilets in the catacombs. I start in the direction of the whistling kettle to ask where to go, but I spot a door down the hall and decide to help myself. I pad down the hallway, clicking on the light to find a powder room decorated in white lily everything— wallpaper, lily-scented candle, even a toilet-seat cover with a giant flower embroidered on it.

My eyes are half-shut when I finish up, washing my hands and splashing some water on my face. I leave, heading back down the hall, past a large bookshelf stuffed with an eclectic mix of scholarly tomes, academic journals, and gardening magazines. I stop, sifting through the reading material; apparently, Headmistress Koehler takes her gardening more seriously than we ever knew. Stuffed between a few issues of *Country Gardens*, though, is a paperback copy of Homer's *The Iliad*. Like the one in Polly's things. I lift it, riffling through a few pages, refamiliarizing myself with the epic poem. Inside this copy, there are a few annotations.

I flip some more pages, noticing one line has been repeated in the margins, every few books of the poem: *Fate is in the gods' hands.*

At the end of the book, sketched on the blank last page in red ink is a checkered game board. But the pieces aren't knights, queens, and rooks; they're people. Some drip tears, some blood. Only one stands victorious, sword raised above his head.

The words from King Lear boomerang back into my head: *they kill us for their sport.*

I push the book back into place, but something else catches my eye. The book beside it on the shelf: *Hero Worship and*

Transcending the Body. I remember the title from my Google search. An icy chill, worse than anything I experienced down in the catacombs, wracks my body now.

The author of the book is Alexander Wells.

As in Torrey-Wells Academy.

The annotations. The patron god Pelops. The eyes in the catacombs. The society members are clearly disciples. Acolytes in need of a sacrifice. My mind spins, full of too many questions.

But two things are certain: Headmistress Koehler is one of them. And Remington and I have to get out of here.

I slide the book back inside the rack and tiptoe back into the hall. When I reach the living room, Remington and the headmistress are seated, nursing steaming cups of tea. "Maren," the headmistress says, lifting a handmade quilt. I force a smile as I take it, and she gestures toward a third porcelain cup.

"Thanks, ma'am." I add some milk to the tea, wondering how to get Remington alone so I can tell him not to take another sip. "I'm so sorry to trouble you," I say, placing a sugar cube into the cup with a tiny set of silver tongs, "but I don't think I can drink this on an empty stomach. Do you have any crackers?"

"Oh." Headmistress Koehler's head falls back. "How stupid of me. Of course, you're hungry. I left the cookies on the kitchen counter. I'll be right back."

"Thank you," I say as she gets up and scurries from the room. I rush toward Remington on the couch, but there's a knock on the front door.

Headmistress Koehler stops at the edge of the room, twisting back around. "Ah, here we are." She plods over to unbolt the door.

My nerves prickle. Is this cop at the door really on our side?

I reach back to make sure Remington is still there, because I don't know what's real anymore. He takes my hand, wrapping his fingers, warm from the fire, around mine. It's going to be okay. The authorities are here because we have to help them with the investigation. Even if the headmistress is part of this, she has to be worried about the video.

The headmistress tugs the door open and moves to the side. A figure shifts in the blackness of the doorway. Slowly, a foot crosses the threshold, and there in the well-lit foyer of the cottage stands Annabelle Westerly.

Her smile is sharp enough to carve stone.

TWENTY-FIVE

I TRY TO SWALLOW, BUT A LUMP IS LODGED IN MY THROAT. MY mouth is too dry.

"What did you do?" Remington shouts at Headmistress Koehler. He stands, hurling himself between Annabelle and me. "You brought her *here*? Did you even call the cops?"

Annabelle shuts the door behind her and begins to unbutton her coat with the careless grace of someone joining a dinner party.

"Of course," the headmistress says. "I had to tell them that if a certain video surfaces, I have strong suspicions that two of my students are the ones behind the camera."

I slump down onto the couch. "The headmistress is part of it." My vision blurs, the haze of the fire coating everything in the room. I'm too tired. I need to sleep. "She's in the society."

Remington spins around, clutching his temples. He strides toward Headmistress Koehler, teeth gritted. "You *knew* Annabelle was holding students prisoner beneath the school? You've been covering for her?"

Polly's going to die. Jane and Gavin too. We're all going to die. We know too much about this twisted academy.

Annabelle drapes her coat over a piano bench and nears Remington. She reaches out to touch him, but he shakes her off.

Her head draws back. "Remi," she says, making a pouty face. "That's not how you behaved the last time we were together. You know, earlier tonight? During the meeting." She grins coyly, running a finger over her bottom lip. "You seemed to like my hands on you, if I recall."

"She's lying, Maren. She's trying to turn us against each other again."

Annabelle laughs. "Oh dear," she says, looking at me. "You thought he was winning all these challenges based on merit, didn't you?"

"Shut up," I snap. She just wants me worked up. Still, I cringe at the thought of them together, and I can't help but wonder if there was more than that one time from the photos.

She walks past Remington, taking a seat across from me on a mauve velvet wingback chair. "We'll need a few minutes, Headmistress Koehler," she says, waving a hand in dismissal.

Annabelle motions for Remington to take a seat beside me on the couch. Once the headmistress has disappeared down the hall, Annabelle folds her hands and places them on her lap. "It seems you two failed to learn your lesson about refusing the society's tasks."

"Why?" I ask, rubbing my sleepy eyes. "Why us?"

Annabelle shrugs. "By now you've likely ascertained that the Gamemaster's Society is no ordinary high school club. It's no coincidence the academy was built directly on top of the catacombs where the society has met and held its semi-annual tournament for two centuries. Torrey-Wells is where we scout our potential members. And this year, you two were selected as champions."

"Selected?" Remington asks.

"Of course." She notices the tray on the coffee table. "Drink your tea, Maren. We wouldn't want you dehydrated."

I stiffen, and she rolls her eyes. "You worried about poison? If we killed you, there would be no one to compete tomorrow night. Anyway, as I was saying, you two are the society's champions, and yes, you were selected. You two are shining examples of the qualities we esteem: competitive spirit, athletic skills, intelligence. You've managed to surpass all of our expectations thus far. Though at times, when we needed to make *absolutely* certain"—she tilts her head slightly—"we helped you along."

"Helped us *how*?" I ask.

"Maren, you didn't honestly think you beat me at our game of Texas Hold'em."

"I did beat you," I argue. "I had a straight, and you had…" But I don't know what she had. "You folded. You left your cards facedown." Suddenly, I'm dizzy. My head sways, and Remington wraps an arm around me, wiping stray hairs from my forehead.

"Here, maybe you *should* drink something. The tea is fine. I'm still alive." Remington hands me my cup, and I sip the now-lukewarm chamomile brew. Remington continues to run his fingers softly through my hair, and I let my elbow rest on his thigh.

"You're cute together." Annabelle muses, but she's frowning. "As I was saying, your final task is to win tomorrow night's tournament. Make your patrons proud."

"So, tomorrow night, you want us to compete for the lives of our friends," I say. "If I lose, Polly becomes the sacrifice." Across from me, Annabelle remains expressionless. "There has to be another way."

"There isn't," she says lazily. "Just play the game. Be the pieces."

"Be the pieces?" Remington repeats, lifting a hand in frustration. But the image from the book in Headmistress Koehler's hallway whips and flaps in my mind, and suddenly, everything fits.

"Game pieces." I cross my arms, sidestepping in front of her. "The society—the higher-ups—think they're gods, and they're playing with us like pieces of a game set. Lately, our actions have felt predetermined. That the society knew what we were going to do before we did it. They want us to feel that way. They're trying to take away our sense of choice, our sense that our choices even matter. They want us to fall into place in this bizarre, fatalistic establishment that's been right under everyone's noses for centuries."

I glance down, meeting her eyes. "*Champion* means we're like hired knights for the society. Fighting to determine the night's events."

"I thought we were fighting for Polly and Jane," Remington mutters, running a hand through his curls, sights still trained on Annabelle.

"They were the bait," I say. "Annabelle lured us in and kept us here by dangling them in front of us. And when our game is done, they'll sacrifice one—maybe both—of our friends in their ritual."

"She's insane," Remington says. Suddenly, he's on his feet, lunging at her across the table. She lets out a noise before Remington's massive hand covers her mouth, the other pinning her down on the floor. She thrashes, kicking the table leg and knocking my teacup to the floor. "Maren, get something to tie her up," Remington growls.

"Wha—we—" But it's the only way. If we let her walk

out of here, Polly, Jane, and Gavin will be left to her diabolical devices. I yank a shiny pink table runner out from under the tea tray and rush over to gag her. She snaps at me, letting out another scream before I secure the knot.

Steps thud down the hallway, and I move to grab a poker from the fireplace. "What's going on in here?" Headmistress Koehler calls, entering the room.

"Sit down," I command, brandishing the poker at her.

She hesitates, clearly considering disobeying and making a run for the door.

"Do it!" I shout, swinging the iron rod in a full circle. Finally, she consents as Remington forces Annabelle back into the chair, wrapping her arms around the back of it. I tear the ribbon off some sort of bird ornament hanging from the wall and help him bind her wrists.

Now Remington turns on the headmistress. "Don't make a move," he snarls. "You two are going to tell me where Polly, Jane, and Gavin are being held. Right now."

Headmistress Koehler's eyes widen. "I—I don't know," she says. "Only the Gamemaster knows."

"Of course she's the only one who knows." I glance at Annabelle, not wanting to touch that gag and give her another opportunity to bite off my fingers.

"Oh," the headmistress says, blinking. "Annabelle isn't the Gamemaster. Is that what you thought?"

A cold, numbness washes over me.

I reach for the armrest of the couch to steady myself. Across the room, Remington's forehead wrinkles.

"What do you mean, she's not the Gamemaster?" he demands. "Who is?"

I peek again at Annabelle. Above the gag, her blue eyes glint nefariously in the firelight.

"I'm not at liberty to say." The headmistress draws her elbows inward, inching herself back toward the far corner of the couch.

I stomp over, ripping the gag from Annabelle's mouth. "Who is it?"

Her lips settle into a thin line. "I'd rather die than betray the Gamemaster," she coos with the air of someone lounging on the Caribbean sands.

"Then tell us more about these *patrons*. I'm assuming they're the reason for the camera in the cell."

"Smart girl you have there, Remington. Perhaps I was wrong to select you as my champion."

Remington's chiseled jaw slackens. "What does that mean?"

"We've all chosen sides," she says, like it's obvious. "I've backed you, whereas the Gamemaster has backed Maren. Our beloved hostess and fearless academy leader"—she tosses a knowing glance at Headmistress Koehler—"well, I won't give her allegiance away. Every society member supports a champion. They like to watch from their place on high.

They interfere. Like Athena and Zeus in battle, they meddle. Perhaps you've noticed?"

A sick feeling rolls through my stomach as I think back to the security cameras stationed everywhere. How the one at my dormitory door fizzled out at just the right moment. To Dr. Yamashiro's class. *They like to watch.* We're their entertainment. "Every society member?" I ask, the words barely audible over the roaring fire.

"You're wondering if your precious Holt has been helping or hurting," she says, mouth poised in a frown of pity. "Don't worry so much, Maren. He's been on your side from the beginning."

The sickness pushes into my throat now, and I choke back a gag. All that talk about finding the Gamemaster. Playing *freaking cornhole* to get an invitation. He went so far as to hand me pebbles on my way into the meeting. Gavin made it seem like he was trying to help me find Polly when really, he was helping the society.

He set me up.

"That's why I had to remove him from the situation tonight," Annabelle continues. "He was working against my champion." Her eyes brush over Remington possessively.

"Do they all know? About the sacrifice?"

"They'll know tomorrow night."

"They won't go along with it."

"Won't they?" Her lip curls. "Now that they've felt

divinity in their veins? The taste of ambrosia lingering on the tongue? They wouldn't do anything to keep it? They wouldn't do whatever I asked of them, for another taste?"

I think of my father, of his failing business, of his shame and disappointment that he couldn't provide for me. If Polly had never been in the equation, and the society came along, offering to fix it all—if they'd assured me that neither one of us would ever have to worry about money again, would I have been sucked right in? Like Polly was? My thoughts whip to Gavin next, of his sister, suffering. One win away from Major Supreme, he was already on the path to saving her. He'd already experienced things no mere mortal could possibly fathom. If he had a choice between going along with all of this to cure his sister, and giving it up, what would he choose?

Suddenly, I can't hold back the sensation any longer. Dropping the fireplace poker to the floor, I rush from the room.

In the bathroom, I hover over the toilet. But my stomach is so empty, I only retch until the acids start to tear holes in my stomach lining. I pull myself up, catching the broken blood vessels in my eyes in the mirror on my way out, and return to the living room. My gaze scans the walls for cameras, but there are so many paintings and knickknacks, like that bird decoration I dismantled and used to bind Annabelle; you could hide a camera anywhere.

"You don't look so good, Maren," Annabelle says in a voice that would fool anyone she hadn't locked up in a cell.

"Don't force me to stuff the table runner back in your mouth," I growl, flopping down onto the Persian rug because there's no way in hell I'm sitting next to Headmistress Koehler.

Before I know what's happening, Remington is using Annabelle's gag to secure the headmistress's hands behind her back. "If either of you move a millimeter," he says, grabbing the poker and wielding it at them, "I'll use this on your legs."

Headmistress Koehler nods emphatically. Remington flicks his head toward the doorway leading to the kitchen and I follow, so out of breath I have to steady myself against the doorframe. But even that isn't enough. My knees start to buckle, and Remington grabs my waist before I can collapse.

"Maren, let's get you something to eat."

"You just tied up the headmistress," I say, my vision tunneling.

"I needed to talk to you in private. You know she would've called someone."

"How is this happening? Can we call our parents?" If I called now, my parents could be here in a couple hours.

"We could…" he says. "But what if the headmistress wasn't bluffing? No one but Polly and Jane is actually in that video. The society—headmistress, cops, mayor, whoever's in on this—could easily say we were the ones filming."

"But at least they'd know Polly and Jane are in trouble," I

whisper-scream. "We can battle the society later, once they're safe."

Remington's breath dusts my neck. "Would they be safe? Annabelle isn't the Gamemaster—at least, that's the story these two are feeding us. I thought tying her up would solve all of our problems, but it solves nothing if she isn't the one holding the girls."

I let my forehead dip to rest on his chest, my neck muscles too weak to function. It's been days without sleep while maintaining my grueling lacrosse schedule. "Then we'll have to find them ourselves." I inhale, breathing in the lingering spiced scent of his cologne mingled with sweat.

Back in the living room, I take up the fire poker again. "Annabelle, tell me who the Gamemaster is or I'm going to smash your ballerina feet with this thing."

She draws her lips into a taut line, and my grip tightens around the iron pole.

"Wait," Remington says. "The Gamemaster's identity isn't a secret from the other members. They must know who it is."

"The members know better than to reveal the Gamemaster's identity to the champions," the headmistress cuts in, pushing her shoulders back against the couch cushions. Apparently, being held hostage isn't enough reason to slack on her perfect posture. "It would make toying with them so much less fun."

Annabelle said the Gamemaster was backing me, which means it could be someone who's helped me along at some point. Like Donella, who may've let me win the labyrinth the way Annabelle let me win the card game.

I look at Remington, wanting to get him alone, to voice my suspicion in private. But behind the couch, Remington's head slumps, his brown irises rolling back to reveal the blank whites of his eyes. "Remington?" His entire body crumples, chin hitting the back of the couch on his way to the floor.

I rush over to check on him, pointing my poker at the headmistress. "Don't you dare move."

Over on the chair, Annabelle cranes her neck to look at Remington, whose unconscious head peeks out from behind the couch. "Oh dear, what do you think happened to him?"

Her saccharine tone makes my blood boil. My gaze darts to his teacup, empty on the coffee table, and then to mine spilled on the rug. "You poisoned us."

My head is too tired. The tiredest.

I press my hand to Remington's cheek, but I don't feel anything. Not warmth, not the scruffiness of his jawline. Not a thing. My fingers don't work. And now my face doesn't work. Because I want to tell the headmistress to stay where she is, but my mouth is glued shut.

"Not poison," Headmistress Koehler says, her voice too deep and jumbled. "A delayed-release sedative. A harmless herb from my garden. Engineered by Dr. Theodore Lowell himself. You'll wake up in a few hours."

Over at the door, the bolt turns of its own accord, and

the door swings open. I look just in time to see a familiar face push into the light.

That face. Of course. It all makes sense now.

But my eyelids, too useless and heavy, fall.

My body follows.

TWENTY-SIX

"Maren." The deep voice splits my head in half. I crack an eye open, and the light stings like lemon juice dripping onto my eyeballs.

"Remington?" my lazy tongue manages.

"Still sleeping," comes the same voice. "He drank a lot more tea than you did. You were barely out an hour."

Blinking against the stabbing lights, I force my lids open. *It's him.*

"You're the Gamemaster," I say, as he helps me sit up and slide my back against the base of the couch. He doesn't respond, only finds a pillow to prop behind me for support.

"You let me steal your linchpin pendant at the ball."

He nods and hands me a glass of cold water. I guzzle it

down, trying to dilute the effects of the sedative. The bizarre, buzzy sensation that none of the parts of my body truly belong to me. I don't even care that the water may be poisoned. I have to flush this feeling from my system.

I'd considered Donella, but my brain stopped short of the real master manipulator.

Paul *Lowell*. The society claims nepotism isn't a factor, but Paul's grandfather is a bigshot donor, and Paul happens to be one of the members of the Gamemaster's Society. He not only got into the society on his daddy's coattails; he got to run it.

"You pretended not to know who I was or what I looked like. And now you're going to kill my best friend," I say, incapable of tears, though I want to cry.

"Of course not, Maren. You and Remington will decide what happens to your friends."

"But I can't compete against him," I slur. "I think I'm in love with him." My voice sounds distant, like it's coming from inside the headmistress's broom closet.

Paul smiles over me, pushing a strand of reddish-brown hair off his forehead. "Yes, that has been pretty apparent since the liquor closet."

"You saw that?" Hot embarrassment crawls up my neck.

"Everyone saw that, Maren. It was cruel of Annabelle to play with him, knowing how you felt. The Gamemaster isn't like her, though. The Gamemaster doesn't want to use your feelings for Remington against you." Paul is weird. Why is he speaking about himself in third person? "The Gamemaster values you and wants to reward you for your display of prowess, which is why you've been granted a reprieve until tonight. You're going to walk out of here right now."

"Really? I thought locking me up and doing whatever you wanted was more your style." In reality, this—making sure the game stays on his terms, not allowing us to back him into a corner—is exactly his style.

Paul laughs, like we're old friends. "You and Remington will rest today. Your classes will be taken care of. And tonight, you'll see Polly and Jane."

"Alive?"

He chuckles again. "Yes, alive."

"And I have your word?" I ask, finally remembering that I haven't seen Remington; I've only taken Paul's word that he's still sleeping. I pull myself up by a couch cushion.

"You have my word. Once Remington wakes up, you can both go back to your dorms and recover. You've been through quite the ordeal."

"No thanks to you," I snap, leaving him to peek at Remington, who still lies passed out on the floor. I move to cover him with the quilt, my fingertips lingering on his chest, feeling the rise and fall. I lean closer, his breath reassuring against my skin. Lifting his head, I tuck a pillow beneath it and wander over to the hallway. "What about Gavin?" I ask before I can help it.

"Already in his dormitory bed."

That weasel probably made more promises to get himself released. "Where are the others?"

Paul reclines against the couch, folding his arms back behind his head. "The headmistress is sleeping. Annabelle is staying somewhere safe."

My mouth muscles twitch in satisfaction. I hope he means *safe from me*. The society is obsessed with being gods, but if they fear me—if Remington and I are failing to behave according to their whims—the power is shifting.

People make mistakes when they're scared. And a mistake is what I need.

"What's tonight's game?" I ask, forcing a nonchalance into my voice. Maybe if I can deliver an "old friends" routine to match his, he'll spill some secrets.

"The Gamemaster is still formulating it."

"Sticking with the third person thing, huh?"

Paul only rests his chin on a knuckle, and suddenly, the bizarre drugged-up sensation falls away, replaced by a vivid, sobering fear. Do I have it wrong? Is he simply another minion following orders?

"Do you hate me for what I did at the ball?" I ask, not exactly sure why I'm asking. Despite everything, I must blame myself for the way I led him on.

"Of course not. Your skill in battle was one of the reasons you were selected. We were proud of you."

"Proud, but going to let me have that linchpin no matter what I did."

Paul's head tilts in thought. "One thing about all of this," he says, and I'm not sure what *all of this* means, because he's motioning around the headmistress's living room. Maybe he means the fact that while we had Annabelle and the headmistress contained, somehow, those two still managed to get a message out to the society. "While we know the big picture—while we will intervene if things run off course—there is so much left to be determined on a smaller scale." I scan the room again, scan Paul's clothes for one of those pin cameras. "So...did I know you were meant to have the linchpin? Yes. Did I know you'd attempt to get it from *me*? Not at all. And when you asked me to dance, part of me did hope you really just wanted to dance." His cheeks flush the way they did at the ball when I asked about his last name.

I glance up, half-expecting the molding on the ceiling to shift and form the two eyes from the fresco in the catacombs. Somewhere in this room, the society must have metaphorical eyes on us.

A low groan sounds back behind the couch, and I pad over to kneel beside Remington. "Hey, shh," I say. "Don't move too fast. Take it easy."

"Maren?" he mumbles, his voice hoarse with sleep.

"Yeah." I take his hand, and, leaning down, place a kiss on his cheek.

At this, his eyelids flutter open, eyes shining as they struggle against the light. "What happened to me?"

"Turns out the tea was some sort of herbal sedative. We were both knocked out."

He squints up at me, trying to lift his head. "Then why aren't we back in a cell?"

I dig my fingers under his back to help him up, the way Paul helped me moments ago. When he's situated against the side of the couch, I turn to search for my leftover water, but Remington catches my arm and pulls me toward him. He hesitates a second, his stare latched on to mine.

Then he kisses me. I startle, unsure if it's a thank-you or a we-might-die-tonight kiss, but his lips are warm, and his hand on my cheek blurs whatever sharpness of mind I'd regained in the last few minutes, putting me back in my drug-induced state. Remington is undoubtedly feeling it too, because his body sways beneath me, and he has to pull away to catch his breath.

I turn to find my glass of water, and Paul is sitting there, watching us like we're a riveting television program. "I'll explain later," I tell Remington quietly as he notices the other presence in the room with a head-jerk. "The Gamemaster has granted us a reprieve until tonight."

"*He's* the Gamemaster?"

"Uh, sure. Maybe?" I hand him the water glass. "I have no idea."

"So what?" Remington asks, taking the glass. "We spend this *reprieve* here, I'm assuming. Where this freak can watch us?"

"Not at all," Paul says without flinching at the name-calling. "The door is unlocked. You may see yourselves to your rooms."

Remington casts him a tired glance. "You're going to trust us," he says dryly, "out there."

"The Gamemaster is certain you won't try anything." Paul stands and walks over to the front door. "Go on, get your rest." His gaze fastens on my fingers entwined in Remington's. "Spend time together. I have a feeling that after tonight, you two won't be quite as"—his lips twist—"close."

He holds the door open for us, and I resist the urge to demand what he means by that. Speaking to Paul is getting us nowhere. And my head is pounding, a remnant of whatever special herbs the headmistress stuck in our tea. "Let's go," I say, standing and tugging on Remington's hand.

He nods, but his legs are too unstable and I'm not strong enough to pull him up. "Come on." I help him try again until he's on his feet, blinking like he's dizzy, leaning an elbow on the couch. I dip my shoulder beneath his arm for support and trudge toward the door. We have to get out of here before Paul—Gamemaster, crazed acolyte, whoever he is—changes his mind.

I grab my backpack from the foyer floor and sling it

on. As we cross the threshold, I hold my breath, waiting for Annabelle to pop out of the dark. But it looks clear, so I nudge Remington to the steps.

"Oh, and you'll find the dining hall available for your convenience," Paul adds, his figure a silhouette behind us in the bright doorway as I crane my neck to glance back. "The Gamemaster understands you must be famished."

"Thanks," I mutter wryly, taking the steps as Remington seems to be regaining equilibrium. His weight transitions off of me. One after another, we hurry through the garden.

Ahead, the orchard is shrouded in mist, filled with the sound of crickets. It stands like an army of monsters beneath the watery moonlight. We push ahead in silence, unwilling to chance a word until we've placed some distance between ourselves and the cottage. Once out, we round the pond, our feet sloshing through the mud and goose droppings on the bank. My heart thunders in the open space. It will be sunrise soon.

"So what's the plan?" Remington asks, keeping pace at my side. "You aren't really going back to your dorm—or the dining hall—where they can keep tabs on you."

"They can keep tabs on us everywhere. They're always watching us. Even in the headmistress's living room." Ahead, a puddle glistens in the moonlight, and I hop it, landing on the slick, silty ground.

Remington, either unsteady on his feet or past caring,

clomps straight through it. "So we're just going to give up, like they want us to?"

"They don't want us to give up," I say. "The opposite, in fact. Paul said he's pleased by how much of a fight we've put up. The society finds us entertaining, and as long as we stay that way, we're safe." I duck an overgrown pine branch, and Remington swats at it. We slip into the shadows between the fitness center and the health building. "But Polly and Jane aren't. So we'll have to come up with a plan." Remington opens his mouth to argue, but I cut him off. "We can't afford to put our trust in the wrong person again. So we'll have some food and some non-drug-induced sleep, and then we'll decide what to do."

"We're really going to waltz into the dining hall? Was I the only one who heard the horror movie music playing while Paul told us the place would be open for us? As in *only us*? You and me, alone in that massive dining hall they invited us to. Without working phones, by the way."

"I heard the music," I say, scanning the final walkway between this cluster of buildings and the dining hall. Remington catches up with me, and I slip my hand into his. "It had *The Shining* vibes, like, if the Carpenters were also providing vocals for the score."

"That was it!"

"Only I'm so hungry, I don't even care if this is the part where the society finishes us off and bakes us into tomorrow's menu while the ghosts of the Carpenters serenade us. I'm eating leftover dining hall food, whether you join me or not." The wind kicks up the spicy scent of the daphne shrubs bordering the dining hall as I release his hand and veer up the path.

Remington growls and kicks a rock, which clanks against a sprinkler. I scold him with a glance, and he ducks his head into his shoulders. "Of course I'm coming." He marches behind me as I try the door, which, unsurprisingly, opens.

The place is dark and still. It's also surrounded by windows; turning on the lights would be a mistake. Instead, we maneuver our way through the tables and chairs to the kitchen to scrounge up some leftovers. When I reach for the handle, Remington tugs on my arm. "What's that?" he whispers.

At the back of the room, beams of light play over the wall. They flicker and oscillate across the shadows. Like fire.

TWENTY-SEVEN

WE TIPTOE TO THE BACK, STOPPING TO PEER AROUND THE corner, to get a view of the small windowless alcove where Remington and his bros usually sit.

Only the long table has been replaced by a small round one set with a white tablecloth and candles. A figure steps from the shadows beneath an enormous framed portrait, and I jump. "Please," says the male figure, whom I now recognize as one of the rotating dining hall chefs, "Have a seat. The Gamemaster has asked me to attend to you."

"Um, I think—you know, we were just going to grab some leftovers from the kitchen."

"The kitchen is locked to students. But I can whip up anything you like, provided the kitchen has the ingredients, of course."

"You were right," I whisper to Remington. "The Gamemaster is going to re-poison us."

"Only we're not going to sleep this time."

"Nope. We should probably—" I pitch a thumb over my shoulder, and my stomach's protests rumble through the empty hall.

"What about a pizza?" the chef asks. "I've already kneaded a batch of dough. It will be ready in minutes. In the meantime, sit down, relax." He uncorks a bottle and begins to pour some bubbling liquid into two glasses. "Compliments of the Gamemaster."

I glance at Remington, whose hand is stretched over his face. But I'm lost to the pizza powers that be. "The Gamemaster can't poison us," I say. "If we die, who will compete in the finale?" I hurry over to the table, grabbing for a glass.

Remington places a gentle hand over mine. "Maybe some water first?" he says to the chef, who nods and scurries off to the kitchen. Remington quirks his lips at me. "At least until you get some food in you?"

"I thought it was sparkling water," I lie. He makes a good point though. I'm light-headed as it is. Our chairs have been placed across the table from each other. Remington drags one right next to mine, settling down in it. "You think they're watching us now?" This alcove is out of view of the corner camera; still, I glance around, scrutinizing the portraits and the intricately carved molding in the dim light.

"We are the society's source of entertainment. It would explain why the Gamemaster went to so much trouble with this setup." He gestures at the cloth napkins and the candelabras. Breaking his own rule, he lifts a glass and takes a swig. "Enjoying yourselves?" he asks loudly, swirling the glass over his head before clanking it down onto the table. "Sick freaks." He takes a napkin and stuffs it into the neck of his coat. "Not sparkling water, for the record."

"Duly noted," I say, lifting a brow at his new accessory.

"They wanted us to be fancy, didn't they? Here, allow me." He reaches over, lifting my napkin between two fingertips and making a show of tucking it inside my collar. I swat at him as he leans over me, his fingers resting on my skin. The playful glimmer seems to seep from his eyes. Dark and intense, they fasten on mine.

I lift my face to whisper in his ear. "Remember, they're watching." My wrist grazes his thigh as our cheeks brush, and suddenly, it's hard to catch my breath.

The chef arrives with two glasses of water and a charcuterie plate, and Remington pulls back, giving my napkin one last necessary adjustment before sitting up in his chair.

We dive in before the chef manages to back away, gulping the water and stuffing crackers and cheese into our mouths. Normally I don't care much for cured meats, but right now, I'm layering salamis and prosciuttos up and practically swallowing them down whole.

I wash it all down with a few too-fast sips of champagne, feeling the effervescent burn in my throat and eyes. I cough and Remington laughs. He dangles a cracker in front of me like I'm a feral cat in a cage. I laugh too, taking slower sips of champagne now, letting it warm me from the inside. And I push back the thoughts of Polly and Jane, who likely haven't had a bite of real food in weeks, much less a spread like this.

The chef arrives with our tomato- and basil-topped pizza, and before I know it, I've scarfed down three slices. "The chef should abandon this place and open up his own pizzeria," I say, wiping my mouth with a fancy napkin.

"You're just hungry. You'd probably say the same thing about summer camp cafeteria pizza."

"Summer camp?" I take another gulp of champagne. "Surely, Remington Cruz doesn't spend his summers at camp."

He shrugs, holding his glass by the stem and letting it tilt lazily. "Occasionally. Doesn't everyone?"

"Not me. Summer camps mean lakes, and I don't get along very well with large bodies of water."

"Afraid of the lake monster, huh?"

My gaze flicks to the wall, and I lean in closer. "More like I almost drowned in a pool when I was nine, and I've sort of never gotten over it."

"Oh." Remington straightens, setting down his glass. "I'm sorry, Maren."

I wave him off. "It's fine. My hair got stuck in my grandparents' pool drain, and I couldn't get free. I passed out, and my cousin rescued me. She basically had to rip a massive chunk of my hair out, but I lived to tell the tale." I make a silly face. "I've tended to steer clear of pools and oceans and even lake monsters, adorable as they may be, ever since."

He smiles and reaches over to place his hand over mine. It's warm, and his eyes are concerned as they linger on me. But none of it keeps me from blurting, "Why did you take the ribbon?"

Remington's brows furrow. Slowly, his fingers slide off of mine. "What?"

"The ribbon, down in the catacombs. You said you weren't going to play Annabelle's game, but on our way out, you took the advantage to the finale and stuffed it in your pocket."

He falls back in his seat, hands clutching the table's edge. After a moment, he reaches into his jacket pocket and removes the red ribbon. He balls it up in his fist before dropping it in front of me. "This is what you're so worried about? Here. Have it."

"No, I don't—I thought we'd decided not to play by the society's rules. So I'm just wondering why you felt inclined to take the ribbon for yourself."

"Take it for myself," he drones. "That's what you think."

"What am I supposed to think, Remington? Only one

girl lives if we play their game. You took an advantage. What could that possibly mean other than if it comes down to it, you're going to make sure you win?"

"I don't know why I took it, Maren," he says, throwing his hands up. "I guess in the back of my head, I thought maybe we could both figure out how to use it. I'm in this *with* you. Don't you see that?"

A knot of guilt forms in my throat. Back in the cottage, he was the only person in the world I could trust. The only person who felt safe. Why am I pushing him on this? Why am I trying to make an enemy of my only ally? "I'm sorry," I say, nudging the ribbon back over to his side of the table. "I trust you. I'm just tired."

"I don't want it," he grumbles.

"Take it." I let my hand fall open on the table, the way Remington did the last time we were in here together. A new treaty. It lays empty, and that lump in my throat starts to grow, so I can barely even swallow. My fingers begin to curl forward, hope siphoning out of me.

But the warmth returns as his hand reaches mine, pressing my fingertips flat against the table. "I'm tired too. But we have a lot left to eat." When he looks at me, a half-smile on his lips, I feel as weak as I did in the liquor closet the night of the dance.

Once the pizza and the entire bottle of champagne have been consumed, Remington and I thank the chef and thread through the dining hall, unsteadily. I catch Remington smiling at me as he holds open the door, and a wave of fear washes over me. "We can't be…" I motion from myself to him. "Like this for tonight's finale."

"We won't be," he assures me, tucking a strand of hair behind my ear. "We'll drink plenty of water and sleep it off."

I step out into the early morning air, and the flower-lined walkway starts to spin. In the distance, the sun's infant rays highlight the horizon. Evening lockdown will be over soon. My bed is so far away.

I shut my eyes, feeling my body rock until Remington steadies me.

"You'll never make it back to your dorm," Remington says, and I wonder if I accidentally spoke aloud, my mind muddled by the champagne. "Stay with me."

"Out here?" I slur.

He shakes his head. "My dorm is much closer. No one's up yet. We can sneak you into my room."

"Don't you have a roommate?"

"Not since the first society meeting. I had a particularly irritating roommate this year. You know Sam Walker?"

I nod, and Remington helps me up the path to his dormitory. Everyone knows Sam, better known as Walker the Talker.

"Well, when we were promoted to Minor Supreme, he suddenly"—Remington shrugs—"moved rooms."

"Are you sure he didn't get killed, Remington?"

He grins. "I'm sure. He got this notice that he needed to change rooms, and if I weren't constantly out on society business, I would be enjoying a peaceful living situation for the first time in years."

"I didn't get anything except for that blackmail video after the first challenge," I grumble.

"Well, you did attempt to defy the society, so..."

"Are you sure you can get me in there?"

"A few weeks ago, I would've said 'not a chance,' but we're society now. Even if we get caught, it'll be by some creepy security guard who's been paid off. Might as well take advantage of it before we bring these bastards down."

Sure enough, Remington's dormitory lobby is empty when we make it through the doors. The clock on the wall reads 5:14 a.m. Remington leads us into the stairwell up to his floor, and after checking the hall, he ushers me into his room.

The inside looks basically the same as mine: a bunk bed, a desk pushed against the wall, and one window, through which sunlight now pours.

"Here." Remington tugs his blanket off the bottom bunk and flings it out over the empty mattress on the top, along with his pillow. "Try to get some sleep. I'll work on getting our phones charged—I've got an extra charger around here somewhere."

"Thanks." I begin to climb the ladder, but, dizzy from the alcohol, I swing out and tumble down onto Remington's rug.

"Are you okay?" Remington whispers, helping me up.

"Mmhmm." I start to giggle.

"Hey, hey, nooo. You cannot laugh like that in here."

"Like what?"

"Like...like a girl! Like *not me!*"

"I'm sorry," I mouth, but more giggles burst out, and I slap a useless hand over them.

Remington's expression is pinched in a mixture of frustration and near-laughter.

"Let it out, *Remi*," I say, trying and failing again to sound like Annabelle as I stand, pushing my shoulders back and doing my best ballerina impersonation. "Your *you* laugh will cover my *not-you* laugh." I try for a pirouette or whatever it's called when you stand on your tiptoes and spin around.

It does not go well. In an attempt to stop myself from falling again, I knock a book off Remington's desk.

"Maren," he whisper-snaps right as, sure enough, someone from the next room pounds on the wall. "It is five in the morning."

"I think the Gamemaster poisoned me again." I lower my head in contrition.

"That must be it." His lips twist back a smile. "Come here." He leads me over to the ladder, and this time, he stands beside it until I'm nestled securely in the top bunk. "Good night, Maren."

"Good night." I tug his blanket up higher. "Remington?"

"Yes?"

"What do you think the finale will be?"

He hesitates at first, and the bed creaks as he lowers onto the bottom bunk. "Let's hope it's a challenge that relies heavily on lacrosse and football skills, so we can crush everyone."

"That would be good," I say, my words slowed by oncoming sleep.

"And for the record," he says, so quiet that it's like he's talking to himself as darkness pushes in, overtaking my consciousness, "your *not-me* laugh is the best sound I've ever heard in this room. Leagues above any sound Walker the Talker ever produced. Also, I loved your ballet routine. Annabelle should be worried about her spot in the spring performance."

"Thanks," I mumble, a smile on my lips as I drift off.

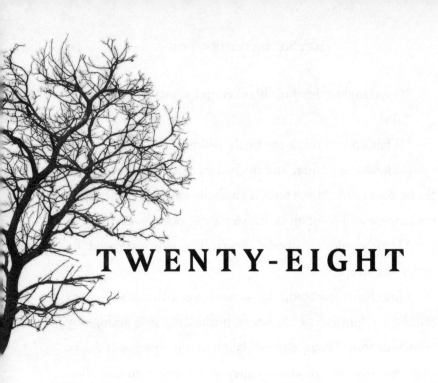

TWENTY-EIGHT

WHEN I WAKE, THE HEADMISTRESS'S DRUG AND THE champagne seem to have left my system. Only a trace of headache lingers. I lean over the bars to check on Remington below, but the bed is empty.

Sitting up, I scan the rest of the room. He's gone.

Why would he leave?

My brain lists possible reasons, starting with "he went to the bathroom" and ending with "he made a deal with the Gamemaster, my life for Jane's." When the door clicks open, I back against the wall, ready for society minions to try to handcuff me.

But it's Remington, who begins unbuttoning an awkwardly bulging coat. Soon, a variety of hidden sandwiches and fruits tumble onto his desk. "Morning," he says, noticing me watching. "Or late afternoon rather."

"Already?"

"Four fifty-six p.m. to be exact. We still have time. When I woke up, there was an invitation—addressed to both of us, by the way, just to make it clear that they knew we were together. The meeting is at midnight."

"When I woke and you were gone," I say, overwhelmed by a sudden need to confess my treacherous assumptions, "I thought—I guess I thought maybe you'd..."

"Been kidnapped while you slept?" He arches a brow. "It's fine, Maren. Whatever you thought, it's my fault for being so closed off before. And whatever you thought, it wasn't true." He points to the spread on the desk. "I was grabbing food from the dining hall."

"My hero," I say, one foot already on the rungs. Once I'm down, Remington hands me a glass of water, and my awareness of our close proximity—of the fact that Remington is showered and dressed and I'm still in yesterday's clothes, filthy from tunnel crawling—hits me like sprinklers in winter. He moves closer, but I gulp down some water and plop into his wheeled desk chair, spinning out and away from him. "Can I have the red one?" I ask, pointing to the fruit.

"Red what?"

"Apple. I don't like the green ones."

He shrugs. "I can't tell the difference."

I laugh. "They taste nothing alike."

"No, I mean, the colors."

The memory of the jeweled chalices filters back into my mind. Remington standing in terror, relying on me to tell him which chalice was which. I glance at the waxy red apple beside the Granny Smith green. "So, they both look gray or something?"

"No, they just look the same." He places both apples in my hands. "I can make you some coffee in the kitchen."

I push off the floor with my foot, sending the chair rolling toward the wall. "I'm good. You don't think there's any way you could sneak me out of here, do you?"

"Now?"

"Don't I deserve one last hot shower before the society kills our friends and possibly us?"

"No one's getting killed. We won't let them. That's why we have to decide what to do with this video before we head out. The headmistress made it clear the society has its claws in the police force, but there's got to be someone we can send it to for insurance. Who could take the society down?"

"Local news?" I suggest. "As long as they don't leak the story before Polly and Jane are safe."

"We need someone to hold the video for us in the meantime. Someone who will get it into the right hands if we…" His gaze trails away from mine. *If we don't make it out of tonight's meeting.* "Someone we can trust."

"I might know someone," I say, my insides so weighted by guilt they're practically crumpling on top of themselves. "But I'll need to speak to her in person."

———————

Some of Remington's too-big clothes and a beanie sufficed as a disguise to get me to the stairwell and out of the dormitory with only a couple of glances. After a quick shower and a change of clothes, I head back out, following the path to the dining hall.

I tug my phone from my backpack, newly charged as I slept. I've been ignoring the twelve texts and five missed calls from Gavin. Rage burns now in my chest, in my head, in my throat; I actually considered him a friend. The emotion blurs into the sizzling swell of embarrassment that I believed—for a second in the catacombs when he looked at me—we might even be more than friends.

But all he ever wanted was to make the Gamemaster happy. He might not know the extent of the society's evils, but he used me. And now he thinks I'm just going to forget about everything he put me through, because, for once, he got a taste of what it's like to fall out of the Gamemaster's good graces.

Still, I couldn't help the sense of relief that settled over me when I saw his texts. Despite everything, some pathetic part of me wants him to stay safe.

I text him to leave me the hell alone and enter the dining hall where I'm meeting Jordan for dinner.

Inside, Remington is already seated at a table in the back, ready to play lookout. The dining hall, with its constant chatter, seemed like the only place I could speak to Jordan without the society listening in.

I grab a tray and head to the roasted chicken and potatoes station, having learned to go into these society functions on a full stomach. After adding a helping of corn, I thread through the diners until I find smiley-faced Jordan off in a corner.

"Hey!" She leans in, lowering her voice. "You missed the last meeting. What happened?"

The words *I was sick* dance on my tongue, but I swallow them back. "That's what I wanted to talk to you about." I look over my shoulder, scanning the diners at nearby tables. I scoot my chair in until the table jabs me in the stomach. "I have to apologize to you. I haven't been honest." Jordan's bubbly expression falters, but I press on. "The society isn't really about fun and games. It's dangerous, and the only reason I invited you was because they forced me to."

Jordan opens her mouth, but I cut her off. "Do you remember Polly St. James?"

She eyes me warily but nods. "You and Polly were attached at the hip before we met."

"Right. Well, she met Annabelle, joined the society, and then the society kidnapped her. They've been forcing me to complete these tasks, threatening to kill Polly if I don't comply." Jordan's eyes widen, and all I can do is shrug pathetically. "Inviting you to a meeting was one of my tasks."

Jordan's gaze sinks to her plate of chicken and green beans. "Annabelle?" she finally asks.

"Yes, her. But more importantly, the Gamemaster, whoever that is."

"You don't know who it is?"

"No idea. Probably a Form IV, but to be honest, I'm not even sure it's a student. The point is, the society brought me and Remington in to get us to compete against each other. It's all this elaborate challenge devised to determine a sacrifice for some sick ritual." Jordan's eyes flick up, narrowing skeptically. I lean in. "Jordan, they're planning to sacrifice a person. Polly, or this other girl, Jane. Remington's ex."

She shakes her head. "I don't know, Maren…"

"I have proof they've been holding Polly *and* Jane in the catacombs. I'm hoping you'll find it in you to forgive me, and that you'll help me get these guys."

She digs her fingers into the hair near her temples. Her lips twist, in disgust or thought—maybe both. "Can you show me this *proof*?"

"I already emailed it to you. Will you help?"

After a painstaking minute, she asks, "What do you need me to do?"

"If everything goes to hell at the finale tonight, and

Remington and I don't make it out, spread the file. Send it to the police in the next county, the media, your parents, the entire school—as wide as you can spread it. The society has its claws in most of these avenues—we have to get it to so many people, they can't possibly cover their tracks. If they're backed into a corner, they'll have to spare Polly and Jane in order to avoid murder charges."

"So..." Jordan starts, her skin taking on a green hue as she pauses to absorb it all. "If something happens to you at tonight's meeting, you want me to send the video to all these people."

I start to nod, but something—a disturbing sensation slithers up my stomach and lodges somewhere at the back of my throat. "I didn't say it was a video," I whisper, my voice barely emerging over the lump. "I said *file*." *How did Jordan know?*

"Oh," Jordan says, the pink rushing back into her cheeks. "I guess I just assumed. Was it a photo? Something else?"

"No," I say, clearing my throat. "It was a video." I'm being paranoid. The society made me this way. She just assumed. How many types of proof could there be? "So you'll do it? You'll help?"

Jordan sighs. "I mean, I want to, but what if they come after me too?"

I grit my teeth. Why did I ever think meek little Jordan would agree to this? "They're being tortured, Jordan." The words come out fast and low, like a growl. "Watch the video. They've been held against their will for weeks. If I weren't certain the society would retaliate, I would send the video out myself right now. But I have to show up to the game tonight. It's the only way to buy time for Polly and Jane."

Jordan swirls her food around with a fork. "I'll do it," she says, curling her fists determinedly.

I exhale so hard the corn on my plate stirs. "Thank you. I knew I could count on you."

But suddenly, it's the last thing I'm sure of. Because that uneasy feeling is still there, coating the back of my throat as I try to chew my potatoes.

TWENTY-NINE

When I step down into the antechamber tonight, thin cloak covering my shoulders, the cold drives in hard, past my skin, past my layers of fat and muscle and tissues, past my innards. The cold, a brutal reminder of the last time I was down here, seems to penetrate my soul.

Remington follows in my wake, never more than a couple inches from me. I'm not sure how he's become the only person I can trust in this school, but even the sharpness of my nerves and the jittery feeling in my stomach dull slightly with him here.

The torches cast a fiendish luminance around the room as the rest of the members trickle in. I spot Jordan, already situated against a wall, and she nods faintly at me. Almost the way Annabelle nodded at me on the performing arts center 'steps. In fact, Jordan's hair even looks like Annabelle's, heated into submission, uniform waves adorning her clavicles.

I hope, if I fail to beat the Gamemaster tonight, Jordan can find it in herself to be brave and expose the society. And looking at her now, a sudden straightening of the shoulders, a severe line where a nervous smile used to be, a confidence that Jordan Park didn't have a few hours ago—I think she just might pull through.

There's a tug on my elbow, and I turn to find Gavin, looking tired and pitiful in his rumpled cloak. "Maren, you came."

"Of course, I came. Thanks to you, I'm stuck in this sadistic society until Remington and I free the girls."

"Maren, please—"

"I can't believe I ever thought we were friends."

"We are friends!" He rubs at his bloodshot eyes. "And I thought we could be—why do you think I followed you all the way through the catacombs last night? I was trying to protect you."

"Save it for someone you didn't lure into this mess."

"If you'd let me—"

Remington barrels through us, shoving Gavin aside. I toss him one last scornful look before wandering away, Remington at my side.

Annabelle is stationed at the front, as usual, surrounded by delicacies. But something about her dress—the simple fabric, the lack of show—thrusts my senses into alert mode.

She's no longer the pinnacle of the society. Earlier in the tournament, she got to play the host and leader. But the charade is up.

The Gamemaster is about to take charge.

I scan the room, finding Paul, half-obscured behind a pillar, conversing with Dallis like he doesn't have a care in the world.

A few feet away, Donella gazes up at Annabelle, like she's ready to head into battle at the call. She would certainly make a formidable Gamemaster. But she stays put.

Behind the silver display table, Annabelle clanks a spoon against a wineglass. "Welcome to the finale of the Gamemaster's Tournament. Tonight, in a special quadrennial ceremony, we all have the honor of paying homage to our fearless leader and gracious provider." Spindly legs of terror centipede through my stomach. She means the sacrifice. "Now, to announce the game. Without further ado, I present your Gamemaster."

Applause echoes through the chamber. I examine the crowd again as my heart yo-yos, falling all the way down and springing up into my throat.

My gaze whips to Jordan, who stands, back pressed against the stone. Suddenly, she flicks her glossy hair back behind her shoulder and steps forward.

Gavin taps my elbow again, another futile attempt to talk to me. When I ignore him, his hand moves, fingers gently gliding down to catch on my wrist.

"Get lost, Gavin," I say, craning my neck to follow Jordan, my heart hammering in my rib cage.

"Maren, I need you to know," he whispers, still trying to pull my attention toward him. "I had to do it, for my sister. You understand, right? And I had to make everything fair. There will be a stage that's exceptionally difficult for you, but I know you. You'll pull through." In confusion, I finally look at him, finding his teeth clamped onto his lower lip. Eyes narrowed, fingers still cuffed like a loose bracelet around my wrist. "And you'll win. I made sure of it." He nods, like we have this understanding, even though somewhere beneath my desire to help him, I hate Gavin Holt with every ounce of me.

"Do I have to hit you harder?" Remington snarls, stepping between us.

But I wave him off, slowly inching my way back in front of Gavin. "What are you saying?" I ask, his face blurring as I stare so hard it's like I'm looking through him.

I turn, certain I've missed the Gamemaster's grand approach to the front of the chamber, but Gavin's words stop spinning and ricocheting off the walls of my mind, finally settling.

Just when it all makes sickening sense, he leans in to kiss me on the forehead and spins around, striding through the clusters of society members to take his place on high.

THIRTY

"Thank you, Annabelle," Gavin says, his voice the same stupid voice from chemistry, his dopey smile the same one he used to get me to cover for his pajama fiasco. My legs go numb, so I can't even flee this dungeon. I sway, bumping Remington, who tenses at my side as he watches Gavin.

My shoulder finds his chest, and he pulls me in closer. "It's going to be okay," he whispers into my ear. "Whatever he throws at us, we'll beat him."

I'm not so sure about that.

"As Annabelle said, tonight is the tournament finale. I think you're all going to enjoy this one. I've been working on it all year." He beams at the crowd. "Would our champions please step forth?"

THEY'RE WATCHING YOU   313

Begrudgingly, we join him at the front. Meanwhile, Dallis—guess Gavin wasn't lying about being friends with him—passes out the goblets, starting with Remington and me. We stand side by side before the entire society, our ridiculous cloaks matching theirs. I restrain my empty fist as Gavin lifts a glass, toasting "the brethren," who gaze back at us in reverence. Their champions. What an honor.

Paul's eyes snag mine, and shame mingles with anger. I was an idiot to think he was the Gamemaster; still, I wish it had been him. I could almost wrap my head around the idea of Paul, this guy I once danced with, being the sadist behind the scenes. At least it wouldn't have been my nerdy lab partner, the guy I almost kissed in a dark passageway. The guy who actually made me feel bad for kissing someone else.

"And now, brethren, drink. Drink to your chosen champion." Around the room, each goblet is raised in either Remington's direction or mine, too swiftly for me to follow, and then the ruby-colored liquid is drained.

In a brazen show of defiance, I lift my goblet to Remington, who, not missing a beat, tilts his at me before downing its contents. I follow suit.

Gavin glares at us momentarily. "Annabelle," he says, tipping his head toward what I now realize is a vintage film projector on the ground, "if you will."

Wineglass in hand, Annabelle flits over to turn on the

projector, which clicks and casts a gritty picture against the
stone wall. The picture plays out, showing Polly, bound and
gagged. Her eyes bulge pleadingly, almost like she can see me.
Beside her, Jane sits against a stone wall, equally restrained.

Remington's body flinches against me.

The projector clicks off.

"Our champions will compete a series of challenges in an
ode to their initiation, where they both proved worthy of our
order. Obtaining the final game piece will result in the victory
of one champion"—his eyes lower as he fiddles with the hood
of his cloak—"and the imminent death of the other."

Death of a champion? But Remington and I are the
champions. A low tide of murmurs ripples through the
chamber; a horrible numbness spreads through me. My
goblet turns over, stem barely hanging from my grasp as the
dark red dregs drip onto the floor.

"Not to worry," Gavin says, motioning for the crowd to
quiet down. "The loser will experience a fate far better than
life. Our devotion and sacrifice bring us all closer to divinity; however, tonight's offering will achieve completion the
instant their soul leaves this world." This elicits a renewed
buzz of elation from the room.

"Now, champions. Allow me to introduce your patrons."
With this, his hands flick to the archway behind him.

In stumbles Polly, hands bound behind her back. Dallis
follows closely, gripping the back of her black dress and

shoving her farther inside the chamber. My insides go cold. I'm looking at a ghost.

"Polly!" I scream, rushing toward her, swatting at anyone who challenges me with my empty chalice. Remington is in tow, but we're blocked by Paul and the other minions.

Before me, Polly has managed to stand upright. Her face is stoic, head held high. I feel a tiny burst of pride that she hasn't allowed these people to break her.

Jane staggers in next, also bound as Donella prods her along. A pink gown flutters in stark contrast to the ratty gag around Jane's mouth. At my side, Remington's tension is palpable.

The gags are removed. The girls seem remarkably sturdy, considering how long they've been kept underground with little light, food, or warmth. Unease trickles through me as I track Polly's movements, noting the muscles that I'd assumed had atrophied after so much disuse in that tiny cell.

The feeling intensifies. Because even the pallor to her skin has suddenly vanished, replaced by a rosy glow.

The bindings on both girls' hands are removed next, but Polly makes no effort to push through the guards to get to me. Off to their left, Gavin crosses his arms.

There's a tap on my shoulder. Reluctantly, I wrench my eyes off the girls to find Annabelle behind me. "What the hell is going on?" I hiss at her.

But she only grins, and when I turn my attention back to the front, Jane's newly freed hands glide down to her dress.

She pinches the pink fringe and curtsies to the crowd, sending a wave of dizziness through me.

The chamber bursts into applause. Polly, somewhat stiffly, performs a bow. The goblet falls from my grip with a crash, glass shattering against the stone floor.

My vision swerves and staggers. When the noise finally dies down, Gavin's eerie laugh drifts through. "Lovely," he says, gazing at the girls admiringly. "One of these beautiful ladies will be announced Gamemaster Elect before sunrise."

"What is he talking about?" I whisper to Annabelle.

"You still think we were holding these girls captive?" Annabelle asks, words muffled by chatter. "Polly and Jane are your patrons. They selected the two of you to champion them. They believed in you, that you'd fight for them. So that one of them could become the next Gamemaster."

"But you—" Beside me, Remington glances at Jane, his expression pained. "They didn't choose this. They were kept in a cell!"

"Were they?" Annabelle's head tilts. "Or was that simply the story we chose to tell?" This time, when she sneers, I have to resist the urge to slap her pretty face. "Do Polly and Jane look like they've been kept in a cell?" she asks. "They've been living in a vacant faculty cottage."

No. "But she—I heard Polly scream. I saw blood."

"You certainly saw something," Annabelle says, her gaze veering to Polly.

"You tricked me?" I say to my best friend, who still can't look me in the eye. I reach out, slamming my open palm against the display table, rattling the glasses. "I thought I was fighting for your life. And you were hiding out, enjoying some sort of sick vacation in faculty housing?"

"You *were* fighting for a life," Annabelle says, frowning. "Your own."

Polly couldn't have tricked me. She *wouldn't* have.

But a terrible thought claws its way into my brain. *Unless it was all contrived. Unless Polly was simply playing the ultimate part.* I think back to her skittishness that day at the Commons. Her nonsensical words: *Chess isn't going so well. It's not just pieces and a board. It's...more. Too much, maybe.* She knew I'd recognize the fear in her eyes, that I wouldn't be able to let her disappearance go.

I want to show you something. Meet me at the fountain. I missed her. I hoped that meeting at our fountain held meaning, and she knew it. She used it to reel me in, and like a hungry, desperate fish, I clamped right onto her pointy hook.

Beside me, Polly stirs. "I'm sorry," she says. "I—I did something bad a couple weeks into the school year. In chemistry. I was caught. They were going to expel me. But Annabelle rescued me. She made the school forget everything, and she showed me that things could be even better if I became a member." Her voice carries a dreamy lilt. "When I showed promise in the Games, Gavin showed me the possibilities if I became Gamemaster." She finally looks at me, her face glowing with a delirious glee. "Maren, Hollywood—my dream since I can remember—would be one blip on my timeline if I became Gamemaster. If we win tonight, I'll be a god."

I stare because I don't know what else to do. An image from the photo collage flashes in my mind—Polly, auburn hair tied up in a messy bun. Sitting on a dirty bench downtown, chomping on a pack of off-brand potato chips from the dollar store, fingers covered in salt. When I speak, my voice is empty, weak. "Polly, what did they do to you?"

"They didn't *do* anything to me!" she shouts, her body shaking. "They rescued me! They gave me a future!" Defiantly, she reaches toward the display, tearing off a hunk of bread. "They're my family."

"They're going to kill me."

Polly shakes her head, too fast, too hard. "I knew you could make it this far," she says, still chewing her bread. "I knew you'd do it and that we'd rule the society—the entire school—together. I've been making sure. Gavin's been making sure. You're our champion."

"But Annabelle is helping *them*." I flick my chin to where Remington stands stiffly beside Jane. "Your *friend* has been doing everything in her power to get me to fail. She doesn't care if I die, Polly."

"You won't," she says, still shaking her head maniacally. "You can't."

I back up, and the crowd begins to part. Remington takes three, large, cautious strides backward. I cast a glance at the trapdoor, and the members are so caught up in awestruck wonder that it seems like they may let us wander right out of here.

But Gavin's gaze fastens to mine, that cavalier quality from a moment ago replaced with concern.

"The finale will take place all over campus," he adds once the chatter has subsided. "In order to save yourself, you must be the first to retrieve the final game piece. Anything goes, obviously." He runs a hand through already disheveled hair and mumbles, "Not that our lovebirds would resort to *anything*."

Or maybe it's hurt, that look in his eyes.

Mentally, I run through Gavin's last rules. What would save one of us while killing the other? Is he going to strap one of his explosive devices to us and make us fight for the code to disarm it? I rack my brain, my gaze sliding over the black cloaks, the faces, the hors d'oeuvres and glass goblets.

"The instrument of death is already working," he says, the arrogance slipping from his voice. "Already in your system."

A trickle of ice moves from my fingertips up to my neck. *The wine.*

My gaze snaps to the glass shards glimmering over the stone floor. The second we let our guards down, believing they needed us healthy in order to compete, they slipped something into our drinks.

I peek at Remington, whose face is ashen, jaw fixed. Suddenly, his elbow cocks back. He launches the goblet, which flies at full speed. Its base grazes Gavin's head.

Gavin simply smiles like the delinquent he is, wiping a drop of red wine off of his neck. Unperturbed, he continues. "You will compete for the antidote. There is only one dose, so sharing isn't an option. In roughly an hour, you will feel and act merely drunk. Not long after, disorientation will set in, along with confusion. At the two-hour mark, the hallucinations will begin—visual and auditory. And then, well, basically it's all downhill from there. Seizures, psychosis, respiratory failure. I think it's safe to say you'll want to finish the task before the two-hour mark. Let's see," he says, pushing up his cloak sleeve to glance at his watch. "One a.m. Ultimately, it will be your bodies that decide how much time is left. Oh, and don't bother with the messy business of disgorging. Your blood has already had plenty of time to absorb the toxins. The guards posted along the gates have been instructed to bring you back to us if you try to escape. Even if you could get to a hospital in time, they won't have the antidote. Dr. Theodore Lowell engineered this plant, which only exists on our campus. A deadly nightshade hybrid he liked to call *Atropa divinus*. You might call it *belladonna's* faster-acting cousin. Dr. Yamashiro and I created its antidote ourselves."

I kneel down, grasping a stray shard of glass. "I don't

believe you. How do we know you're not playing another trick on us?"

"You only have to look at Remington's eyes," Gavin says solemnly.

I turn to find Remington squinting at the piece of glass in my hand, which digs sharply into my palm. He looks up, and I startle. Because his pupils have expanded to blot out nearly all the brown of his irises.

"It's the atropine," Gavin says. "You may experience some blurred vision and light sensitivity. I apologize for that."

"Light sensitivity?" Remington growls. "I think it's the psychosis and death you should be apologizing for!"

"Well, you won't die right away," Annabelle says, brushing past me to join Gavin at the front. "Whoever of you doesn't win the antidote will simply be rendered useless, at which point we'll be able to conduct the ceremonial ritual." My stomach flips. I think the light-headedness and shortness of breath may have already started, or it could be the nerves. "But you don't want to waste all your time chatting." She chuckles. "Come, champions. Join me so your society can send you off properly. Whether from here or afar, be assured. The brethren will be watching tonight."

Watching. Riveted on their chaises while we decide who lives and who dies. I tread through the crowd, taking no pains to avoid knocking elbows on my way to the front. An acute pain in my hand reminds me I'm still gripping the shard of glass, and everything in me begs to take a swipe at Gavin's face with it.

A hand tugs on my forearm, and when I sling a withering glare at the offender, Jordan's made-up, glossy eyes lock on to mine. "Maren," she whispers, but I twist from her grasp before she can give herself away.

"Do it now," I mouth before striding the rest of the way, Remington in tow.

Gavin is a monster. Either we find someone on the outside to stop this, or one of us dies. Waiting is no longer an option. I only hope Jordan comes through.

I wait for Gavin's next words, a sense of utter helplessness coiling itself around my limbs. Despite my act of rebellion, there can only be one victor.

Remington or me.

There's no way to win this game.

THIRTY-ONE

"CHAMPIONS," GAVIN SAYS IN HIS OFFICIANT'S VOICE. "I'LL be needing your phones." Casually, he motions to the display. When Remington and I make no effort to obey, Gavin's shoulders droop. "We can't start the game until I have those phones," he pouts. "You don't want to sit around and die in here, do you? That's so boring."

I sigh through my teeth and dig the phone from my pocket, sliding it across the display. Once Remington has done the same, Gavin grins and produces two pocket flashlights. "You may use these as light sources. And one more thing. I've been informed someone may have an advantage in tonight's finale. If that's the case, you must play it now."

That familiar dread creeps up my back. I peek at

Remington, who tugs the red ribbon from his pocket without hesitation. He marches up to the front of the chamber.

This is how it's going to be. He's given up on any hope of working with me. I'm on my own.

Remington dangles the ribbon in front of Gavin, who scrutinizes it as if inspecting the strip of shiny fabric for authenticity. Apparently satisfied, Gavin digs into his robe to remove a small scroll. "Use this whenever you like."

Remington takes it, hand hovering in midair for a moment. His knuckles glow white in the torchlight as his fist tightens around the scroll. Tiny pitter-pattering steps quicken in my chest. He's going to destroy it. Another show of defiance—another demonstration of our unity.

But he tucks it away inside his robe, and the light steps slow to a deadening halt.

"It is now time to begin," Gavin says. "Only the game sprite knows where you will find your first game piece." His brows waggle mischievously. "Oh where, oh where could she be?"

I glance around the chamber, my feet still pinned to the earth. Time stops. Part of me wants to slump down onto the stone and give in. To let the poison wreak its havoc on my body. I can't compete against Remington. Not when his life is at stake.

The other part of me wants to follow through on this deep desire to slug Gavin in the mouth with this shard of glass. But that's as good as ensuring my death, so I let it fall to the ground.

Then there's a third part—the smallest piece of me—that's aware of what I have to do and willing to do it. That's the part that glimpses a wink of sparkling gossamer wings. A hint of fluorescent blue in the darkness, like a dragonfly's wings. It dips down through the trapdoor before disappearing back up in the old cathedral. It's what wrenches my feet from the ground and sparks me to action.

But I'm already seconds behind Remington. In a game like this, those seconds might as well be days.

Once I'm up inside the old cathedral, the other society members' cheers and chants fading behind me, the sprite has already disappeared outside. But I catch a ripple of Remington's cloak sliding out through the makeshift door.

A piercing pain wedges itself in my chest.

He's playing. Trying to beat me so he can live, despite the consequences for me. When I inhale, the sharpness intensifies, and my steps are staggering. But on the next breath, the pain lessens. By the third one, I'm already sprinting after him.

Outside, the cold stings my face as I search for Remington's black cloak, which has blended into the night. I start to run, even though I have no idea where he or the sprite went, until a branch rustles off to my right. A blur of motion gleams beneath the lampposts, and I follow it downhill toward Horton Pond.

Ahead, Remington takes a sharp turn before the pond, and I follow, my shoes slipping in the sludge on the bank. I catch myself before falling in the mud, but I've lost Remington again. After the grass, I take the pathway, hoping it's where the game fairy headed.

Sure enough, footsteps slap the cobblestone, and the lampposts highlight Remington's figure just as he disappears inside the Arthur Aquatic Center.

My stomach somersaults. *No.*

I've never been inside this building before. This is what Gavin meant by having to make the game fair. He added a challenge I can't possibly complete. Definitely not before Remington. Gavin must've obtained my admission essay—or managed to hear my whispers last night in the dining hall. He learned about my fear of water, and he's using it against me.

Clenching my teeth, I push through the doors, finding myself inside an enormous, humid facility with bleachers lining two sides. Immediately, the scent of chlorine sends my head spinning. The Olympic-size pool, complete with lane dividers and starting blocks, is right in front of me. The dizziness hits so hard I press my back against the cold wall to keep from falling in. Across the pool, the sprite stops before the exit door at the back. I watch the cracked and distorted version of her gesture with two hands around the facility before waving goodbye and flitting out the door.

"Maren!" I hear Remington's voice, but I have to shut my eyes to stop the room from moving. "Are you okay?"

"Mmhmm," I mumble, even though nothing about me or this situation is okay. I didn't even realize I'd slid to the cold floor. But here I am, my palms pressed into the slip-proof tile. I reach up to rub my scalp, which is suddenly sore where my hair was ripped and pulled at when I was nine years old.

Remington comes closer, leaning down to whisper, "It's going to be alright. But can you help me figure out what we're supposed to be doing?"

We? "You left me." I keep massaging my scalp. "You took the advantage for yourself and left me."

"Sorry about that," he says, not sounding very sorry at all. "But remember this is all a source of entertainment for them. We have to act like we're competing."

"Likely story," I accidentally say aloud.

"Look, all I want is to get you out of this place and to safety, but we have to play the game." His lips purse and then he mouths, "Did you do what we talked about?"

I nod. I tasked Jordan with getting the video out. Only Remington doesn't know I already pulled the trigger on the whole thing. "It's happening now," I whisper, finally opening my eyes.

He blinks, but a look of understanding comes over him.

Maybe someone out there is still free of the society's web. If not—if my decision to expose the truth about the society

explodes in our faces—we'd better hurry up and figure out
how to save ourselves before we both die.

"Okay," I say, using the wall to push myself to my feet.
"What are we looking for?"

"That's the thing." Remington stands at the edge of the
pool, peering down into the blue water. "They didn't say, and
that fairy pretty much pointed to the entire place."

I head to a set of bleachers, wobbling a little as I teeter on
the small border between the water and the seating. I scan the
tops of the benches before moving around to the back. Then I
climb over and duck beneath the metal legs in search of some
clue, some instruction to guide us.

"There's something in the bottom of the pool," Remington
says, pointing. "Make that two somethings. In the shallow
part."

Before I can react, Remington is flinging his cloak and
shirt onto a bleacher seat. He kicks his shoes off and takes
two loping steps to the edge. He dives down, reaching the
bottom to retrieve the first item. As he surfaces, taking in that
first breath, I finally suck in some air too.

Remington glances from the small object to me, his
expression grave. I know what he wants me to do. I have to
try. I have to make it seem real.

I don't let myself think about it. I know how to swim. I
used to do it all the time. I kick off my shoes and approach
the water, shutting off my thoughts; if I think about it, I'll fail.

I plunge in, the water a cold shock that strangles me as I swim for the item at the bottom. But a few feet down, I start to panic. My mouth opens despite my efforts to keep it shut, letting in the disgusting water. Flailing, I grab for the ends of my hair, certain they're trapped, though I'm nowhere near the drain.

I surface, gulping in air and water all at once.

Remington's figure is hunched on the side of the pool. His look pleads, saying what he can't shout in front of the cameras.

I inhale, slow and deep. Then I dive back down again, forcing my eyes open against the stinging chemicals. The water pulls against my jeans. I reach for the small object, my lungs screaming, about to burst.

My fingers curl over the tiny bottle, and I flip my body, pushing off against the bottom with my feet.

I burst through the surface, wheezing in a painful breath and coughing up the water still trapped in my lungs. I dog-paddle to the side, where Remington seems torn between helping me up and standing his ground. He flicks his chin toward the bottle clutched in my fist.

"It's not the game piece," he whispers, daring to sidestep closer to me. "It's down there."

I've already uncorked my bottle, dropping the rolled paper into my palm. I read the message, even though I don't have to. Because I know where the game piece is.

Your first game piece lies behind the door at the
bottom of the sea.

The drain.

That bastard.

Pins prick over my scalp, and I hunch over to catch my breath. "I—I can't."

"You just did so well," he pleads. "Think of it like taking a very cold bath." He forces a smile.

"I take showers."

Remington gnaws on his lower lip. "The society has no rules. *Anything goes.* But they'll be on to us."

Before I can ask what he means, Remington is hurtling himself back into the pool. I peek, watching his arms yank and turn as he unscrews the cover, and hunch back down again.

Then a horrible thought thrashes my mind. The filtration pump is still on. What if he—? I dart around the pool's edge, searching for the pump, unable to watch him get eaten by the drain, which is identical to the one that nearly killed me.

Finally, I spot the series of pipes attached to a cylindrical nozzle. I sprint to it, alarms blaring in my head when I realize it's not a simple on/off switch. There are various knobs, dials, and timers, and fear of somehow turning the suction higher while Remington's arm is in there freezes me where I stand.

I reach out, placing my hand on the switch that looks

most promising, pulse thumping in my neck. But behind me, water splashes and I spin around to find Remington breaching the surface.

The drain didn't kill him. He swims to the side, and that crippling fear that it's my turn takes hold of me.

Maybe he left the cover off, at least. I remove the elastic from my wrist and tie my hair back out of my face.

Seated on the edge of the pool, huffing, Remington throws his T-shirt on over his dripping wet body.

"I know," I grumble in irritation. I've got to face my biggest fear. And I will, even if the drain kills me before I get the chance to save myself.

Remington gets up, sliding an arm into his coat sleeve, whatever he found at the bottom of the drain clenched in his fist. Once his shoes are on, he tosses one last look back at me before heading out into the night, leaving me alone with my watery grave.

I stare down into the unnaturally blue water, the horrible realization wrapping around my throat: Remington just abandoned me to my worst fear.

THIRTY-TWO

I WATCH WHERE HE VANISHED THROUGH THE DOOR, AND THE sensation coils tighter, squeezing.

I can do this. I have to. But when I turn to face the pool, my vision goes foggy like the windows in this place.

My mouth is dry. Too dry. I may have only minutes before the poison starts to take hold of my mind.

I take off in the direction of the back door. In the distance, a shadow flaps like a massive bird over the grass in the moonlight. Remington. He isn't waiting for me to complete my task. Beneath my bare foot, something squelches. I glance down, where a damp, half-rolled piece of paper lies on the tile. Stooping to pick it up, I unfurl it some more and read:

The owner of this scroll may skip one task.
Somewhere near you lies a gilded box. Find it and
retrieve your game piece.

—VOD

Victory or Dust. Remington wasn't abandoning me. He gave me his advantage. Blinking away my bleary vision, I scan the room for a hint of gold. The advantage says it's a box. With a jolt, I sprint toward the lockers lining the far wall of the building. Sure enough, one of them has been painted gold.

Only there's a lock dangling in front. I grab it and pull, letting out a growl of frustration when it doesn't fall open. How am I supposed to get the game piece if the box is locked?

I take a deep breath, ready to turn back around and face the pool, when my gaze catches on the lock. There's something strange about it; instead of numbers, there are letters.

Like a million grains of colored sand falling into perfect place to form an image, the answer comes to me. The signature from the scroll wasn't a signature at all.

It was a code.

I reach for the lock and spin it clockwise until it clicks on V. Then around counterclockwise to the O. Finally, holding my breath, I let the dial settle onto the D. I yank on it, my breath whooshing out along with the satisfying *pop.*

I toss it to the ground, pulling open the door. Inside, there's another rolled clue, along with a tiny bronze object.

I scoop them both out, already making my way toward the back door. Unraveling the note, I read, careful not to slip as I pass over the last few tiles. GO TO THE PLACE WHERE YOU LEARNED HOW BONDS ARE FORMED AND BROKEN.

Bonds? My brain snaps to Polly, to the financial aid meeting at Henning Hall, where we met. I stuff my wet feet into my sneakers and head out the door in the direction of the Hall. But I stop before making it to the grass, my shoes skidding on the cobblestone path. The hall is where Polly and I first met, but it's not where our friendship ended. No single location could encompass the way our friendship faded to a not-quite end.

How bonds are formed and broken. There's more than one kind of bond. Maybe this clue isn't referring to the ones between people, but rather, the ones between elements. Which I learned about in the chemistry classroom.

I start moving again, pausing at the doorway to peek at the bronze object. It looks like the ornamental top of a skeleton key.

The game piece. We're building a key. And Remington just gave me my first half.

Outside, the cold night air freezes my clothing, which whips and flaps like sheets of ice against my skin. There's no sign of Remington, so I head straight through the athletic fields, my feet flying over grass and then pounding over hard dirt. Far ahead, Remington's figure is a vague blur, ascending

the hill beneath the silvery moonlight. But once he's crested,
I lose sight of him.

I press on, my breathing ragged as I bull through a copse
of trees and sprint up the path to the Lowell Math and Science
Building.

An acidic taste lurks at the back of my throat. Gavin is
making us compete in the place where he and I first got to
know each other. Back when I believed he was a smart yet
absentminded, slightly accident-prone goof.

Inside the cylindrical building, I lope up the nonfunction-
ing escalator. Up on the top floor, a light turns on. I leap onto
the steps, following the glow to find Remington standing in
the doorway to my chemistry classroom.

"The next piece is here somewhere," Remington says,
rubbing his temple as he scans the room.

"Let me guess, we have to mix the chemicals that will kill
us if the poison fails."

"Don't give the Gamemaster ideas." Remington searches
Dr. Yamashiro's cluttered desk, shoving papers and knickknacks aside.

"Why did you help me back there?" I whisper, walking
the edge of the room, fingers dusting the windowsills and
cabinetry.

"So you didn't have to go down there again."

"But I thought—"

"It wasn't even a decision." His voice is tired and worn.

A suffocating silence follows his words. It coats the air. No, this isn't the decision. It's the one at the end that counts. And if we can't figure out a way to save both of us, how are we supposed to choose?

I continue skimming cracks and crevices, looking for an envelope—the society's preferred method of communication. Instead, my fingertip brushes a set of small boxes stacked in the bookshelf that normally houses various chemistry tomes. I drag them out, noting the linchpin symbol printed on the top.

"Here!" When I start to lug the boxes out, a wave of dizziness slams into me. I squint down at the boxes in my hands, which tumble down to the floor, landing with a crash.

Remington skirts the desks to join me. "Maren, what happened?"

"I don't know where I—why am I here?"

He stares at me, concern in his black eyes. Why are his eyes so black? And then I remember. The poison. Gavin mentioned disorientation and confusion. On the floor, Remington handles the boxes, which are still intact. I squat down as he unhinges the lid to the first one, revealing a mass of jigsaw puzzle pieces with a single card on top.

"*Solve to reveal the location of the final game piece,*" I read aloud, tossing the card aside. "So...we just have to solve a puzzle?" That seems easy enough. I scoot away from Remington so our pieces don't get mixed up, and dump the contents of my box onto the shiny tile. The pieces display an array of dots that join together in an impressionistic version of a leaf here, a branch there, maybe? But there's something off about the colors.

It hits me as Remington groans. The pieces, the dots—they're all shades of green and red.

"They all look the same," he snarls, slamming a fist down onto his pile. The pieces fly in every direction.

He's right. It's basically a color blindness test cut up into tiny bits. This is what Gavin meant by giving me a surefire way to win. If I wanted to, I could solve my puzzle, find my game piece, and take the antidote while Remington continued to stare at his pile until time ran out. Guilt bites at the back of my brain. He could've kept the advantage for himself. But I was too much of a coward. "Stay calm," I tell him. The water from my soaked jeans pools and bleeds around me, but I've already connected three border pieces that possibly make up the edge of a pond. "We only have to finish one."

He moves to peer over my shoulder, his wet hair dripping onto my pile. "What can I do to help?"

"Let me think," I say.

He backs up, pacing the room as I gather the rest of the forest green pieces into one pile and the reds and oranges into another. The harsh lines of the red family resemble some sort of building, possibly the location of the second half of the key.

But a few minutes later, I have the dark green area half-finished, and a small series of blue dots emerges in the center. The number 4.

"What does this number mean?" I ask, still working on finishing up the treescape. Once it's done, I have the number 2.

"The cards," Remington says suddenly, thrusting his in front of me. "The back is a coordinate map of the school."

"And it will lead us directly to the other halves of our keys." But I heard the way my own words just slurred together.

Panic throbs in my head, in my hands, threatening to take over. I inhale, letting the breath trickle out slowly. I'm so close. I dig through the red pieces, lifting a burnt orange shade and clicking it in place. The number 7. I continue sifting and sorting until the likeness of the academy boathouse materializes, along with a lime-hued number 6. One more coordinate to go.

The sound of glass clinks over in the supply cabinet. "Hey," Remington says. "Dr. Yamashiro has a bunch of herbs in here. *Valeriana officinalis*. Some of this stuff looks like plants in the headmistress's garden. Let me—" He cuts off, and when I peek, he's moved to one of the student computers. "Here. Google says this plant can be used as a mild sedative. But this other one, *Eschscholzia californica*, that's a poppy. As in opium? Wait, no, wrong species. But this one does have medicinal properties, like to help with depression and insomnia. Do you think Dr. Yamashiro keeps more of the antidote somewhere in here?"

"Doubt it," I murmur, trying to focus.

"Well, I'm going to look." He starts rifling and banging around, the noise competing with my own scattered thoughts.

The last are blue-green shades, which I'm assuming to be Guffman's Pond behind the boathouse. I try the first one, but it's not a fit. After a quick shuffle, I have the right side of what could either be a 3 or an 8, which means I need at least one more bit of the pond. "Toss me a pen," I call to Remington just as I find the piece, a teal shade with the lighter blue wing of a duck on the top and some of the left side of the 8 on the bottom.

I turn to see that Remington has successfully broken into Dr. Yamashiro's filing cabinet. Papers are scattered about the floor and the desk. The pen lands beside me, and I scribble down 427 and 68 on the side of the card with the map, then trace the latitude and longitude with my finger. "Looks like the game piece is somewhere on the boathouse dock. Let's go."

I'm already on my feet, but Remington remains hunched over a page on the desk. "*Atropa divinus*. These are his test trial notes for the antidote." I hear it in his voice now too, the way the words lull and drag, blending and twisting together. "Forty-one rats died. Subject forty-two was treated with activated charcoal, which slowed the toxin's effects, but ultimately, the subject couldn't be saved. Then on the final batch, called AAD43, the rat lived."

"One rat survived? He didn't repeat the trial?"

"It's better than no rats, I guess." He digs through another drawer. "They must've created more than one dose of the stuff. The question is where did they put the rest?"

"Remington," I say, bouncing on my toes in the doorway. "We have to hurry."

"I know." But he doesn't stop his mad search. He knocks a few vials to the floor, and loose herbs drift down to the floor. "But we don't even know the keys will be together. I didn't finish my puzzle."

The thought jabs at the back of my jaw like a stray chicken bone. "They were together in the last challenge."

"But what if the Gamemaster wants to make sure we separate this time? What if my puzzle leads to different coordinates?"

I glance down at his scattered pieces and throw a hand into the air. "Even if that were true, we don't have time to solve another puzzle."

When Remington looks at me, I swear, his head just lifts right off his neck and floats over to the window.

"Maren?" the floating head asks me, drifting closer now. "Maren?"

I can't answer it. Instead, I try desperately to swat it away.

"Maren!" Remington's arms are around me before I can fight him off. He holds me for a minute. "Maren," he whispers into my ear. I glance up at him, finding his head right in place where it usually is. "There's only one antidote. You should go. The poison is affecting you faster. I still have time to look for this AAD43."

I turn to face him, and he bends down until our cheeks brush. "Where are you supposed to look? The cameras are all over campus. They'll know if you stop playing by their rules."

"I know," he says. "I'm hoping it's in here somewhere. And if not, maybe everyone will be so focused on the cameras along Gavin's finale course, they won't think to look for me until it's too late."

Tears sting now. "If you don't find it," I whisper, "wait for me in the place where we first..." I push up onto my tiptoes and press my lips to his. A reminder. His poison-dark eyes meet mine and flicker with understanding. The bushes behind my dorm, where we first kissed. One of the many places I questioned his loyalty. A gush of sadness fills me. "I'll find you. I'll get you help."

"I will. Now hurry up." He nudges me toward the door, but I turn, kissing him again. I shut my eyes as our lips meet, and it brings back that first kiss, and before that, the memory of the hidden liquor closet where I first felt that magnetic tug. Where I first wanted his lips on mine.

A thought snags my breath, and I pull away. "The liquor closet," I whisper. "Remember, on the top shelf above the booze, there were a bunch of weird medicines."

"You're right," he says, and I think I catch a glimmer of hope in his midnight-black eyes.

"But Paul said there's a camera inside. Be careful."

He nods, turning back to the desk, and I race out of the building, scrambling down the staircase. The moon casts a milky rinse of light over the athletic fields and the plum orchard beyond it. I weave through until I reach the wooden planks of the boathouse dock on Guffman's Pond. Producing the flashlight, I shine it over the boards, pilings, and a couple of motorboats floating in the water. At the end of the dock, I hop down into one of the boats, feeling around beneath the seats. It turns up nothing, and when I try to climb back onto the dock, the high-pitched sound of some sort of siren creature calls to me from the black sea. My heart rams into my ribs.

You heard nothing. Nothing's there.

I lower into the next one, swaying as the boat rocks with my momentum. My light flits over the bottom of the shell. I bend to check every nook and cranny. When I spot a tackle box beneath the last seat, my hopes soar.

Inside is a rolled note. I unfurl it to find the bronze barrel of a key attached to the bit. Then I dig into my pocket to retrieve the ornamental half, wobbling as the boat sways. The seat is damp, but I lower onto it, screwing the two halves of the key together. Relief spirals through me.

But a moment later, it coils back down with nauseating

speed. Because inside this already-rocking boat, my legs are starting to feel wobbly, like they're made of gelatin.

I heft myself back onto the dock, scraping my palms on the splintery planks and dragging my useless legs up behind me. Once on solid ground, I shake out my legs and stretch the note open beneath the flashlight. TAKE YOUR KEY TO THE PLACE WHERE THE DEAD BECOME IMMORTAL, TO THE PLACE WHERE WE WATCH.

The catacombs. But it doesn't provide a specific location. I'd need fifteen *hours* to search that place. Or another coordinate.

And the back of this note is blank.

Breath suddenly shallow, I force my feet to move toward the place where this all started, the ghastly dungeon below the earth.

The place where, if I make it in time, I'll be cured.

I only hope Remington is having luck finding his own cure.

THIRTY-THREE

THE STILLNESS OF THE ANTECHAMBER SUCKS MY BREATH away, using it a moment later to play a silent tune that makes my neck hair stand on end.

It's empty. No hooded figures huddled around waiting for me. They really must be lounging around somewhere, watching the show.

Finding my feet again, I stride through the passageway to the next chamber, the only direction you can possibly go until the fork ahead.

After that, I have no idea where to go. I take the staircase down like we did the night we searched for Jordan, running over the note in my head. This is "where the dead become immortal," right? As in they live on because they're buried in a fancy sarcophagus? And "where we watch" must refer to wherever the society has a screen set up, streaming the feed of Remington and me bumbling over campus like blind rabbits.

But I pass through the next chamber and my gaze skims the etchings of the teeth-bared charioteer. Suddenly, I know exactly where to go.

Where we watch. The Gamemaster isn't referring to "we" as the society; he's referring to "we" as the gods. Sitting on high. The massive eyeballs looking over the tiny humans as they shed one another's blood.

The fresco. The one I saw painted above that horrid bone table on the night Jordan played princess.

My steps accelerate as I retrace the path Remington and I took that night. Adrenaline buzzes in my ears—in my entire body. My awareness of the space is suddenly heightened, my mind its own map. When I hit a fork in the tunnels, I make a sharp right, and my heart pushes into my throat.

A hooded figure blocks my path. One with red devil eyes. Panic swells in my throat. I can't breathe. The figure races toward me, draped in black, like Death approaching.

But I blink. And it's gone. The corridor is clear. It was another hallucination.

Struggling to suck in a full breath, I stumble, bracing myself against the wall. My nerves prickle as spindly, hairy legs crawl over my hand. I shriek and shake off the thing, which skitters across the floor. My entire body quivers, and I have no way of knowing if that spider was real or just another figment of my poison-rotted mind.

I reach the top of the staircase, the creepy eyes staring down on me. Only this time, they follow me and watch as I pass by. *It's not real. It's not real.* Wheezing, I throw myself into the door. It's unlocked. Relief swirls through me, and I stagger inside.

The room is lit by two standing torches. There, against the wall, is a glass case displaying a single dark-green vial.

I stagger forward, jamming my key into the lock and twisting with all my might. It clicks. I tug on the door and thrust my hand inside to remove the vial.

In my grip, the vial stops looking like a vial. It starts to grow legs. It whispers to me how bad of an idea it is to drink this stuff.

I can't listen to it. I pop the cork off, letting it bobble on the floor by my feet. Then I down it in one uncoordinated flick of the wrist.

The liquid—a nasty, bitter syrup—burns my tongue and throat as it goes down. I'm still so thirsty. I'd do anything for a glass of water.

When the last drop goes down, my head feels tired. The chamber is moving, like there's an earthquake. I need to lie down. To make it stop. I start to slump against the wall but force myself back upright. *Remington.* I promised to save him.

I take a second to steady my breathing. In and out. The rocking of the room slows. This antidote might actually be working. At least Gavin told the truth about one thing. Still, I have to get out of here. I start in the direction of the open door, but a dark shadow pushes into the doorway. The torchlight flickers.

Another hallucination?

"I knew you could do it," comes a voice, which seems very real. Very familiar.

The shadow steps forward into the light. The hood falls back, revealing Gavin's green eyes, flooded with relief.

He's blocking my way out.

———

"Maren!" Polly pushes past Gavin to get into the room. "You did it! I knew you would!"

Her radiant, gleeful expression brings on a new bout of dizziness. "You're welcome," I say, the words tying up together. "Now get out of my way."

Jane peeks in now, face pale. "So, it's over?"

"Guess your friend isn't as badass as mine," says Polly with a shrug, slinging an arm over me. I shove her off with what little strength I have and careen away.

"But Remington..." Jane's gaze diverts to the empty glass cabinet. "You won't really..."

"You know it's necessary." Gavin shifts in front of her, placing his hands on her shoulders and frowning like a father forced to dole out a consequence.

"Well, where is he?" she asks. "He never even made it to the boathouse."

"His location has yet to be determined," Gavin says. "We know he wandered off course after failing to complete his puzzle. I'm assuming Maren whispered a fake location to him—well played, by the way."

"Thanks," I mutter, trying not to collapse.

A boyish grin slides over his lips and he reaches out to steady me. "Annabelle's checking the other campus cameras. Once he's found, we'll bring him in for the ceremony."

A surge of fear spikes in me. They're searching for Remington. How am I going to get out of here, find him, and get help before the poison does too much damage?

"Well, you don't need me anymore," I say, attempting to slip past them.

"Of course, we do," Gavin says, incredulous. "You have a seat at the winner's feast. There are food and drinks in the next chamber." He pats Jane on the shoulder. "It's not customary, but you may accompany us. Some wine will help ease the sting of tonight."

"I should be in a hospital," I press. "Not at a feast. I really think—"

"Maren," interrupts Gavin, turning to face me. "That antidote is better than anything the hospital can provide. I tested it on myself. I told you that I'd never let anything happen to you. In an hour or so, you'll hardly remember the experience. Stay with us for this celebration. If after tonight, you truly can't remain a part of the society, you're free to go. I'm hoping you'll come around, though. And I hope you'll..." He clasps my frigid hand in his warm one, squinting down at me through his frames.

I tense, pulling in a deep breath and considering bulling past him. But I'm still too weak and disoriented. I have to send a message. Even if Gavin returned my phone, though, I wouldn't have a signal down here. I'll have to wait until I get my strength back to fight my way out.

I exhale, lowering my head and squeezing his hand in return. "Fine, let's go have a party." But Gavin barely has a chance to smile before the sound of footsteps thunders just outside the door. In the hall, a massive shadow shifts over the corridor wall.

Remington lurches into the doorway, holding on to the frame as if for dear life.

THIRTY-FOUR

PANIC BLARES IN MY EARS LIKE A FOGHORN. HE DIDN'T FIND the antidote. So what is he doing *here*?

"Remington!" Jane pushes through us to throw her arms around him. But he wrenches away.

"Maren," he says, stopping to gasp for breath. A look of disgust crosses his face as he takes in my hand wrapped in Gavin's before I release it. "Come on."

Gavin sidesteps in front of me. "That's not quite how this is going to go."

"I'd like to see you try to show me how this is going to go." Remington releases the door frame and takes a lumbering step toward Gavin, who easily dodges Remington's veering fist.

"Please," I whisper to Polly and Jane. "If you two buy us some time, I can get him help before it's too late."

"You don't need him," Polly says. "Neither of you does. And I'm not giving up my new title for him. Besides, if not him, someone else will have to die. We can't just skip the sacrifice. We could lose everything the society has built."

"You can't really believe that," I hiss.

Polly rolls her eyes. "Even if I wanted to help, I wouldn't be able to. You think we're alone in here?" She points to the corner of the ceiling. "They're watching our every move. The moment you two run, half a dozen society members will be on you. And he's not exactly in any condition to put up a fight."

She's certainly right about that. Having given up on subduing Gavin, Remington sinks to the ground. His complexion is sallow, eyes still that unnatural black, and I can hear the sound of his strangled breathing from across the room.

Still, making a run for it could be our only option. Maybe if I can help him to his feet, whatever adrenaline is left will combine with his athlete's drive to make it out of here.

I pad toward him, still unsteady myself, but a voice drifts in from the corridor, nearly knocking me sideways.

"There you are." Behind me, Annabelle glides into the room, pushing back her hood and shaking her glossy blond locks out. "Remington, you made my job so much easier."

Remington growls, flashing a row of what appear to be

blackened teeth, and lunges for her. She hops, dodging his efforts with a giggle. I squint at Remington, but his mouth is shut. Am I still seeing things?

I must be, since no one else seemed to notice Remington's teeth.

"But I am disappointed in you," she says, wagging her finger like a stern dog owner. "You had so many fans, and I was your biggest one. There are a lot of disappointed faces in the viewing room. Though," she adds, gaze falling on me for the first time, "I must say, Maren. You were rather ruthless. Allowing Remington to give you his advantage and then finishing up the course all by yourself. You'll always have a place here, you know. How does Major Supreme sound?"

"Sounds like a bunch of culty cultish crap. You really think Pelops will bless you if you kill someone tonight?"

"Oh Maren," she says, pursing her lips, "he already has. Which is why we'll continue living as gods among men, while you're thrown out of Torrey-Wells for insufficient funding. Or worse, depending on how you behave at the end of all this. Now, if you'd all follow me, we must proceed with the night's events."

"Please," I beg, tears flooding my eyes as Remington's strong body just lies there. "I know you don't want to do this. Just because your dad is"—I bite back the horrible names I want to call him—"*society* doesn't mean you have to live this way."

But Annabelle ignores me, inspecting a red fingernail in the gauzy light.

"Are we just going to leave him here?" Jane asks, looking down at her ex with a mixture of concern and fear.

Gavin sighs, rubbing his face. "You can bring him to the feast. I know you and Maren will want to say your goodbyes. Besides, the more incapacitated he becomes, the easier the ritual will be."

"Thoughtful of you," I say, attempting to rush over but losing equilibrium.

"Don't trouble yourself," Annabelle says, grabbing my wrist. "Jane will help him. Come along." She prods at me, soon joined by Polly, until I relent, turning down the corridor after Gavin.

My skin squirms as I allow Polly to support me through a bout of dizziness. We pass the horrible fresco of the eyes, following Gavin, who removes a large wooden beam lock, apparently meant to keep things in. My tongue sticks to the roof of my parched mouth and my stomach flips. It's another trick. They're planning to lock us both inside.

But we enter the chamber, finding it fit with a long, wooden table and chairs. It's set with eight white plates, accompanied by chalices filled with red wine. A spread of various breads, cheeses, and fancy cakes fills the center.

Annabelle moves to the opposite side of the table and takes a seat. "Please, sit," she says, raising a chalice and taking a sip. "Congratulations to the champions." She flashes that knowing smile I'd like so very much to punch off her face.

"Thank you so much, Annabelle," I coo, unhooking my arm from Polly's and dropping into a seat near the door.

Jane helps Remington into a seat on the corner, placing herself between us. The pathetic way his eyes keep darting about the room stabs at my heart. He's seeing things.

"Eat up," Gavin says with a frown.

"I think I've learned my lesson about the society's diet," I say.

"Oh, you're all being silly." Annabelle picks up a white wedge and pops it into her mouth. She washes it down with a swig of wine. "See? Not poison."

"That's what you said in the cottage."

Polly is already scarfing down food like she really has been kept in a cell all this time. She grabs a cluster of grapes and begins plucking them off and popping them into her mouth, one by one. On my other side, Jane guzzles red wine.

My lips curl in disgust. Look at them. *The gods*. Drinking wine while the rest of us fight for our lives.

I turn back to Polly, to the friend I've missed with my whole heart this semester. With everything in me, I will her to look at me, to snap out of this terrible fantasy. To take my hand so that together, we can help Remington and flee the catacombs for good.

Instead, her stare, full of that enraptured shine, is

fastened to Gavin. "Polly," I say, leaning closer to whisper. "It's not too late to get him out of here." I flick my head in Remington's direction, helplessness gripping me as I watch him reach out and snatch for something that isn't there. "No one has to die."

"Of course someone has to die!" Polly's eyes brim with that feverish glow. "Don't you see? This is the small price we pay to have everything we could ever desire."

I grit my teeth and pound a fist against the table, sending a wave of water from the pitcher splashing onto the table. Now that I've seen the tall glass pitcher sweating in the center of the table, ice cubes floating at the top, there's nothing I'd like more than to gulp it all down. Though most of my symptoms have subsided, the thirst is as bad as it was an hour ago. But it's too risky. I cast a glance at the doorway behind me. Where exactly are these other society members? If they're watching from another level, I might be able to outrun them. Except Remington would never make it. I'm not even sure he still grasps what's happening as he swats at another invisible fly.

Then his gaze snaps to mine. And his pupils—they're no longer too big and black.

Maybe it's another part of the poison's process. But his eyes flick pointedly toward the door, and a tiny bud of hope blossoms in me. I just can't let anyone else catch on. "How will you explain his death?" I ask as Polly nibbles on a bite-size white cake.

"We'll do what we've been doing for centuries," Gavin says, the awkward quality I found so endearing replaced by cool indifference. "We'll make it go away."

Jane takes another sip of wine, nodding along.

At the end of the table, Remington's fingers crawl across the table toward a slice of cheese, which he takes and examines. My bloom of hope withers, especially as he pushes aside a fork like he's disgusted by it.

"Oh dear," Annabelle says, and my heart sinks. We're out of time.

Remington grabs for a wineglass now, and I don't even bother telling him to drop it. He can't get much more poisoned than he already is. But his gaze whips to mine, followed by a barely perceptible glance at the knife in front of him.

The air, taut with fear and nerves, snaps. Before the others can blink, he's on his feet, knife in hand.

Annabelle reacts the quickest, reaching for a plate. She hurls it across the table, and it whizzes just between Jane and Remington. Blood pumping, I grab my knife and dive off my chair and onto the floor, crawling toward the wall. With his left hand, Remington tosses his wine in Annabelle's face before smashing the stem against the table. He brandishes his makeshift knife at Jane, who seems to freeze in place, horror creating hollows in her cheeks.

Gavin is already skirting the opposite side of the table, headed for Remington and gripping his own blade.

I back up, holding my knife, watching as Remington tries to pass Polly, who refuses to budge. "I'll use one of these on you if I have to," Remington growls, a weapon in each hand.

"Remington!" I shout, getting to my feet. But I have to turn away as Gavin comes up behind me. I scream, swiping at him with my knife. He mimics the move, and I jump back, barely evading his blade against my chest.

Gavin pauses, a look of shock crossing his face at how close he came to slicing me open. His green eyes flash down to the knife and back up again, narrowing as they fix on me.

To our side, there's a shriek and a clatter. Gavin's attention diverts, and I slip out into the doorway, watching as Annabelle clambers straight over the table, snarling like a wild animal and heaving herself at Remington. He shifts, and she lands stomach-first on the chair post.

Gavin tears past the doorway to help, and my knuckles dig into the stone archway so tightly they hurt. Polly's lying on the floor, her glass broken into fragments beside her; I have no idea what state she's in. Red wine—maybe blood— covers the stone and seeps beneath the table.

Above her, Jane has suddenly come alive. No longer petrified, she grabs a metal fork off the table.

Desperate, I lunge for the water pitcher. It's heavy in my weakened hands, but I bring it back and swing with all my might. A sickening crack resounds as it hits Gavin's skull. He stands still for a moment before reaching back to touch his head. As his hand comes away coated in blood, Jane shoves her chair across the floor with a screech, slamming it into Remington's shins. He cries out and crumples onto the chair. But he recovers, black teeth bared, smacking her in the face with a plate and pushing past a still-dazed Gavin to get to me.

I duck into the corridor, Remington close behind. Annabelle's shouts still echo through the chamber as we push the door shut. "Get the beam!" Remington calls, throwing all his remaining strength into holding it despite the pounding from the other side. I find it propped against the wall and drag it over. Hefting the splintery beam, I slide it into place.

"Let's go," Remington says, grabbing for my hand.

I take it, and together, we hurtle through the corridor as fast as our faltering legs will take us.

Nearing an open door, we skid to a tiptoe. "So," I hiss, "you did find the antidote?"

Remington releases my hand. He peeks inside the chamber, and, finding it empty, presses on. "No," he answers, huffing. "But I broke into the health center and found some charcoal." That explains the black traces on his teeth. "It took time. But I think it's absorbing some of the toxins."

"So you were faking?"

"Not most of it. Back in that first chamber, I really couldn't stay on my feet." The hall ends up ahead, and Remington stops, holding an index finger to his lips. But his breathing is so labored, anyone in the room would hear us out here.

"Then you still need the antidote," I whisper. "Why did you come back?"

"For you." He checks around the corner and then turns, meeting my eyes for the briefest second. "I knew they wouldn't let you go without their sacrifice. I was hoping the charcoal would help enough for me to get you out of here. And if not..."

He would've let them take him. So that I could go free.

We pass through the hauntingly silent chambers until Remington halts. At first, I think he's hallucinating again or about to collapse, but he glances from side to side. "It's too easy."

He's right; it feels like a trap. But we can't just sit around, waiting to be found. My fingers graze his sleeve as I push ahead, the map from the night Jordan played princess imprinted on my brain. I lead us through the remaining passageways, until finally, we fly through the empty antechamber to reach the trapdoor.

I scramble up the ladder, Remington close behind me. When I enter the old cathedral, my heart stops.

We're surrounded. Figures in black robes form a circle, blocking every possible angle of escape.

Remington inches up behind me, threading his fingers through mine. I squeeze back.

At the far side of the cathedral, the wall creaks. A large beam of light swings at us like a laser, and I shield my eyes.

Something moves over by the members' entrance, and the light whips away, zigzagging over the society members and drawing nearer to us.

It's over. We'll never be able to fight this many of them. Remington's struggling for air and I can barely stay on my feet.

I squint at the approaching shape, blinking until Jordan's pale face and black hair zoom into focus. "They're over here!" she screams, waving at whoever's back there.

More footsteps now, like thunder over the ancient cathedral floor.

Uniformed figures burst into view, shouting and grabbing at the hooded people, raising their guns. My breath snags. I lift my hands, kneeling down on the floor, and Remington falls in line behind me.

The police continue wrangling, their shouts jarring in the dead of night. But I exhale, releasing a ragged, anxious breath, and inhale sweet relief.

She did it. Jordan actually did it.

THIRTY-FIVE

FIVE MONTHS LATER

I TRUDGE BACK TO MY DORM ROOM, WET SANDALS SQUISHING
over the carpet, towel wrapped around me. The key card buzzes
me in, and I open the door, immediately dropping my shower
caddy.

Shampoo oozes over the floor, a slick tile now that Polly's
rug has been removed. The cold slime hits my toes, but I'm
focused on the envelope. The one someone slid beneath the
door, addressed to Maren Montgomery.

It can't be.

After the police stormed the old cathedral, we learned that
Jordan had also alerted the local media, who were stationed

outside, ready to get the story of the prestigious academy run by a bloodthirsty cult.

By the time Jordan convinced the police to uncuff Remington and me, Remington was in bad shape. Despite my objections, we were both sent off in an ambulance, leaving Jordan in charge of one last important task: tracking down another dose of the antidote.

After some rest and fluids, I was fine. Remington, on the other hand, had to battle. Doctors say the only thing that kept him alive was the charcoal. It bought him some time, which they managed to extend with fluids and other medications. A few hours later, though, he took another turn for the worse.

That's when Jordan showed up with the antidote she stole from Dr. Yamashiro's cottage while he was in police custody. She had to sneak it past the hospital staff, who never would've let Remington ingest the questionable concoction. Not long after, Remington's doctor got to claim responsibility for his patient's miraculous recovery.

Jordan, Remington, and I were interviewed extensively by the police. We explained that we'd been held against our wills, that we'd unwittingly participated in the poisoning of Alicia Jones. That some of our teachers were aiding and abetting these criminals. And that no one was guiltier than the headmistress herself, who drugged us when we came to her for help.

It was difficult to weed out the society members from

innocent faculty. We only had two names, but we knew there were more. Detectives eventually made a deal with the headmistress: a reduced prison sentence in exchange for the complete list.

We all know it's not a complete list. Just the Torrey-Wells members. And maybe not even that. Because I'm standing over an envelope exactly like the ones I used to receive. Like the one I found in Polly's chess set that started this whole mess.

When I bend down to pick it up, my phone buzzes on my desk, causing me to kick my already leaking shampoo bottle.

I take a deep breath, right the bottle, and pick up the envelope. I plod over to my desk to find a text from Remington. **Get my anniversary card?**

Growling, I slam the envelope down on the desk. But I can't resist for long. I tear it open and read the handwritten note:

> Roses are red
> Or are they green?
> Would you care to join me for dining hall pizza,
> Oh fair, ferocious queen?
>> Love,
>> R

I set the card down on the desk and grab my phone, dialing his number. It rings once, and he picks up. But I already heard his ringtone echoing out in the hall.

I rush over, slipping in the puddle of shampoo I never cleaned up before wrenching open the door to find Remington in the doorway, cringing.

"What are you doing?" I whisper. "Get in here." I pull him inside, dragging him past the fallen shower caddy to the bottom bunk. Then I push him onto the bed and stand over him. "We're not in the society anymore, Remington Cruz. You can't sneak into the girls' dormitory and expect to get away with it. How am I going to get you out? And also, what anniversary?"

Remington only grins up at me. "After everything we've been through, you're scared of breaking the *no boys in the girls' dorms* rule?"

I cross my arms and glare down at him.

"Okay, fine. Five months ago today, I realized there wouldn't be much water in my future."

"Because there's a drought coming?"

"No, because you hate water. And I love you. So now I hate water." I refuse to smile because of the card prank, but he adds, "Also, five months ago today was the day I realized your eyes weren't red like a demon's; they were green."

My mouth threatens to curl, so I smash my lips together. "The card was bad form, dude."

"Oh, come on, you loved it. That burst of adrenaline followed by the world's cutest poem. How did you ever manage to score a guy who knows you so completely and perfectly?"

"Guess you learned from knowing nothing about your last girlfriend—namely, her very peculiar religious beliefs."

"No more peculiar than your bestie's."

When the school board replaced the headmistress along with the bad faculty seeds, it also notified my dad that my tuition through Form IV was paid in full due to my trauma (read: to avoid further litigation). Polly and Jane, along with most of the other society members, were able to use their newfound wealth and connections to blame the headmistress and get off with counseling.

I haven't spoken to Polly since the day she came by to clear out the rest of her things. She was, understandably, moved to a dormitory across campus, far away from me. "You can keep the coat," she said, gaze on her cardboard box.

"Thanks." Part of me was grateful because I still didn't own a nice coat; part of me wanted to take her offering and stomp it right in front of her. I haven't touched the coat since that day. I'm not sure I ever will.

Before she left, Polly stopped in front of the door, large box in her arms. I thought she needed help, so I brushed past her to get the door. But she didn't pass through it. Instead, she continued to stand there, breath heavy as she faced the hallway.

My heart hitched as I waited for her words. There wasn't hope for us; I knew that. I would never be able to trust her again. It didn't stop the memories from tumbling through my head, though. I was still stuck, my brain half-trapped in our fantasy of a friendship. I'd left the photo collage up on the wall, for heaven's sake. It was like I couldn't move on until we'd had *this*—whatever this was.

She turned to look at me then, mascara starting to smudge as her eyes teared up. Her chest rose and fell, and my throat tightened. I was about to invite her to sit down when she hefted the box of belongings higher. Without so much as a glance back, she strode out of the room.

I still pass her on campus, see her in the dining hall, sit beside her in classes.

She and Jane might've been able to buy their way to freedom, but everyone knows about their former extracurricular habits. Not long after the police shut everything down, the local paper printed an exposé, naming the society members currently at the academy—students and faculty. They also dropped some names of former members. The list included politicians, a private university president, a pharmaceutical company owner, a film director—even the princess of a small island.

All of these accused members issued statements of denial. But I heard the pharmaceutical company owner and the director made considerable donations to charitable organizations shortly after the exposé was printed.

I know they're out there. I can only hope that since the local police chief was fired, Remington, Jordan, and I will be safe here until graduation.

One thing is certain. I will not be stepping foot in those catacombs again. I knew the tunnels were old. I never fathomed they could be as old as the ones in Paris. Apparently, they were constructed gradually, over the course of half a century. Investigators are still down there, digging, uncovering secrets—and bodies—the society managed to conceal for ages. I don't think even Gavin knew the half of what had gone on before he took over. He doesn't have to worry about any of that now that he's in prison.

I called him over the summer. Not because I was worried about him, but to ask about his sister. He thinks as long as he stays loyal—meaning he refuses to give up more names—the society will continue to help her. He still believes they care about him, that they're family.

And he still thinks there's hope for us. That I could somehow love him after all the suffering he put me through.

"Seriously, how are we going to sneak you out of here?" I ask Remington.

"Um," he says, twiddling his fingers, "dress me up like your tall new roommate?"

I glower. "I've decided I like living alone." It's not completely true; Jordan and I have talked about rooming together next semester There aren't many people I trust enough to share a bunkbed with these days.

But I trust her. I'm not sure she and I will ever have the tight friendship I once believed I had with Polly. After everything we went through, though, Jordan and I have grown close. I betrayed her—sacrificed her to the society for Polly's sake—and she saved my life anyway. She saw past the allure of the society, past my shortcomings, and did what was right. She's loyal and brave in a way Polly never was.

"Ooh, I've got it. Don't sneak me out." He lifts his scarred eyebrow, and I punch him. But he takes my arm, tugging lightly.

"I hate you, Remington." But I let him walk me closer.

"I know." He slides his arms around my waist. "We've come so far from the days you used to think I was going to tie you up and abandon you to the cult."

I lean in and press a finger to his lips before he can ruin the moment any more. "Maybe by the time our next five-month anniversary rolls around, I'll only strongly dislike you."

He grins up at me, drawing me closer still. "May the gods grant your request."

ACKNOWLEDGMENTS

THERE ARE SO MANY PEOPLE TO THANK FOR TAKING THIS book from a tiny seed of an idea to the final, polished book that readers hold in their hands. To my fantastic editor, Wendy McClure, thanks for loving this story, for your brilliance, and for always being such a joy to work with. To Eliza Swift, thank you for believing in my stories and for giving me a chance. My thanks go out to Madison Nankervis, Chelsey Moler Ford, and the entire Sourcebooks team. Thank you to Liz Dresner and Esther Sarah Kim for the perfectly chilling cover.

My endless gratitude to Julie Abe and Laura Kadner. You two are there for everything, and I don't know why you put up with any of it. May your lives be forever filled with cupcakes and unicorns. Thanks to Laura, Julie, and Madeline Dyer for reading my early drafts. To Suzanne Park, Alexa Donne, and Dana Mele—thank you for telling me how to do all the publishing things. I would be lost without your guidance.

To my wonderful agent, Uwe Stender, thank you for your enthusiasm, knowledge, and tireless efforts behind the scenes.

Much love and gratitude to my parents, George and Rebecca Kienzle, for supporting my dreams since the day I was born. Thank you to my Ichaso family and to my Lewis family for your encouragement. To my church family, thank you for your prayers and for always asking how the book stuff is going.

Matias, thank you for being the most supportive husband a girl could ask for. Thank you for all the hours you've spent brainstorming with me, for all the drafts you've read, and all the millions of little things that mean everything. Kaylie, Jude, and Camryn—thanks and hugs for all for your love, encouragement, and patience with me. Kids, keep writing your amazing stories.

To the readers, book bloggers, and influencers, thank you for your support.

Finally, all gratitude and praise to my Lord and Savior.

ABOUT THE AUTHOR

Chelsea Ichaso writes twisty thrillers for young adults, including *Little Creeping Things* and *Dead Girls Can't Tell Secrets*. A former high school English teacher, she currently resides in Southern California with her husband and children. You can visit her online at chelseaichaso.com or on Instagram @chelseaichaso.

FIREreads

❀ #getbooklit

Your hub for the hottest young adult books!

Visit us online and sign up for our
newsletter at FIREreads.com

 @sourcebooksfire

 sourcebooksfire

 firereads.tumblr.com